Bill Knox began his writing career as a young Glasgow journalist. Married with a grown up family, he is now a full-time author. He has been a crime reporter, motoring correspondent and news editor.

He has made many contributions to radio and television and was well known to Scottish viewers as the writer and presenter for twelve years of the Scottish Television police liaison programme *Crime Desk*.

He won the prestigious Police Review Award for the crime novel which gave the best portrayal of police procedure, *The Crossfire Killings*.

Bill Knox's work is published in ten languages, and his world sales exceed four million copies.

DEATH BYTES

A very different murder arrived on Detective Superintendent Colin Thane's lap. Different because it took place in broad daylight beneath the windows of Glasgow High Court, two of the chief witnesses were law lords, and the attractive woman who was killed had links with the high-tech world of computer chips — a world where rich pickings waited for the ruthless. The truth about what was happening was hidden in a strange mix of old craft skills and new technology, presided over by a feisty American woman executive, holding a final balance while others died.

BILL KNOX

DEATH BYTES

Complete and Unabridged

ULVERSCROFT
Leicester

First published in Great Britain in 1998 by
Constable & Company Limited
London

First Large Print Edition
published 1999
by arrangement with
Constable & Company Limited
London

British Library CIP Data

Knox, Bill, *1928 – 1999*
    Death bytes.—Large print ed.—
    Ulverscroft large print series: mystery
    1. Thane, Colin (Fictitious character)—Fiction
    2. Police—Scotland—Fiction
    3. Glasgow (Scotland)—Fiction
    4. Detective and mystery stories
    5. Large type books
    I. Title
    823.9'14 [F]

    ISBN 0–7089–4160–5

Published by
F. A. Thorpe (Publishing) Ltd.
Anstey, Leicestershire
Set by Words & Graphics Ltd.
Anstey, Leicestershire
Printed and bound in Great Britain by
T. J. International Ltd., Padstow, Cornwall

This book is printed on acid-free paper

For Michael and Debbie

Once again, I admit that this fiction story varies in some procedural detail from the real-life Scottish Crime Squad's operational methods.

The detective officers concerned prefer it that way. They have told me why, and the reasons are good!

BK, Glasgow

1

Four more days, and Police Constable E694, Kidd, David, could hang up his uniform for two whole weeks and go off on annual leave. Goodbye, Glasgow and city grime. Hello again, Spanish sun, sangria, and whatever else bachelor luck might turn up . . .

Four more days! Dave Kidd tried hard to concentrate on the immediate task of completing yet another plod around this same small circuit of city streets, as decreed by his sergeant.

'Keep doing it until when, sergeant?' he'd asked.

'Until you're told to stop,' he was answered.

'Until when' had already lasted from the start of his shift until midway through this Tuesday morning in June. The sun was bright in a cloudless sky, he was already sweating enough to make his uniform shirt cling to his back, and Constable Kidd had had enough.

Aged twenty-two, medium height and build, with short fair hair and freckles, Dave Kidd had recently finished his probationer period in E Division, where the local hard men allegedly chewed iron nails and spat rust. His feet felt sore. He had lost count of the number of times he'd made this clockwise slog around his appointed circuit.

Set near to the heart of Glasgow, it began at the junction where the grubby tenements of the historic, bustling Saltmarket looked towards the red bricks of the City Mortuary. From there, the way continued down Saltmarket and past Glasgow Green to the traffic lights of the Albert Bridge and the broad, lazy flow of the River Clyde. Make a right turn before the bridge into Clyde Street. On the Glasgow Green side, a scrawny scarecrow of a woman still lay in a drunken sleep among the grass and ground-hugging bushes near the river's edge.

Dave Kidd had no idea when she had arrived this time, but every cop in E Division knew Old Aggie. She was harmless, but tended to be explosively noisy when wakened. So why disturb her? Old Aggie was so often there she had become part of the scenery. A part that didn't register any more.

Later, a lot of people were going to regret his decision not to disturb her.

The next set of traffic lights along Clyde Street was at the Victoria Bridge junction with Bridgegate, a street which was a mix

2

of the old, the demolished, and gap sites, all flanked down one side by the high stone arches of a railway line.

He turned into Bridgegate. Straight ahead, on the south side of a little spur called Mart Street, was the main reason for this endless patrolling — the landmark bulk of the new High Court of Justiciary. The High Court was in session, with all that meant in terms of judges and lawyers, witnesses and juries, accused, the inevitable interested public, and all the vehicle traffic they generated.

The courthouse, a honey-coloured stone building, was a modern legal beehive where only the most serious criminal cases were heard. It had taken three years to build at a cost to the taxpayers of £28 million. For the money, the city had gained a complex of four new courtrooms in which justice could be administered while backed by the latest in information technology and electronic security. Externally, the package had come complete with floodlights, ornamental railings and even a garden filled with flowering shrubs, the tall, cool greenery of young trees, and a feature fountain. The main entrance to the complex had a wide expanse of polished marble floor, backed by a high atrium.

Yet total contrast existed a stone's throw away from that eye-catching entrance, behind

3

a high metal fence which ran like a boundary along the other side of the Mart Street spur. Courthouse visitors could gape across at the chaos that Glasgow's citizens knew as Paddy's Market — a down-at-heel street market where almost everything could be bought or sold.

A fringe of tiny shops traded busily behind the fence from a bazaar-like collection of one-time garages or railway arches. The rest was an area of waste ground where a market stall could be a trestle table filled with discarded crockery, or an opened cardboard carton filled with old shoes. The last few times round, Dave Kidd had noticed that one space was occupied by a teenage girl in denim jeans, squatting patiently on the ground and trying to sell her sole stock — a single length of cheap cotton cloth. Elsewhere were rusty refrigerators and ancient TV sets, displays of old watches and jewellery, mounds of second-hand books and tapes.

Paddy's Market traded anything to anyone. With simple rules for most occasions.

Cash only.

No receipts.

No guarantees.

Each time round, Mart Street was where Dave Kidd met and passed Peter Florian, his neighbour constable who had drawn the matching anticlockwise duty. Florian, a fat, slow-moving veteran heading towards retirement, nodded each time they passed, then kept ambling on.

This time Florian was late and hadn't arrived when Dave Kidd reached Mart Street. Added to the heat of the day, a gusting wind had appeared from the west, sending surprise clouds of grit and dust swirling across Paddy's Market and everything around. As he slowed, looking around for his fellow constable, another cloud of dust swept across Dave Kidd and stung at his face. He cursed, turned his back to the wind, and rubbed a hand across his eyes.

He first saw the woman as his vision cleared. Tall and thin-faced, her long, raven black hair tied back in a simple ponytail, she was leaving the market and coming out into the street through an open gate in the fence. Probably in her thirties, she wore a dark blue skirt and a lightweight white cotton jacket. A black plastic tote bag was slung by its strap over her left shoulder, and she seemed to be arguing with a figure in black motor-cycling leathers and a red crash helmet.

Caught by the sheer anger on the woman's face, the young cop watched as the couple walked a few paces together. Then Black Leathers, face totally hidden under the crash helmet, grabbed the woman by the arm and brought her to a halt.

By then, they were maybe thirty yards away from him. Suddenly, the expression on the woman's thin face changed from anger to disbelief, from disbelief to horror. For an instant, she stiffened as if in shock, then she seemed to sag. Sheer instinct taking over, Dave Kidd started to move towards the couple.

As he did, a whole sequence of events came together. Black Leathers let go of the woman, who staggered, then screamed in a way that cut through the air. A motor cycle ridden by a second figure, also in black leathers and a red crash helmet, came out through the gate in the fence. Engine popping busily, the machine halted beside the other man, who swung on to the pillion seat. Instantly, the motor cycle began howling up through the revs, and then it was moving, rapidly gathering speed. Now there were other shouts and screams.

Chasing on foot was useless. Dave Kidd gave up as the machine weaved a fast, noisy way past the people and vehicles around, while his mind registered that the crash helmets worn by both rider and passenger were marked with narrow double bands of white — and that the pillion rider now clutched the raven-haired woman's black plastic tote bag.

For a moment, he'd almost forgotten the woman. He looked round, in time to see her collapse against the wall of the High Court building then slump slowly towards the ground.

Bewildered, uncertain, Dave Kidd swung his attention back towards the speeding motor cycle, then it had vanished from sight round a bend in the road. A police whistle was shrilling, and he realised that it was his own. Then there was the suddenly comforting sight of the bulky Peter Florian thudding along the street towards him.

The woman lay motionless. Down on his knees beside her, he saw the way her black hair had come loose from her ponytail, the way her white cotton jacket had fallen open. Dave Kidd saw the rest, and briefly closed his eyes.

'What the hell have you got, Dave?' Newly arrived, panting, the other constable looked down, then drew a deep breath. When he spoke, it was meant as no blasphemy. 'Sweet Jesus.'

Dave Kidd forced himself to look again. She had been wearing an embroidered white linen blouse under that cotton jacket. A red spread of blood was oozing from a small, neat stab wound under her left breast. The force of the blow and the way it had cut through the blouse had forced some material into the wound.

'Peter.' White-faced, knowing he was trembling, Dave Kidd turned to his fat, veteran companion. 'Is she . . . ?'

'Dead?' Florian had already stooped, checking for a pulse at the woman's throat. He nodded, stood upright again, and quietly crossed himself. 'Bad luck, boy. You've landed a murder.'

It was the first time Constable E694 Dave Kidd had ever seen death close up. He swallowed hard.

'Steady, boy,' murmured Florian, dragging out his personal radio, ready to summon help. 'Remember the audience.'

Dave Kidd looked over towards Paddy's Market. The few seconds that had passed had been enough for that busy area to almost empty. Even the girl with her single length of cloth was leaving. It was to be expected. There were always plenty of people who didn't want to know, with their own reasons.

'Damn them,' said Dave Kidd bitterly.

'Not there,' said Florian softly. He gave the smallest of gestures up towards the building above. 'Worse.'

Dave King raised his head, saw, and

froze. Two floors above them, two men stared down at them from one of the High Court windows, eyes unemotionally sharp with professional interest. They had removed their traditional white horsehair wigs, but they wore their red velvet robes trimmed with white ermine fur.

'Oh God,' said Dave Kidd.

It looked like he'd got himself two serious witnesses. Two he recognised from TV and newspaper photographs. One, almost bald, was Lord Lewis, the Lord Justice General — the most senior and most feared of all the High Court of Justiciary's law lords. Lord Kirk, the other judge with him, had a tight, frowning face and believed that the civilised world had come to an end when convicted prisoners could no longer be sentenced to the galleys.

The two judges moved back out of sight as Peter Florian finished using his personal radio and lowered it.

'We stay, we don't touch, we don't even breathe on anything, son,' he reported wryly. Then he sighed and thumbed over his shoulder towards the red brick of the City Mortuary. 'Well, it's close enough to where they'll take her.' A thought struck him. 'You're due off on leave at the weekend, right? Spain?'

'Majorca.'

Dave Kidd looked sadly at the dead woman lying on the ground, blood still slowly spreading from that wound. Blown along by another gust of wind, a scrap of crumpled wrapping paper from the market had draped itself against her face. He stooped, lifted the paper, and tossed it aside.

Somehow, he didn't think he'd be on that charter flight. Not now.

Goodbye, Majorca.

★ ★ ★

A bureaucrat somewhere, probably looking into his Civil Service issue crystal ball between sacred rounds of golf, had decided there were potential money-saving reasons why Wednesday should be decreed as M for Move Day for the élite Scottish Crime Squad.

So this was Wednesday, and it was all happening. Ever since early morning, convoys of police vehicles and hire vans had been ferrying the final loads of equipment from the Squad's previous home to this new and customised location on the outskirts of Glasgow. The telephone service, including the dedicated lines had been switched over at exactly 7 a.m. Seamlessly, one set of radio

10

equipment had taken over from another.

'And everything self-destructs at midnight.' Detective Superintendent Colin Thane made it a murmur under his breath as he stood in the middle of the general chaos which was intended to become the reception area at the Squad's new headquarters.

'Sir — ' The warning yelp came almost too late as a detective constable staggered past carrying several cartons filled with files.

Everybody, including detective superintendents, was being put to work. He had carried his own share of cartons earlier. Now he was having a break while the action continued around him. Even in the middle of it all, he was easy enough to spot.

A tall, grey-eyed man in his early forties, with strong, regular features, a humorous mouth, and thick dark hair in need of a trim, Colin Thane was wearing a lightweight blue lovat suit with a white shirt and a plain knitted blue tie. His home scales might show he had become a couple of pounds or so overweight, but he retained most of an athletic build which went back to younger days when he had been a reasonably rated entrant in the annual police boxing championships. That, he told himself, was before he had gained a wife then, following that, two children, a dog, and a mortgage.

11

The casual thought went. What had to be the same telephone had begun chirping again and wasn't being answered again — there were plenty of telephones around, but nobody could discover where this one was located.

He yelled a fresh plea. 'Can't someone find that damned thing?'

'Trying, sir!' A policewoman went scurrying past, aiming a glare at the back of his neck. Colin Thane might be second-in-command of the Scottish Crime Squad, but she was already coping with a score of other tasks. Her personal priority was to find the key to the door of the women's washroom, left locked by some idiot.

Two men in overalls struggled through the confusion, wheeling in a heavy steel cabinet on a trolley and followed by a harassed foreman brandishing a layout plan. An electrician was using a power drill in one corner, other people were coming and going, and all the time the same telephone kept chirping.

'Do you think hell might be something like this, sir?' asked a sardonically amused voice at Thane's elbow.

'Hell is better organised, Francey. I guarantee it.' Thane grimaced at the man who had joined him. Thin, in his mid-twenties, he had thick black hair and a thin

12

straggle of a bandit moustache. 'Why are you here? You're supposed to be making sure we leave nothing behind!'

'I got bored.' Detective Inspector Francey Dunbar gave an unabashed grin. Wearing faded denim trousers and a grey rollneck sweater, Dunbar was leaning on an old silver-topped cane he had bought in a junk shop. It was no affectation. Dunbar was still recovering from a car crash in which another Squad officer had been killed, and now walked with a heavy limp. Maybe always would. 'I thought I'd see how my elders and betters were getting on.'

'And?'

Dunbar's grin widened in a pretence at innocence. 'No comment, sir.'

'Well, you've seen,' said Thane stonily. 'So now you can get back.'

Dunbar's reply was lost as one of the men with the trolley and the steel cabinet tripped, yelped, and went sprawling. A wild grab to save himself simply brought the cabinet toppling and man and metal hit the floor with a deafening crash. That brought a total silence all around — even the mystery phone had stopped chirping. Complaining, rubbing his shoulder, the man swore pungently as he was helped to his feet. He kicked viciously at some loose sections of carpet before pouncing

13

on a broken length of phone wire, holding it up.

'What idiot left this like a flamin' tripwire?' he demanded.

The removal team got the cabinet back on its trolley while the general bustle resumed. But Francey Dunbar had vanished, and a moment later Thane saw why. Jack Hart, the Squad commander, had appeared from somewhere and was shouldering a way towards Thane through the reception area chaos.

'What's going on, superintendent?' demanded Commander Hart bleakly. A man in his early fifties with high cheekbones, thinning grey hair and a lined sad-eyed face, he looked around with something close to despair. His usually quiet, almost lazy-sounding voice had an unaccustomed edge. 'Can't any of these people answer a telephone? I gave up — it was quicker to come down.'

'We've had problems, sir.' Thane decided it was better to leave it there.

'I should be surprised?' The Squad commander was a neat figure in a charcoal grey suit, an immaculate striped shirt, and a carefully knotted silk tie. But a streak of cream paint smeared one sleeve of his jacket. Hart sighed and lowered his voice. 'Tell me about it, Colin. I've a secretary trying to

14

coax her word processor back to life with a nail file. I broke a window lock trying to get fresh air. I can't find half the things I know I brought over, and my damned coffee percolator won't work.' He paused to draw breath. 'Well, you've got a chance to escape from it. Come up, I'll explain.'

Thane followed Hart across the reception area then let him take the lead on the stairway which led to the upper floor. After years of existing within a cramped single-storey block, the Squad had at last moved to this new headquarters building where two floors meant more space all round — almost twice as much as before — and allowed a suite of conference rooms, a variety of duty rooms, offices with glass divider screens, and much more, all with fitted carpets throughout. Computer terminals had taken over from typewriters.

All the way up, the bare-walled stairway smelled of new paint. A selection of government issue plants in plastic pots had been dumped on a half-landing. Further on, a security door with a keypad lock had been left open at the top of the stairway. Thane's office was along to the right, the Squad commander's domain was to the left, and Thane followed Hart into the Squad commander's outer office, where a plump, smartly dressed brunette in her forties was at her desk and working on a dismantled electrical switch.

She heard them arrive and looked up.

'Winning, Maggie?' asked Thane.

'Don't even ask.' She turned to Hart. 'You've got to speak to Crown Office, commander. They said please.'

'Please means urgent.' Hart's lined face hardened. 'I'll call them now. But block everything else. And be careful with that switch.' He took another step towards his private office, then stopped and cleared his throat hopefully. 'Uh — percolator working yet?'

His secretary looked at him in a frosty way that was its own answer.

'I only asked,' said Hart hastily.

'I'll tell you when, commander.' Rank held no privileges with Maggie Fyffe, a cop's widow.

Hart beckoned again, and led Thane through into his private office, which was large and suitably executive style. The Squad commander's new desk, bleached walnut in colour, was relatively tidy. A prized antique police helmet had its place on top of one filing cabinet, a photograph of Hart's wife sat on another, and most of an entire wall of the office was covered by a map of Scotland from

16

the islands of the north and west down to the English border. A scatter of different coloured pins each had their own meanings.

'I'll make the call.' Hart went over to the desk, settled in his swivel chair, then picked up a telephone. 'This won't take long.'

Once the call was connected, most of the talk came from the other end of the line. Hart's monosyllabic replies told little, and Thane turned away, going over to the room's large main window and looking down at another small convoy of vehicles arriving with what had to be some of the last equipment being moved. As the convoy came in, a couple of empty vans drove out.

Put simply, the Scottish Crime Squad had totally outgrown its previous home. This new location was still south of the Clyde, still close to the city's high-rise skyline, and near to both the M8 and M77 motorways and to Glasgow International Airport, yet an outsider saw only one more anonymous, uninteresting redbrick building surrounded by a security fence and among a widely spaced scatter of almost identical neighbours. It could have been anything from a warehouse to an industrial unit. Except for one building which housed a Customs and Excise unit, most of the others were exactly that.

'Yes. Superintendent Thane is with me

now.' Hart's use of his name made Thane look round; the Squad commander winked in his direction then he listened and replied again. 'Hell, Thane knows all that. And he'll be on his best behaviour. I guarantee it.' He hung up, sat back, and gave Thane a wisp of a grin. 'Crown Office wanted to be sure you can be diplomatic.'

'And?'

'I lied,' agreed Hart. 'I said yes.' He gestured Thane towards a chair. 'Park yourself.'

Thane dumped a carton of books from a chair on to the floor, sat, then waited while Hart again read through a fax message which was top of the papers on his desk. Whatever was going on, the fact that Crown Office were involved meant it mattered. They represented the ultimate authority behind all criminal prosecutions in Scotland. Their staff were all top civil servants with government issue leather briefcases.

He watched Hart use a small gold propelling pencil to underline two points on the message. In the police world, Hart ranked as a detective chief superintendent. Next step up — if he wanted it — he'd be an assistant chief constable.

A posting to Scotland's élite Crime Squad was a chance any cop dreamed about. It was a small unit, the total strength of only about ninety men and women hand-picked from Scotland's eight police forces. Most served for three years then were scheduled for rotation back to their parent forces. Most fought tooth and nail against that return.

The Crime Squad's ways of working, often a blend of undercover work and surveillance, were hard to match. Free from local ties or regional boundaries, financed by Central Government, they regularly chose their own target operations, keeping a deliberate low-key profile. They had no custody cells of their own, no suspect was ever brought to their building. Often the first that a local force might know the Squad had been visiting was when prisoners were brought in along with a polite request for a receipt.

'Right.' Finished, Hart tossed the fax sheet aside, built a steeple with his fingertips together, brought them up under his chin, and looked across at Thane. 'You read today's major incidents digest?'

Thane nodded. The digest, produced by National Criminal Intelligence, was down-loaded as a print-out. Only major incidents from the previous day made the digest, each rating a few lines. But the digest's value was the way it kept police forces in touch with happenings outside their own territories.

'Including a woman murdered outside the new Glasgow High Court building?'

'Yes. Her tote bag was snatched. Probably a mugging that went wrong.' Thane looked at Hart with a wary suspicion. 'Why?'

'It may be that way. But there's an outside chance she could interest you.' The Squad commander gave a slight shrug. 'When her body was stripped for autopsy, they found a piece of DIY style jewellery around her neck.' He lowered the fingertip steeple. 'A thin gold chain, Colin. One with a microchip mounted as a pendant.'

'Real?' Thane frowned.

'Real,' confirmed Hart. 'Not an imitation. So then some smart alec from E Division happens to remember a special request we circulated to all forces. That we wanted to know about any crime report that even mentions computers — and particularly microchips.'

'Then E Division cried hooray?' suggested Thane resignedly. 'And they're trying to unload their murder on us?'

'The way they put it, we're welcome to get involved,' corrected Hart drily. 'Do you remember who wanted that special request authorised?'

Thane nodded sadly. He had.

'Can you also remember who talked

me into agreeing?' Hart didn't wait for an answer. 'Strathclyde force headquarters suggested we take a look.' He made a noise close to a sigh. 'We started it, I had to say we would. Then Crown Office come scurrying on the line. Officially, this is now a joint Crime Squad and Strathclyde investigation. You're designated as running the show.'

'Me?' Thane made it a startled protest. 'But — '

'It gets worse,' said Jack Hart grimly. 'I was conned, Colin. What Strathclyde didn't say first time round was that their E Division have two witnesses you're going to love. They're High Court judges.'

Thane swallowed. 'They saw — '

'It all,' agreed the Squad commander. He had been holding down the makings of a wry grin. Now he let it surface as he thumbed at the telephone. 'Crown Office says try to treat them as ordinary witnesses. But stay on your best behaviour.'

'Like don't bounce them off walls?' suggested Thane bitterly.

Jack Hart gave a grunt and a nod, and pushed a printed fax across his desk. 'That's an update from E Division — they've now got a name for their body. One of their people will meet you at the City Mortuary at noon, and the judges will see you at their lunch break.'

'At least it's different.' Sighing, Thane took the fax. 'Suppose it remains looking like a simple mugging that went wrong?'

'Then we drop it,' promised Hart. 'I make noises about our workload, and — ' He didn't finish as a loud bang, a bright flash, and a startled yelp came simultaneously from the Squad commander's outer office.

'What the hell?' Alarmed, Hart came catapulting out of his chair. 'That's Maggie — '

When they reached the outer office there was blue smoke in the air around Maggie Fyffe's desk, mainly coming from where a power lead had blown out of a wall socket. Blackened and scorched, the other end of the lead was still plugged into a chrome coffee percolator. Still shaken, the Squad commander's secretary was cursing with a splendidly rich feminine ferocity.

'Are you all right, Maggie?' demanded Hart anxiously. 'What the hell happened?'

'You wanted your coffee, didn't you — sir?' She glared at him. 'I tried to fix the plug, what else — sir? So I damned nearly get blown up. And since when was I paid to be anybody's bloody electrician?'

'Shocking,' murmured Thane sympathetically. 'Be more careful next time, Maggie.'

'Out,' snarled Hart. 'Concern noted. Don't make things worse.'

Thane grinned and left. Once clear of Hart's office, he went along the corridor to his own new office as second-in-command. It was considerably smaller than Hart's, and a pile of cardboard boxes, contents overflowing, had been dumped beside the window. A slim, attractive redhead in her late twenties had been making an attempt at sorting through the boxes, but broke off and looked round as he entered. Detective Sergeant Sandra Craig was wearing one of her usual blue denim working outfits with a wisp of white scarf and black Cuban-heeled boots.

'Forget the unpacking,' said Thane shortly. 'It can wait. We're making calls.'

'The High Court mugging? I heard, sir.' Which meant Maggie Fyffe. His sergeant hesitated and indicated her denim jeans. 'What about these? I can change — '

'No, you'll do.' He thanked God the time was long past when High Court dress codes even demanded that women officers gave evidence wearing hats. 'They're judges, yes. But this time, they're witnesses. There's a difference.'

'Yes, sir.' A twinkle showed in his sergeant's ice green eyes, a chuckle edged into her husky, charm-school voice. 'Fine. As long as they know it.'

Sandra Craig collected her leather shoulder-bag, then followed Thane out of the room and down to the turmoil of the ground floor. Ploughing a way through, they went out into the courtyard parking area almost hidden in the middle of the building. There was a light rain in the air as they crossed towards Thane's car, a black two-litre Ford Mondeo which had cost him a few favours to the Squad's transport pool sergeant.

'You drive.' Thane tossed the keys to Sandra Craig.

His sergeant shook her head and pointed. The Ford was blocked in its space. A patrol van was parked across its bows with the rear doors open and the interior packed with more of the Squad's removal. Two conscripted traffic wardens were unloading its contents at a speed considerably slower than that of any average snail.

'My wheels, sir?' Sandra Craig pointed to her white Volkswagen Golf, parked a few spaces along, and unobstructed.

Thane growled and took back his keys. Unlocking her own car, his sergeant slid behind the vehicle's steering wheel, started it up, then set it moving as soon as Thane had settled in the passenger seat. The new electronically controlled security gate purred open as they rolled towards it, then the white Volkswagen was through and had snaked out into the main road traffic flow. A few moments more, and it joined the M8 motorway route in towards Glasgow.

Sandra Craig drove in the smooth, deceptively easy style which she'd acquired on her way to passing the full police pursuit driving course. That had been at Tulliallan, the Scottish Police Training College, where her all-round grading had confidentially marked her out as a future advanced promotion prospect.

The light rain had ended, the road was drying again, the sky was clearing. Colin Thane watched as the redhead flicked off her car's wipers as a lead-in to a quick blend of gear-change and acceleration. That took the Golf rocketing past both a slow-travelling truck and a rust-bucket old station wagon.

'About these judges, sir — ' Sandra Craig gave Thane a quick, inquiring glance as she settled the Golf back into the flow of motorway traffic — 'how much did they see?'

'The lot, they think.'

'That should help — if we're lucky,' she mused. Briefly, her hair glinted like rich copper in the returned sunlight. 'What have we got on the woman?'

'Not a lot.' Thane hauled out Jack Hart's fax message and read it again while the Golf travelled on.

Jane Tamsin, aged thirty and divorced, had lived with a widowed cousin — but had failed to come home the previous evening. The cousin had become worried after hearing a morning TV news report that the woman killed outside the High Court building remained unidentified. She had contacted the police — Jane Tamsin worked part-time for a firm which specialised in architectural heritage salvage from old buildings, and Paddy's Market was a place the woman visited regularly, scouting for finds among the junk on its stalls.

Jane Tamsin's body had been identified by her cousin at the City Mortuary at nine thirty that morning.

'And the two on the motor cycle?' queried Sandra Craig, taking one hand from the wheel so that she could bite at an apple. 'Anything more on them, sir?'

Thane shook his head. The machine had probably been a 600 cc Ducati, possibly stolen, and with phoney plates. A computer check with the national vehicle register at Swansea showed that its registration number belonged to a heavy goods vehicle in Yorkshire.

But the real reason he was on his way to the City Mortuary wasn't Jane Tamsin's death. It came down to the little microchip pendant she had been wearing.

The world now depended upon new technology for most things it did. New technology depended on microchips — semi-conductors — and needed them by the million from cheap and simple switch controls to tiny sophisticated miracles that could run factories or fight wars. There was money waiting around the world for any criminal able to supply advanced design semi-conductors. Computer chip theft had graduated to armed hold-ups and vicious hijacks, and the Scottish Crime Squad had recently been presented with it as a general operational target.

So far, it had been a long haul. They had notched a few reasonably spectacular results, mainly linked to other target investigations. Then had come Thane's notion of circulating an all-forces request for any crime report that even mentioned computers. And now, thanks to that notion, the Squad was being hemstitched into what had all the signs of being a simple four-by-two murder investigation.

There were easier ways to win friends!

Thane realised Sandra Craig had spoken and was waiting on an answer. He grimaced.

'Sorry. That didn't register. Say again.'

'Nothing important, sir.' The way she spoke meant it was. 'I asked if you'd heard about last night's Federation meeting — '

'No.' Thane's membership had ended abruptly with his last promotion. The Police Federation was closed to ranks of superintendent and above. Suddenly, he remembered. 'Election night, wasn't it?'

She nodded, took another bite of apple, and beamed. 'Unanimous vote. I'm the Squad's new delegate.'

'I hope you'll all be very happy,' said Thane sourly. The election had been caused by Francey Dunbar resigning. The Federation's official role was mainly consultative and they couldn't take any kind of industrial action. But throughout Dunbar's spell as delegate he had excelled at stirring trouble with a long spoon. Thane had an uneasy feeling that it might be the same with Sandra — she wouldn't remain idle. 'Any priorities, sergeant?'

'I've a few to consider, sir.' She said it demurely. 'Still, the earth won't catch fire — not straight away.'

'Warn me when it does,' said Thane resignedly. 'I've some leave due, so I can get far away.'

They left the urban stretch of the M8 at

28

Glasgow Cathedral interchange slip and made their way down from there past the historic medieval church with its twelfth-century crypt and thirteenth-century choir. That meant threading through the usual coaches loaded with tourists. But soon after that they drove in the cramped unloading yard at the red-brick rear of the City Mortuary, stopping next to a parked Eastern Division CID car. The car had two Eastern officers standing beside it.

Introductions were brief. Detective Chief Inspector Tom Radd was middle-aged, balding and lanky, with a Technicolor taste in neckties. His number two, a detective sergeant named Alex Paulson, was medium height, fat, moon-faced, and totally content to offer a handshake and stay quiet.

'Straight question, superintendent.' Radd didn't waste time on preliminaries. 'The way I heard it, you're taking over on this murder. Have I got that right?'

'Maybe yes, maybe no.' Thane saw a glint of suspicion in the balding man's watchful eyes. 'I'll nose around a little. We may have a shared interest, we may not. For now, we workshare whatever we get. Happy at that?'

Radd exchanged a glance with his moon-faced companion, then gave a nod. 'Reasonably, sir. There's not much to add to what you've got — no trace of the bike, no trace of either man.'

'A complete vanishing act,' said his fat sergeant lugubriously.

Thane nodded, looking around. From where he was standing, with his back to the mortuary building, he could see the sun glint on the stonework of the High Court and transform the jetting water of its fountain to bright silver. Beyond, on the western edge of the courthouse building, to judge by the number of people around, it seemed to be business as usual again at Paddy's Market.

'We had another try for witnesses over there,' said Radd, reading his visitor's mind. He scowled. 'It was three wise monkeys time with most of them. See no evil, speak no evil, hear no evil.'

'And they're good at it,' muttered his sergeant, then was silent again.

'Heavy caseload back at the ranch?' asked Thane sympathetically.

'Heavy enough.' The Eastern DCI nodded gloomily. 'We've a couple of good, old-fashioned family style stabbings. There's a new solo hold-up merchant trying for the *Guinness Book of Records*. And at the top of the tree we've a major touch of the Group Disorders . . .'

'Amen,' said Sandra Craig piously.

A long-retired Chief Constable had created

that particular label, had insisted it be used to describe gang fights. It remained ever since. Forget the numbers involved, forget the weapons they might be using, forget the injuries and the occasional deaths, they went into Glasgow's annual statistics as Group Disorders.

'How bad?' asked Thane.

'Two distinct gangs, fighting over territory with a drugs background. The home team are Shettleston-based, the outsiders are moving in from Balornock. So far, we've one dead, two critical, three in intensive care, ten arrests. The invasion team tried to use a home-made rocket launcher.'

'Education has its benefits,' said Thane mildly.

'Trouble is, we know our rocket scientist heads up his side and has his personal bodyguards. But that's as close as we've got — we haven't even a name. Just that he's threatening he'll be back. Still, to hell with it.' Radd dismissed the problem and reached into his jacket pocket. 'I think this is what you want, superintendent.'

He brought out a small, labelled glassine evidence envelope and passed it to Thane. Its contents were a thin gold chain and a small pendant. A crudely shaped metal mounting surrounded a tiny fingernail of

31

almost translucent material which glinted silver in the sunlight.

Silicon, cheap and commonplace as a mineral, became treasure-house in value when refined into the raw material of the computer world. But why use it as jewellery? Thane sucked his teeth for a moment, baffled. Then he shrugged to himself. The answer — if there was an answer that mattered — would have to wait.

He added his signature to the others already on the evidence label, keeping the provenance record unbroken, then tucked the envelope in his inside jacket pocket.

'Sir, everything we've got seems to say this started out as a mugging then went wrong,' said Radd cautiously. It paid to go carefully with strange superintendents, in particular a Scottish Crime Squad superintendent. 'You don't see it that way?'

'I haven't heard enough to see it any way,' admitted Thane drily. 'But it won't hurt to keep the options open for a little.'

Jane Tamsin's clothing had gone to Strathclyde's forensic department for a routine full examination. The Eastern Division men handed over a thin bundle of photocopied statements, including those already taken from the two High Court judges.

'Do you want us to wait on, superintendent?'

asked Radd. 'The mortuary team know to expect you — and I could use the time.'

Thane frowned. 'Who did the PM?'

'Doc Williams.'

'Then I won't need my hand held, and there's no need to wait.' Doc Williams was a senior police surgeon. He and Thane regularly worked together. 'I'll see him now — then cope with the judges.'

'Good.' Tom Radd looked relieved. 'I'll be back at Division if you need me. And thanks.'

He beckoned Paulson. The two Eastern men said goodbye, left and climbed into their car. As it drove away, Thane turned and Sandra Craig followed him into the mortuary building.

They were half-way along a spotlessly clean, brightly lit corridor when a wall hatch opened and the duty attendant stuck his head out and gave a gnome-like grin.

'Nice timing, Mr Thane,' he invited. 'I've put the kettle on.' His beam extended to Sandra Craig. 'Fancy a cuppa?'

'Sorry, Freddy. No time,' lied Thane. He knew how and where the grey-haired Freddy's cups were washed and how metal autopsy spatulas were used as spoons. 'Maybe later.'

'Look in anyway,' urged the attendant.

33

'I've a new joke for you, Mr Thane. You'll love it — that's a promise! Wait a moment.' His head withdrew, they heard him use an internal phone, then the handset tinged down and he reappeared. 'Doc says come on through. Second door on the right.'

They went along a corridor where the air had a hospital smell laced with something more. The second door was marked 'Private'. Opening it, they went through into a large room with white tiled walls and floor. In the middle, two autopsy tables with stainless steel tops and floor-level drains were surrounded by clustered equipment. One table, still stained from recent use, was being hosed down by a male attendant who wore overalls and rubber boots and who was humming a tune under his breath. He saw them, gave a friendly nod, and hosed on.

For a moment, there was no one else in sight. Then Doc Williams, immaculate, dark-haired and aged about fifty, emerged from behind a screen at the other end of the room. The police surgeon had been changing his green hospital style jacket for a clean one, and completed fastening buttons as he came over.

'You're looking well, Colin,' Williams told Thane cheerfully. 'Too healthy for my trade!' His grin switched to Sandra Craig. 'Can't

34

you get rid of him, sergeant?'

'I'm working on that, Doc,' she said solemnly.

'Keep at it.' Williams winked. Then he faced Thane again, his carefully cultivated humour giving way to cool professionalism. 'Jane Tamsin, the woman killed at Paddy's Market?'

Thane nodded.

'She's different, interesting.' The police surgeon raised a questioning eyebrow. 'Want to see her?'

'I'd better,' said Thane unemotionally.

'Donny, a moment, please.' Williams signalled. The mortuary attendant turned off his hose, laid it down, and wheeled a trolley forward. It bore a shape covered by a white cotton sheet.

'Thank you, Donny.' The police surgeon drew back the sheet in a surprisingly gentle way, uncovering the naked body of a woman. He laid his right forefinger on a round and livid puncture wound below her left breast. 'Cause of death, and very neatly done!'

Thane saw Sandra Craig's mouth tighten, heard her quick intake of breath. The redhead still had to learn to conquer her sense of outrage when faced with violent death. In a way, Thane hoped she never would. Face impassive, he took a step nearer the trolley

35

and looked down at Jane Tamsin's body. This woman, with her blue-black Spanish gypsy hair, her strong features, that slim build and muscular thighs, had been handsome in life. Which meant she would be hard to forget — and that might be a help.

'Scars or distinguishing marks?' asked Sandra Craig resolutely.

'She was mildly into body piercing,' offered the police surgeon. 'Navel — done a while back, a keeper ring in place — and there was a silver nose stud in her left nostril. No surgical scars or other marks.' He paused for a moment. 'For my official report, she was a well-nourished female in good health. She had good overall muscle tone and was sexually active. Stomach contents show she had a light breakfast maybe four hours before death — coffee, toast and orange juice. A moderate amount of alcohol had been consumed the previous evening.'

'How moderate?' demanded Thane.

'Balance blood alcohol content against normal burn-off rates and we're probably talking a few glasses of wine.' Doc Williams shook his head, forestalling the question. 'Enough for a mild hangover, Colin. Nothing more.' He paused again, this time showing his teeth in a humourless professional smile. 'Want to move on to how she died?'

'Yes.' Thane had kept a grip of his impatience. 'Please.'

'I'll show you.' Doc Williams led the way across the tiled floor to a viewing screen. He switched it on, then fed an X-ray negative into the holding slot. Its grey, back-lit image offered its secrets, and the police surgeon used a small glass rod like a pointer. 'Here we have the left side of her chest area — ' the glass rod moved ' — and the stab wound ran from here to here. Very narrow, very deep.'

He removed the X-ray negative and substituted another. The same grey outlines were there, but now crossed by a thin, straight line of hard black. 'That's how deep. Exactly 158 millimetres — we used a number six plastic knitting needle as a probe. The length of blade that penetrated would be less, of course. Probably about 140 mil. long — flesh compresses under impact. The blade went in under her ribs, penetrated the anterior wall of the heart, then kept on going.'

Sandra Craig moistened her lips. 'Some kind of stiletto?'

'A good guess, sergeant — and you're on the right kind of track,' murmured Doc Williams. 'This weapon was very narrow, fairly long and sharply pointed. Much stronger and thicker than a knitting needle — we used that only because one was available.' He was in a pleased, professional mood. 'Then to make absolutely sure of penetration depth our people carried out a full chest CAT-scan examination. That was before continuing with the remaining — ah — normal procedures.'

'Thorough, Doc. Like always.' Thane knew that a little praise went a long way with the dapper, dark-haired man. 'Can you make a guess at it?'

'Yes.' Williams almost purred. 'Probably a steel spoke from a motor-cycle wheel, one end sharpened to a fine point. The other end bound with electrician's tape or similar, as a handle.' He demonstrated with the glass rod and the palm of his hand, apologetically using Sandra Craig as a model. 'Your killer has the weapon concealed in the sleeve of his jacket. He lets it drop down into his cupped hand, like so, and — '

The redhead gave a startled gasp as the tip of the rod jabbed hard under her ribs.

'Sorry, sergeant. A necessary illustration,' murmured Williams. 'You'd still have a few seconds, maybe even more — but for practical purposes, you'd be already dead.'

'You've seen this before?' asked Thane.

'Heard about it.' The police surgeon switched off the viewing screen. 'It's a favourite South African township gang method in muggings — but they usually attack from the rear, and they use sharpened bicycle spokes. Any resistance from a victim, and there's a single jab into the spinal cord. The poor devil concerned lives but is paralysed for life.' He gave a careful frown. 'This wound is larger in diameter, so more likely a larger spoke from a motor-cycle wheel.'

With a motor cycle already a feature in the case, it wasn't too much of a leap into the dark. Thane accepted the premise. 'How much strength behind it?'

'Plenty, going in. But it could need even more to haul it out again. Suction, Colin.' Williams illustrated by making a loud sucking noise through his pursed lips. 'That's the reason a bayonet has a groove down both sides of the blade — one twist, it comes out clean from whoever you've stuck, and you're ready for your next customer!'

'Oh God,' said Sandra Craig softly.

It might be stomach-tightening, but it was true. Thane knew he could leave the rest for the official autopsy report, nodded to his sergeant that they could leave, and was set to follow when the police surgeon stopped him.

'Colin — ' Doc Williams spoke quietly and grimly — 'this is outside my area, and I know it. But nail this particular bastard.

The way this woman died was vicious and cold-blooded.' His mouth tightened. 'From the slick way it was done, I'll guarantee it wasn't his first killing. I wouldn't expect it to be his last.'

Thane nodded but said nothing, then he followed Sandra Craig out of the room. Behind them, Jane Tamsin's trolley had already been taken away and another of the city's current crop of sudden deaths was being pushed towards one of the stainless steel tables.

Outside in the corridor, heading towards the exit, they discovered they couldn't escape so easily. At the sound of their footsteps, the same window hatch opened again and the same grey-haired attendant beamed out.

'Still no time for a cup of anything?' he asked hopefully.

'Sorry, Freddy.' Thane shook his head.

'Another time, eh?' The man grinned. 'Well, here's that laugh I promised.' He paused for effect. 'Did you hear about the ugliest man in town?'

Thane gave a gentle smile. 'Whose mother only had morning sickness after he was born?'

They got past while Freddy was still scowling. It was a point of honour for police to know the mortuary attendant's latest joke.

It was two days since a Central Division sergeant had spent most of an off-duty hour telephoning round about 'the ugliest man in town.'

Outside, the sky overhead was unbroken blue and Thane and Sandra Craig walked across to the High Court building with the sun warm on their backs. A gardener was recovering two emptied beer cans someone had thrown into the water feature fountain beside the main door. Someone else had tried to erect a sales display for team supporters' shirts near the entrance pillars and a large constable who had ripped it down was looking around for the vanished culprit.

They went in through a large revolving door and across a marble entrance floor fit for any five-star hotel. The Courts Commissioners had gone for quality in the whole complex's construction. The marble was Golden Flower, quarried in India then polished in Italy before it came to Scotland. The cream stonework came from Yorkshire, the sunlight shone down from a high glass atrium roof. The traditional dark varnished woodwork which had featured in centuries of Scottish courts had been banished for pale Swiss pear veneer or light maple.

Thane still hadn't got used to the changes, still had a wild vision of a high-kicking

41

chorus line of dancing lawyerettes exploding down one of the stairways in a can-can style musical number. He saw his sergeant give him an odd look and sobered down as they went over to the reception desk, where a line of airport style information screens gave details of judges, trials and courts.

'We were told about you, superintendent,' said the duty receptionist, an attractive woman with a dark blue skirt and jacket uniform. 'Lord Lewis and Lord Kirk are both in court. You've to wait.'

'How long?' asked Thane resignedly.

'Until they're ready,' said the receptionist blandly. 'Until their courts rise for lunch.' She gave a fractional, women-against-the world smile towards Sandra Craig, in a way that made it clear that law lords could eat mere detective superintendents as a starter course. 'I'd back Lord Kirk. The word is he has a weak bladder.'

The airport screens showed Lord Kirk was in Court Three, the case was HM Advocate against a name Thane knew, a company director charged with attempting to murder his wife. A black-gowned court officer slipped them into the courtroom by a side door and they settled in two of the chairs kept for visiting professionals while a brief flicker of a glance from the robed figure on the bench showed that their arrival had been noted. Noted, and probably timed.

The court and its layout was a revelation on how much had been changed for a new century. There was a carpeted floor and individual, quietly patterned and upholstered chairs for everyone present, from press and jury to members of the public. Counsel sat around a table bristling with the microphones of a high fidelity recording system which had made a team of shorthand writers redundant. There were built-in TV screens, for showing video-recorded evidence from children and other vulnerable witnesses.

In the middle of it all, sitting between two white-gloved constables in the large, upholstered dock, the man on trial seemed to have both shrunk and aged.

They usually did. Colin Thane let the cross-examination of the latest witness wash over his head while he kept one eye on the creeping hands of the clock on one wall. Almost without realising it, he reached into his jacket pocket and touched the glassine envelope with its gold chain and that microchip pendant.

Thane believed in hunches. Only about an hour earlier he had viewed the death of Jane Tamsin as just another sad incident in a city which saw its full share. Now a tendril of

43

doubt was steadily growing — maybe still without any real foundation. Except that there was the way she had been killed — and there was Doc Williams's warning.

He pursed his lips. The usually unemotional police surgeon had called her killing 'vicious'. It was a word which more and more could be applied to computer crime as the demand for stolen high-grade chips kept increasing. Microchip crime had grown up.

Suddenly, the High Court proceedings were interrupted. Leaning forward, Lord Kirk halted everything.

'Can counsel advise me how much longer this witness's evidence will last?' he demanded frostily. He barely listened to a flustered advocate's reply. 'This seems a good time to break for lunch.'

His long horsehair wig flapping, heavy, ermine-trimmed red robes swishing, he headed out while the court was still rising. Jury and counsel followed while the prisoner was escorted back down the eighteen steps to the basement cells, the public area cleared.

Only Thane and Sandra Craig remained in an empty courtroom when at last the black-gowned court officer looked in and beckoned. They followed him out through the same side door then along a short corridor to where a keypad lock opened

a private door to a small elevator. They
went up in the elevator, which was also
keypad operated, and when it stopped and
opened they had entered strictly judicial-only
territory. All the walls were panelled in richly
polished wood and displayed a framed line-
up of oil and watercolour paintings. There
was thick wall-to-wall carpet underfoot, every
fitment around murmured quality.

'Nice,' mused Sandra Craig enviously.
'How do I get to be a judge?'

'Chance would be a fine thing, sergeant,'
murmured the court officer, a small, round-
faced man who had been a Regular Army
sergeant major with the medal ribbons to
prove it. He gave a sly wink. 'If I find out,
I'll be ahead of you!'

They reached one of a line of polished
maple wood doors in time to hear a toilet
flush somewhere behind it. Their guide
signalled a halt.

'Lord Kirk's robing room.' He waited a
few moments then tapped lightly on the
door and a raised voice on the other side
invited them to enter. The court officer
opened the door and waved them through,
but stayed outside and closed it again once
they were in.

'Superintendent Thane?' The man who
came to greet them was barely recognisable

as the same presence who had presided in Court Three. Out of his wig and robes, Lord Kirk was a small slight man with sharp, ferret-like features and sparse grey hair. He had removed his white cravat and had unfastened his shirt's stiff wing collar. His watery blue eyes switched to Sandra Craig, his voice surprisingly quiet. 'And — ah — Sergeant Craig, correct?'

'Thank you for seeing us, Lord Kirk.' Thane kept carefully to the formalities. 'I'll make this as short as I can.'

'We know why you're here, of course,' said the slightly built judge. 'The Lord Justice General will be along soon. He's finishing a rape case.' The watery blue eyes chilled. 'Peter Lewis doesn't like rapists. Neither do I — if the law allowed, I believe most should be impaled. On rough steel posts, preferably on exposed hilltops.'

Behind the judge, the robing room was fitted out like a small, snug study with deep armchairs, a telephone, and an occasional table. The velvet and ermine judicial robe had been thrown over one armchair. To one side, an inner door revealed a shower and toilet, a large wardrobe, and a shaving point beside a full-length mirror. A gleaming refrigerator stood on the far side of the wardrobe, with what looked like a newly poured glass of white wine on its top.

'We've already given statements, superintendent.' Lord Kirk crossed over and took a small sip of the wine, then laid the glass down again. 'What more do you want?'

'To be sure we understand everything.' Thane looked past him towards the room window. It was small, with a restricted view. 'When you saw the murder — '

'That wasn't from here.' Lord Kirk's ferret face showed approval. 'We were in the judicial library — that's next to our dining area. I'll show you.'

He led them back out into the maple wood panelled corridor, then through another door into a long and bright room which held a balanced blend of law books and computer facilities. Windows ran along most of one side, with the entire stretch of Paddy's Market clearly visible below. Down there, the trading stalls were still busy as ever.

'We were standing here,' said the little judge. 'Something all of us on circuit often do.'

Sandra Craig was puzzled. 'It's not much of a view, Lord Kirk — '

'It's a very good view, young woman,' said a new, deeper voice. Wig discarded but still wearing his robes, Lord Justice General Lewis joined them. 'In fact, it was our deliberate choice. We felt it would give us more of a view of the real world outside.' Tall, bald and heavy-faced, he stood beside Sandra and gave a wry frown towards the market. 'This time, it certainly did!'

'Finished your rape, Peter?' asked Lord Kirk.

'Suitably,' agreed Lord Lewis. 'Yours, John?'

His fellow judge shrugged. 'Trundling.'

Scotland's top law lord let his eyes linger on Sandra for a moment before he turned to Thane. He gave a slight nod. 'We've met before, superintendent.'

'In court, Lord Lewis.' The experience would have been hard to forget, although a few years had passed. 'I remember.'

'I thought you might.' Satisfied, the Lord Justice General nodded then glanced at his gold wrist-watch. 'Can we finish before our other colleagues arrive from their courts?'

Sandra Craig opened the Eastern Division file and Thane got to work, checking through the statements already given by the two law lords. There were some variations, particularly when it came to describing the two men on the motor cycle.

'I've learned a lesson, Thane.' The Lord Justice General scowled a near apology. 'The next time some fool of a witness claims he or she can't remember, I'll be more understanding.'

'Even if it's a fool of a police officer?' Thane couldn't resist the dig.

'*Mea culpa*.' The tall, bald judge grimaced. 'What's your view, superintendent?'

'I don't trust people with perfect memories,' said Thane drily. 'They usually lie.' He considered both judges again. 'So if there's anything you now remember, anything you want to add . . . '

The two men exchanged a frown. Then Lord Kirk's sharp ferret face wrinkled with embarrassment.

'There was a girl — a young girl. Not much more than school age. She was sitting on the ground, selling something — '

'Cotton towelling,' broke in Lord Lewis. He gave a snort of triumph. 'A single roll of it, spread out. She was in her teens and wearing blue jeans — I'd forgotten about her.'

'And that damned motor cyclist drove over the roll on the way out!' Bitterly, Lord Kirk snapped his fingers. 'Thane, she has to remember him!'

'We'll find her,' said Thane softly. He exchanged a glance with Sandra Craig. It mattered. It was the first time the girl in jeans had been mentioned by anyone. 'Thank you.'

They stayed by the window another couple of minutes, talking, looking down at the market. There was no sign of the girl and no other memories were wakened. Then it was time to leave. Both judges walked with them to the elevator.

'Sergeant — ' the Lord Justice General spoke mildly just as the gate was closing — 'remember me to your father. I haven't seen him for some time.'

Sandra Craig mustered a quick smile, then the gate closed and the elevator was moving down.

'He knows your father?' Thane stared at his sergeant. 'Do I get to ask why?'

'They were in the same class at school.' Sandra Craig flushed. 'Sometimes they go shooting together.'

'Shooting.' Thane swallowed and gave up. There was a lot he realised he didn't know about his sergeant. He left it there as the elevator reached the ground floor and they got out. 'We'll split, Sandra. You try a walk around Paddy's Market. See if anyone remembers this teenager with her roll of cotton towelling. I'll get a lift back to headquarters.'

They parted. Thane stopped to greet a lawyer he knew, then was on his way out of the building when the duty receptionist beckoned him over to her desk.

'A call for you, superintendent.' She offered her telephone. Tom Radd, the Eastern detective chief inspector, was on the other end of the line.

'Something I thought you'd want to know about,' said Radd unemotionally. 'The message was waiting on my desk when I got back. We've another link between Jane Tamsin and computers.'

'Like what?' Thane frowned at the receiver.

'She was an assembly worker with a computer firm until three months ago.' Radd paused. 'After her cousin identified the body this morning, one of my DCs gave the woman a lift home. She mentioned it then.'

Thane swore softly. 'Do we know which firm, or why she left?'

'No, and it's like a circus in here. But the moment I've someone free — '

'Leave it. We'll do it,' said Thane.

He hung up on the man's thanks.

2

A new swirl of activity swept around the High Court reception area as one case ended in Court Two and another was called up, production line style. The new name flickering on the electronic board should be worth several tabloid column inches — one of yesterday's football heroes was on a charge of attempted murder, with an indictment which included trying for a penalty goal using his wife's head as a football.

The Eastern Division telephone call had changed Colin Thane's priorities, but he had sent Sandra Craig on her way, and she had already vanished. Hopefully, he pushed a rapid path through the bustle of the sunlit atrium hallway, exited from the building by the main door, looked around, then sighed. There was no sign of his red-haired sergeant. If Sandra Craig had headed straight for Paddy's Market, then it had swallowed her up.

Women, Thane decided, always vanished when they were needed. Sandra Craig had the only car keys.

Still cursing under his breath, he directed

a scowl at a white Rover traffic patrol car which was drawing up outside the City Mortuary. The constable who emerged from the passenger seat and ambled into the stark brick building was carrying a large Despatches delivery run envelope. In a matter of seconds he was out of the building again, empty-handed. By then, Thane had recognised the traffic car driver as a former beatman he knew and had crossed over.

'What's the chance of giving me a lift over to Crime Squad headquarters?' he asked as the other constable got back aboard. He made an appeal to male understanding. 'I've a woman sergeant who has left me stranded.'

'Typical of them. Can't allow it, sir — anyway, there's no problem.' The driver grinned and beckoned Thane into the car's rear seat.

'Crime Squad have moved,' warned Thane, closing the door and settling back into the seat cushions.

'We heard,' said the constable riding shotgun. 'Only this morning, wasn't it?' He paused, watching the traffic as the police car began moving. 'How do you like the change, super?'

'Ever moved house?' asked Thane sadly. 'Believe me, this is worse — a lot worse. I ran for cover as soon as I could!'

The men grinned. Then the driver gave a quick snort and pointed as they drove past a red Ford coupé.

'Mine, Bob!' he declared triumphantly. 'That makes us square — seven all!'

'No way, Ernie.' His companion scowled. 'Game's ended.'

'Like since when?' demanded the driver indignantly.

'Like since we picked up the super,' said the other man flatly. 'I win, seven to six, straight and fair — you buy lunch again.'

'Having yourselves a car spotting day?' queried Thane mildly.

The patrol car twosome exchanged an embarrassed grin and didn't answer. But Thane knew he was right. There was a whole set of traffic cop games for when things became boring on a shift, each a game with its own set of rules. In one, players settled on a make and colour of car, then played what amounted to car spotting and scoring points as they travelled. A variation, for when business was really slack, also began with choosing a make and colour of car. Then the traffic car crew would follow any vehicle that matched their choice. Depending on the players' mood, the next stage could be a simple speed check — or waving down the driver and giving the vehicle a full going over. Provided, of course, it wasn't raining. No sane traffic cop wanted to get out of a nice, dry car and risk getting wet.

Most vehicles had some minor fault, enough to justify a frown and a warning. At very least the driver could be left feeling jangled for the rest of the day. Sometimes — just sometimes — it was genuinely worth while and a stolen car might be recovered or the driver was wanted on a warrant.

Car spotting, traffic style, could be useful!

'I'm buying,' surrendered Ernie as they weaved through another knot of traffic. Then he glanced back at Thane through the driving mirror. 'Super, heard any more about that Ducati from yesterday — the murder bike?'

'Not yet.' Thane shook his head.

'By now, the thing is in the river,' said Bob wisely. 'Bound to be.'

'Now there's a piece of real original thinking,' said his partner sarcastically. 'Thank you, Constable Sherlock MacHolmes!' He made an apologetic noise in Thane's direction. 'Uh — what's happening in the murder, super? Are your mob involved?'

'Involved, yes,' agreed Thane. It was a good word. 'More than that, not a lot . . . not yet.'

The traffic crew took the hint. They

switched to some vague noises about football team form, then were silent until they dropped their passenger outside the Crime Squad's new home. Thane waved his thanks as they drove off, then entered the steel-ringed compound by the security-monitored pedestrian gate and walked to the main building.

'Found your way back, sir!' The woman constable on reception desk duty straightened cheerfully as he came in. She was in her twenties, her thick chestnut hair razor cut short and straight. The style suited her. 'We're counting numbers going out, then coming in — just in case!'

'You're surviving?' asked Thane.

'Even enjoying it.' She smiled and gestured around. 'I think we're winning!'

Thane looked and blinked. She might be right. A scatter of cardboard boxes were still dumped haphazardly over most of the front office area with people continuing to move around them, recovering what they needed. Here and there an odd tradesman was still hammering and banging at things. But the previous chaos seemed to have ended.

Thane glanced at his watch. He'd been gone barely four hours, but the new headquarters was gradually coming together. He could even see a couple of civilian staff already working at their desks, oblivious to what was still going on around them. The fan of security monitor screens above the reception counter was fully operational. A telephone rang and he heard the call answered. Fax machines buzzed and a computer printer was purring.

'Maybe I should stay away more often,' he told the policewoman. 'What happened?'

'Maggie Fyffe got fed up and took over.' Her dark eyes twinkled. 'Girl Power, sir. Maggie says women are better at organising things.'

'I'll bet she does,' said Thane resignedly.

He left her and climbed the stairway up to the upper floor, where the air was still laced with the smell of wet paint. At the top, he avoided an electrician who backed out of a cupboard nursing a power drill. Jack Hart's office was empty. There was no sign of the Squad commander or his secretary anywhere around, and Thane went on past a line of other offices where there was still no sign of anyone in residence.

But when he reached his own office he was surprised. Someone had emptied some of his cardboard boxes, had placed a bright new in-tray centrally on his desk, and had already left some reports for processing. It was clue enough. Colin Thane knew only one Scottish Crime Squad member who felt equally at home with paperwork or an alley-cat style street brawl. Scrawny, plagued by a recurring peptic ulcer which generated an awe-inspiring and thunderous belch, acid-tongued to match, usually needing a shave and a change of shirt, Detective Inspector Phil Moss was both unique and beyond value.

Thane grinned to himself, returned to the corridor and went along to Moss's new office. Moss wasn't there, but he gaped when he went in. Everything in the room was unpacked and in place, from files to wall charts. There was a solid mahogany desk, a piece of furniture which certainly wasn't from any police budget and could only have been diverted from some city politician's office. It came close to Squad commander size. And how the hell had the same lowly, scruffy DI obtained a TV set with satellite and video boxes?

'Your little friend Moss is quirky,' mused a familiar voice. 'But he knows how to organise.'

'Maybe we could hire him out,' suggested Thane, turning.

'Suppose we offered Air Miles?' The woman standing behind him in the doorway gave an amused, throaty chuckle. Tina

58

Redder was a detective chief inspector in her late thirties. Dark-haired, cream lace shirt-blouse tucked into a less than knee-length velvet skirt, DCI Redder was no pin-up. But she did have the best-looking legs in the Squad — and knew it. She was currently heading an operation closing in on a forger who was making better Swiss francs than the Swiss could produce — and making them in between shifts in a South of Scotland weekly newspaper office. Half her team would have died for her, the other half would cheerfully have cut her throat. She probably knew that too.

'Where is he anyway?' asked Thane.

'Moss? He had to go galloping back to our old place.' Tina Redder slouched against the doorpost in a careless way that emphasised the potential delights under her cream blouse. 'There was some kind of panic call from Francey Dunbar.'

'About what?'

'No idea. He just stuck his head in, told me he had to go, then vanished in a puff of smoke.' She considered Thane again, a faintly malicious glint in her hazel eyes. 'And what's happened to your baby sergeant? Lost her again?'

'She's doing a job for me.' Thane ignored the bait. Tina Redder didn't totally like the younger Sandra, and it was mutual. His red-haired sergeant habitually referred to Tina as the Broomstick Lady. 'I left her at Paddy's Market.'

'Maybe someone will take her in part-exchange.' Tina Redder dismissed the thought. 'What happened here is that Jack Hart led an exodus to get something to eat — the canteen isn't working yet.' She shrugged. 'I couldn't leave — I'm waiting on a phone call from Zurich, so I settled for an apple. But our beloved commander said I was to tell you that everything has been ironed out — official — with Strathclyde's ACC (Crime). The media won't be told, but we now call the shots on the Jane Tamsin murder. Strathclyde's troops will assist as required.'

Thane nodded, relieved. Whatever spin might eventually be put on the final credits was incidental.

'Another item. Your wife phoned.' Tina Redder grinned wickedly. 'Seems you were supposed to buy her lunch.' She saw Thane's expression. 'Don't tell me you'd forgotten?' Her grin widened. 'Anyway, you're lucky this time. She said something had turned up at work, so she couldn't make it. I said what a pity, and that I'd pass on the message. You owe me.'

'I owe you,' admitted Thane wryly. Some days, he felt he owed everybody. He had been due to meet Mary for lunch after her morning stint as part-time practice manager at a local health clinic, a lunch meeting they did now and again. But the thought had been knocked out of his head by the rest that was happening. 'Thanks.'

'Part of the service.' Tina Redder eased off the doorpost, moved as if to leave, then paused. 'I think a couple of your people set up camp in the main duty room. If there's anything more, they'll have it.' A slight frown creased her forehead. 'Any hint of a motive for the Tamsin murder?'

'No.' Slowly, Thane shook his head. 'Except that however the killing was dressed up, it was deliberate — more than a case of a mugging that went wrong.'

'Then you're not on the trail of some killer computer?'

'Not yet.' He stayed patient. 'Tina, are you trying to tell me that people think I'm becoming obsessive?'

'No. But don't say I didn't warn you.' She stopped there as a telephone rang somewhere near. Her teeth showed in a quick grin. 'That's my call! Into battle!'

Thane saw another eye-catching display of legs as the Broomstick Lady left. In another moment, he heard her take the call. Left alone, he stood for another couple of moments in the silence of Phil Moss's small office, chewing lightly on his lower lip, frowning.

No, he had no kind of obsession about computer-related crime. What he did have was a perfectly healthy and strengthening hunch. When stolen computer software had first surfaced in the crime pool, that had been a high-tech curiosity. But for more than a handful of years Criminal Intelligence units everywhere had reported steady growth of a crime now running into millions annually.

A new kind of crime usually meant acquiring a new kind of expertise. Anyone could buy expertise when the price was right, like most things could be bought provided scruples didn't cloud the deal. But hell, no, he wasn't obsessive.

At least, he didn't think so!

Thane grimaced to himself, left the rest of the thought there, headed for the duty room, opened the door, and went in. It was a large and bright room, with long windows overlooking the central courtyard, and like everywhere else it smelled of drying paint. From new computer screens and touch-tone telephones, to unscarred desks and unsagged chairs, it looked unreal — unused.

A microwave oven still in its wrappings sat next to a half-unpacked photocopier under an empty noticeboard. For the moment, the duty room's only occupants were two detective constables, both in their shirt-sleeves, neckties loosened, reading newspapers near one of the windows. One of them saw him, nudged his companion, and they both grinned a greeting.

'Lunch break, boss.' The older of the two, a thickset man with cropped hair, set down the newspaper he'd been reading. Detective Constable Ernie Vass had joined the Squad from Aberdeen CID. Before that, he had been moved out of Grampian's traffic department for denting too many police cars. 'All quiet for now.'

'Fancy joining us, sir?' asked his tall, slim companion, who had boyish features and fair, curly hair. Detective Constable Dougie Lennox had come from an Edinburgh CID murder team with a reputation for smooth-talking any consenting female who crossed his path. He gave a lopsided smile. 'The menu choice is soup, soup, or soup.'

'If you can spare it.' Thane saw the small bottled gas camping stove hissing at their feet, a metal cook pot balanced over the blue flame of its burner. The spicy smell of tomato soup caught at his nostrils and he realised how hungry he was.

Hot soup was poured in a large mug like the ones being used by his two DCs. His carried the large-lettered advice 'Be Safe at Night — Go to Bed With a Cop'. Thane took a first, mouth-scalding sip and nodded his thanks. 'Who brought in the stove?'

'Ernie. He used to be a Boy Scout — like in Be Prepared,' explained Lennox, then he grinned. 'Except he forgot to bring the napkin rings.'

Thane grunted. 'Heard anything from Sandra?'

The two exchanged a glance, then shook their heads.

'Or Moss?'

'Yes.' Ernie Vass produced a small, black Dutch cheroot and lit it with a kitchen match struck on the rim of his signet ring. 'He phoned, boss. Something turned up, and he's handling it along with Francey — uh — Inspector Dunbar.'

'Something turned up like what?' demanded Thane.

'No idea, sir.' Vass shook his head.

A vehicle drove noisily into the courtyard. Going over to the window and looking down, Dougie Lennox brightened. 'But we've someone back.'

'Nice timing,' muttered Ernie Vass under his breath.

Nursing his soup, Thane crossed over. Down below, a battered, rusty Land-Rover van had backed into a parking space. As its engine switched off and a lanky man in overalls climbed out, they could hear a dog barking. He looked up, saw them, and nodded a greeting. Jock Dawson, the Squad's dog handler, had first arrived on a temporary transfer then had become part of the Crime Squad scenery.

'Leave him,' said Thane. He took another look, noticed that his own car was no longer blocked in, then gestured Vass and Lennox back to their desk. 'Tell me how things stand here.'

In a very short time, the two men had checked and double checked their way through most things gathered about the murder of Jane Tamsin. Thane couldn't fault what they'd done, as far as it went — which ran from the continued hunt for the Ducati motor cycle to running a complete records check for any known muggers who worked in pairs and had used extreme violence.

'What we've got so far doesn't win prizes.' Thane drained the last of his soup, set down the mug, and wiped his lips with the back of a hand. 'So let's go back to basics.

What's always the first rule in a murder investigation?'

'Uh — if she's married, take a good look at the husband?' Dougie Lennox's deceptively youthful face creased in a frown. 'Or the boyfriend, if there is one?'

'And if not, why not,' suggested Vass, his voice carefully neutral.

'Three words,' reminded Thane grimly. 'Who? What? Why? Who is she, from what kind of background, and why was she killed — if it wasn't a mugging.'

Ernie Vass darted a sideways glance at Lennox. 'You think that way, sir?'

'I'm going to give it a try.' Thane considered Lennox. 'Talk with the two uniformed cops who were outside the High Court. Go over their story and their descriptions. Ask if they noticed a teenage girl wearing blue jeans hanging around at the time or if there's anything else they can add. Ask around for motor-cycle outlets that sell red crash helmets with bands of white. Jock Dawson can help you.'

'We'd settle for his dogs,' suggested Ernie Vass. 'At least they're intelligent.'

Thane ignored the interruption. 'And a priority on your list — or pass it on to Sergeant Craig when she arrives. I want to know more about this 'architectural heritage' outfit that employed Jane Tamsin, what she did, how it tied in with her spending a morning wandering around Paddy's Market. Understand?' As Lennox nodded, he switched his attention to Vass. 'Ernie, you're with me. Have we a name and address for the cousin who identified her?'

'Russo.' Vass made a quick flick through the fax sheets in front of him and found the one he wanted. 'Russo — Mrs Mary Russo, early thirties, a widow, one child. She's a schoolteacher, lives in East Kilbride.'

Thane sucked his lips. He should almost have expected it.

East Kilbride, a post-World War Two town built on a greenfield location, was only about ten miles out from Glasgow. It was a high-tech magnet for new technology — including the computer industry. He'd seen statistics which claimed over forty per cent of all brand-name personal computers built in Europe were made in Scotland, and a great chunk of that forty per cent could be labelled 'Made in East Kilbride'.

'That's where we're going,' he told Vass. 'My car, I'll drive.' He thumbed at the man's smouldering cheroot. 'And that doesn't come with us. Not health, for hygiene. Right?'

Ernie Vass sighed, but nodded.

The route from the city south towards East Kilbride was busy, already picking up the afternoon's home-bound shopping and school run traffic to add to its usual mix of business and commercials. But the day was staying bright, sunlight gleaming from the windows of the new town's housing blocks all around as the black Ford Mondeo passed through. Thane had twisted a few arms to win the Ford from the Squad transport pool, and it had been worth it just to hear the smooth two-litre purr of the sixteen-valve power unit. In the passenger seat, Ernie Vass sat with his eyes closed, a town map on his lap, and pretended to be asleep. It was his usual protection when other people were driving.

The address was at Lamanda Quadrant, in the new town's Murray area. Travelling anywhere in East Kilbride meant roundabouts — through four of them to reach Lamanda Quadrant, travelling along a feeder road from the main town centre then following the map in a right turn past a small line of shops.

'Damn,' said Thane as they took the right turn. He nudged Vass hard in the ribs. 'Trouble.'

Lamanda Quadrant was a curve of cream-coloured eight-storey housing blocks, the high amenity kind where tenants paid high rents, expected elevators to work, and might even turn out for church on Sundays. They wouldn't approve of what they had at that moment — the small car burning furiously outside one block, a fire engine and a police patrol car already in attendance.

'This I could do without,' cursed Ernie Vass as the Ford drew in. He got out first, used his warrant card to flag at an overweight sergeant who came bustling over, spoke briefly to the fire crew who were using foam extinguishers on the vehicle, then grimaced as Thane joined him. 'Torched. Like to guess whose car this is, sir?'

'Mary Russo's,' said Thane resignedly. He looked at the housing block. 'Where does she live?'

'Up there.' Vass thumbed skyward. 'Top floor.' He brightened. 'But the elevator works.'

Among cops, that was always something worth celebrating. Thane nodded and led the way towards the block's entrance. On the way, they went close to the burning car, a middle-sized Peugeot which still showed traces of scorched and blistered green paint. They also passed the fat sergeant, who was muttering into his personal radio. Thane stayed expressionless but knew that jungle drums were busy.

A handful of residents were standing around the entrance door but said nothing, their expressions neutral, obviously not welcoming this small invasion. Inside, the entrance hall was carpeted, there were small tubs of flowering plants, and a tall, bird-like woman was just coming out of the elevator. She frowned at them and quickly walked past.

'It's like we just stood on dog poop,' complained Ernie Vass as he followed Thane into the elevator. 'Don't they know we're the good guys?'

'We're an intrusion,' said Thane stonily. 'Be glad they don't have a servants' entrance — we'd be told to use it.'

The elevator was spotless and smelled of pinewood air freshener. When he pressed the button for the eighth floor, the door closed with gentle sigh. They rose swiftly, and on the way up, Thane quickly reminded himself of what little had been reported about Jane Tamsin's widowed cousin. Mary Russo's husband, a North Sea oil rig worker, had been killed in a drilling accident six years back. A teacher before she married, she had returned to work as soon as her only child, a daughter, was old enough to attend school. That he could easily understand. Teaching school was a good way to earn a living for a widow with a school-age child. Mother and child more or less shared the same school hours and the same holiday times. It still wouldn't be easy, but there were worse situations.

When the elevator door opened at the eighth floor, there was more carpet and a couple of potted plants. There was also an opened apartment door to the left, with a young constable posted outside. The constable stiffened, stuck his head inside the apartment, spoke, and as Thane reached the door a woman police inspector emerged to meet him. She was in her late forties, with neat greying hair, and her tunic had a blue and white police long service ribbon above one pocket.

'Inspector Shaw, superintendent. Shift inspector with the local sub-division.' Her manner was friendly. 'My shift bought the fire call. How did you know about it, sir?'

'I didn't,' admitted Thane. 'Call it bad timing. I came out to talk with Mary Russo about her cousin.'

'The murder. We know about it.' The woman officer nodded her understanding.

'Give me a minute and I'll tell her you're here.'

She went back inside. Thane waited, conscious that he and Vass were being scrutinised by the constable, hearing a murmur of voices in the apartment.

Inspector Shaw returned, beckoned, and the two Crime Squad men followed her in through a modest hallway where a long table displayed a small array of brasswork and pewter animals. At the end of the hallway they passed a glass door and entered a living-room which was comfortably furnished around a dark leather suite of armchairs, a couch and a large walnut TV cabinet. It was carpeted in a rich green Axminster. A woman who had been on the couch rose as they came over. She was in her thirties, plump and medium height, dressed in tailored grey trousers and a washed-in yellow wool sweater which was tight for her build.

'Mrs Russo — Detective Superintendent Thane.' The grey-haired woman officer completed the introductions, then gave Mary Russo a beam of reassurance. 'I'll go and check that Andy is happy.' She glanced at Thane to explain. 'Andy — Andrea — is Mrs Russo's daughter, superintendent. I asked a neighbour to look after her.'

Thane considered Mary Russo as the

policewoman left. Jane Tamsin's cousin had a similar head of jet black hair, but tied neatly back by a narrow white velvet ribbon. Her face was thin, sharing features from the same gene pool as her cousin, and her only make-up was a touch of coral pink lipstick. The eyes which met his own were both bitter and suspicious.

'This can't be easy for you — or for your daughter,' he said quietly.

'I'll survive, and she'll get over it.' Mary Russo gave a shrug. 'Being nine years old is too young to really understand what's been happening.'

'But she knows about your cousin?'

'That she's dead, yes.' Mary Russo nodded. 'Thank God I could get her off to school this morning before I went to see Jane's body.' From her voice, she was struggling to keep control. 'But why are you here, superintendent? Haven't I answered enough questions — or are you going to go over the same things again?'

'Your cousin was murdered, Mrs Russo. Now your car is set on fire outside your home.' Grimly, Thane held her gaze. 'So — yes, I'm sorry. But I've a job to do, to find the people who killed her. The more time that passes, the harder that can get. And the sooner we talk — '

'The sooner you'll catch them, the sooner this will be over, I know.' Mary Russo looked down at the carpet, breaking his eye contact, then stayed silent while she seemed to compose herself again. Then her head came up, she straightened her shoulders, and she gestured towards the armchairs that matched the couch. 'You'd better sit down.' She managed a small smile. 'Both of you. You make the place look untidy.'

Thane and Ernie Vass settled in the armchairs. Vass, producing his notebook but not opening it, slid a hand unobtrusively into his jacket to switch on the small totally illegal tape recorder he always used as back-up.

'Straight question, Mrs Russo,' said Thane without warning. 'Why do you think your car was set on fire?'

'That's what I want the police to tell me,' she said with anger. 'Isn't that supposed to be your job?'

'It is — sometimes we're even reasonably good at it,' said Thane wryly.

'I'm glad.' The chill in Mary Russo's voice grew. 'Inspector Shaw asked that same question. The answer hasn't changed. I don't damned well know. Can you write that down so you don't forget?'

'I won't. That's a promise.' He tried to soothe her down with the feeling that the raven-haired teacher would have the capacity to make life hell for any pupil who crossed her. 'But I need to hear your story again. Mostly about this afternoon.'

'If it helps.' She took a long, weary breath. 'I didn't have to drive in to the mortuary. A police car took me in from here then brought me home again around midday. Andy gets her lunch at school, so I took the afternoon off and just sat around, doing nothing, until it was time to bring her home. I drove to the school — it's also where I teach. So I checked in at the principal's office and told them what was happening. Then I collected Andy at around three thirty, her usual time, and we drove home.'

'Straight home, Mrs Russo?' queried Ernie Vass.

'We stopped at a supermarket.' The woman shrugged. 'I bought a few groceries, then we got home at around four. I parked the car outside the block as usual.'

She told the rest with a brief, impatient precision. Her daughter had wanted to watch TV, she had decided to make herself a pot of tea. But they were still settling when Mary Russo heard a loud revving of motor-cycle engines from street level. The revving died back to a murmur, then there was the sound of breaking glass. Andy had been first to look out, shouted, then her mother came over.

Mary Russo's three-year-old Peugeot, its windscreen smashed, was already on fire and well alight. Two bikers in black leathers sat on their machines beside it. One looked up, saw Mary Russo and her daughter at their eighth-floor window, and waved derisively — then the engines revved again and they left in a squeal of rubber and a scatter of gravel.

Within seconds, they were gone from sight.

'When I telephoned the fire service and police, they already knew.' Mary Russo grimaced. 'We've a nosy bat who lives alone on the ground floor, old Helga Reed. She called them. It would make her day. A whole lot of her damned days!'

Thane's expression stayed neutral. In the police scale of things, a nosy neighbour was usually a good neighbour — except he didn't think Mary Russo was in the mood to be fed crime prevention propaganda. He caught Ernie Vass's eye, thumbed towards the door, and the burly detective constable rose and left. Helga Reed was going to have another new experience to add to her stock of stories.

'These motor cyclists. Could you identify them?'

76

'From up here?' She shook her head. 'No chance — and they were wearing crash helmets.'

'What colour of crash helmets?'

The woman thought and frowned. 'Probably red.'

'Anything else about them?' It was vital he didn't prompt her.

'About the crash helmets, you mean?' Mary Russo paused again, then gave a slow, understanding nod. 'Yes. I think there was some kind of band around the tops — maybe two bands. Both white.' The woman looked at him earnestly. 'But still why, superintendent? Why me? I haven't any enemies I know about — damn it, even the kids I teach probably like me. I don't owe money, I haven't been threatened.'

'I believe you, Mrs Russo.' Thane waited in silence, giving the woman the time she needed to arrive at the inevitable alternative.

'No, not me.' A slow horrified under-standing dawned in her eyes. 'You mean you're thinking of Jane — the way she was killed, the way her killer escaped. On a motor cycle. That there could be a link?'

Thane nodded.

'But — ' she swallowed — 'the police at the mortuary said Jane was killed in a bagsnatch that went wrong.'

'Maybe yes, maybe no. We're not certain of anything. Not yet.' Thane treated her gently. 'Your car being torched — well, that's an old terrorist tactic, Mrs Russo. Like you're being handed a warning . . . '

She took a sharp intake of breath. 'To keep my mouth shut? About what?'

'My guess would be that they're fairly certain you don't know anything that matters. But if they're wrong or if there's something you might remember later . . . '

'Then I should forget it again?' She considered the prospect slowly and soberly. 'I know. You'd say the police could protect me. But for how long? Isn't that the real question — how long? I've a nine-year-old daughter, superintendent. I think that gives me a special right to know.'

'If it happened, we'd do our best. Count on that.' Thane left it there, knowing she was asking a question he couldn't answer, refusing to lie to the woman, concentrating on keeping her talking. 'Can you tell me anything about the bikes they were riding?'

'No.' She shook her head. 'Two wheels has never been my scene — even when I was a teenager. Four wheels and a radio or I didn't want to know.'

Thane rose, walked over to the window, rested his hands on a white plastic sill where

78

two large red Venetian glass vases were filled with dried flowers, and looked down. He could see the fire-blackened remains of the Peugeot in the parking area, shrunk by distance to the size of a burned-out toy. The blaze had been extinguished, only a single thin, greasy tendril of smoke still rose from the car's interior. The fire crew had begun rolling up their hose jets and stowing away their equipment. A tow truck had arrived and was waiting in the background. Excitement over, the audience of neighbours and locals were fading, leaving only some children and a couple of dogs.

The bottom line was simple enough. A torched car was no big deal. There were plenty of areas where it happened every other day of the week.

'You'll get a copy of the police crime report. That will save any hassle with your insurance company.' Thane came back from the window to where Mary Russo waited in silence, her fists now resting lightly on her lap. He sat opposite her again. 'Tell me about your cousin Jane. Begin — well, when she came to live with you and why.'

Once she'd started, Mary Russo answered his questions unemotionally and factually, as if she was suddenly glad to talk about the dead woman. It was something that often happened, as if releasing memories could act like a safety valve for pent-up emotion.

Jane Tamsin had come to East Kilbride almost a year back, moving over from the east coast on the strength of a new job. She had come to stay with her widowed cousin, her only living blood relation, and had rented a room from Mary Russo in the Lamanda Quadrant apartment. They had got on well together, and there had been few problems.

'This job that brought her through to East Kilbride from the east — ' Thane fished carefully — 'have I got it right? Something in computers?'

'Yes.' The woman nodded. 'Jane was on the microchip production line at the Sonnet-Bytes plant — and she was lucky. Sonnet-Bytes isn't large, but they offered one of the best work conditions packages in the town, and they paid well.' One hand moved from her lap, and she ran a fingertip along a seam on the leather couch. 'That was until about four months ago when they lost some big order and she was made redundant.'

'It happens.' But not too often in the microchip world. That much he did know. So had it really been that way? He hid the thought behind a sympathetic nod. 'That would hit you too. If she had been paying you rent . . . '

80

'She had money saved. I told her I could wait, but she didn't miss a week.'

Very carefully, Colin Thane moved on again. 'When Jane died, she was wearing a gold neckchain with a microchip pendant. The pendant looked . . . '

'Home-made?' Mary Russo twisted one of her slight, tight smiles then brushed a loose lock of jet black hair back from her forehead. 'It was. Jane got it as a present from the one man in her life who had really mattered.'

'Do you know his name?'

'Peter somebody.' She shook her head. 'I wasn't told his second name. I think they met when she worked in Edinburgh, but I'm not even sure of that. Or why it ended.' She saw Thane's question coming. 'I never met any of the men Jane dated. She kept her private life exactly that, superintendent — private. Dealing with someone her age, I reckoned it was none of my business if she didn't always sleep in her own bed. We were two adult women under the same roof, we respected each other's privacy — that's why we didn't fall out. But I knew that Peter had been special, very special.'

'Did you get to know any of the people she worked beside at Sonnet-Bytes?'

'One or two — casually, nothing more. I haven't seen any since she was made

81

redundant.' She shifted her feet and smiled at a memory. 'Soon after Jane started there, the plant had a tea-and-buns open day. I was invited along with Andy — first time, only time. We even met Abigail Carson, the woman who is managing director. She's big and blonde and American, and she took quite a shine to Andy — '

'Andy.' Thane stopped her there. 'How much have you told her?'

'So far?' Mary Russo took a breath and let it out as a sigh. 'Just that Aunt Jane is dead, and that it was in some kind of an accident, while she was at work. I know I can't leave the truth too long, in case she finds out from someone else.' She shook her head. 'I'm a teacher. I should know how to handle this kind of thing, but I can't — not yet.'

'It's never easy.' Thane eased her on again. 'Did you know of any new man coming into Jane's life?'

'No.' Mary Russo shook her head.

'Why should she have been wearing that computer chip pendant?'

'Why not?' The woman's patience frayed at the edges. 'I told you, she liked it. Peter had given it to her. Did she need a reason?'

'No, she didn't.' He backtracked quickly. 'But she got a new job.' He paused, puzzled, certain he'd heard a movement behind him, then went on. 'Tell me about it.'

'Why should she tell you anything? And who the hell are you anyway?' suddenly demanded a new rasping voice from immediately behind him. 'Mary, don't worry. If he's some damned reporter, I'll throw him out on his ear!'

Thane turned. The tall, thin man behind him was in his late forties, with a beak nose and small eyes, his bald head sporting only a thin tonsure of short grey hair. His slate blue business suit was teamed with a white shirt and a patterned tie, he had brown pigskin shoes, but the main thing that registered was an aggressive scowl. 'Did you hear me?' The man took a step nearer. 'Get up out of that bloody chair!'

'It's all right, Ken,' declared Mary Russo urgently. 'He's — '

'Police.' Thane finished it for her. 'Detective Superintendent Thane. Scottish Crime Squad.' Without rising, he showed his warrant card.

'I . . . ' The man reddened, his aggression fading. 'I thought . . . '

'Forget it,' said Thane drily. 'My turn.' He glanced at Mary Russo. 'Do you know this man?'

'He's a . . . a close friend, Kenneth Hodge.' She moistened her lips with the tip of her tongue and looked anxiously at the man. 'It's all right, Ken. Really.'

'So let's start again,' suggested Thane. 'Like I say hello, Ken — and how did you get in here?'

'The door was open, wasn't it?' Hodge was defensive. 'I walked in.'

'Give me a moment.' Frowning, getting up from his seat, Thane went out of the room and walked through the hall. The apartment door still lay open, but there was no sign of the uniformed man, and it was the same when he looked out along the eighth-floor landing. But another apartment door was open further along, and when he went nearer, he heard a male laugh then a woman's voice.

Thane swore softly and took a deep breath.

'Constable!' He made it a bellow. 'Out here! Now!'

A noise like a muffled yelp came from inside the apartment. The young uniformed man appeared like a rocket, colour draining from his face, wiping damp coffee away from his lips, one hand still clutching a slab of cake.

'Sir — I — ' The constable glanced over his shoulder in despair as the door behind him clicked firmly shut. 'The woman in there — I — she invited — '

'Leave your post like that again, and I'll have you skinned,' said Thane bleakly, then tried hard to stay grim-faced. The boy in front of him looked as if he should have still been at school — and the nervous way he clutched the cake meant it had collapsed into crumbs. 'Once you're skinned, I'll personally nail your hide to the nearest wall. Understand?'

'Sir.' The youngster nodded unhappily.

'We've a visitor. He arrived while you were gone.' Thane gave the fact a moment to penetrate. 'Your job was to prevent that. Maybe win a medal. If necessary, posthumously. Understand?'

'Sir.' The constable swallowed. 'But . . . '

'But what?' rasped Thane.

'The woman in there, Mrs Cowan — ' the young face twitched earnestly — 'we were talking.'

'There's a surprise,' said Thane sarcastically.

'Superintendent, she says she has seen a biker hanging around Lamanda Quadrant late at night. She saw him pick up Jane Tamsin a couple of times. One night, he brought her home.'

Thane sucked on his teeth. Somehow, he didn't feel totally surprised. 'Can she describe him?'

'No, sir.' The constable suddenly became

aware of the crumbled cake still clutched in his hand. He hesitated, then got rid of it into a pocket. 'Same with the bike, sir. I asked.'

'Tell your inspector, no one else.' Thane gave a slow, approving nod. 'You needn't dwell too much on — uh — the background details.'

He saw relief on the youngster's face, left him, and went back into Mary Russo's apartment. She was still sitting on the couch, but Kenneth Hodge was now protectively close beside her. They'd been in the middle of a low-voiced conversation, one that ceased abruptly as he entered. Awkwardly, Hodge cleared his throat.

'Superintendent, about the way we met,' he said uneasily. 'I was away out of line. But I'd only just heard about Mary's cousin being killed — '

'How did you hear?'

'It was on a news broadcast.' Hodge went on without a pause. 'I came straight here from my office, then I saw Mary's car was burned out.' He showed his teeth in a scowl. One front tooth was chipped and blackened. 'I felt sick. Mary matters to me. In her own way, so did Jane.'

Now eager to be friendly, Hodge talked with little need for prompting. An architect with a small but prospering private practice, he had an office in East Kilbride town centre's Plaza Block and his work mainly involved hotel and ship interior designs. Divorced and English, he'd first met Mary Russo when she'd been at a party with Jane. After that, they'd been going around together for most of the past year.

'But with no ties involved,' emphasised Mary Russo. She gave a quick smile in a way that made her years younger. 'That's agreed.'

Hodge nodded. 'When I — ah — arrived, you were asking about her cousin Jane's new job. I can tell you.'

Mary Russo nodded. 'Ken fixed it.'

'I regularly order architectural salvage materials from Empire Lines in Paisley.' Hodge stroked a hand self-importantly over his bald pate. 'Michael Spring, their boss, owes me a few favours and he knows it.'

So Hodge had told Spring that he knew a reliable woman who had been made redundant. And Empire Lines had a vacancy for someone needed to scout for salvaged materials. Jane Tamsin went for an interview the next day and got the job.

'Paisley?' Thane raised a questioning eyebrow. East Kilbride to Paisley meant clocking a few miles.

'Sometimes she could get a lift across, and there's a reasonable bus service,' reminded Mary Russo. 'She talked of buying a car when she had the money.'

'Wouldn't she have been happier working with another computer firm?'

'Hell, that kind of job doesn't grow on trees.' Kenneth Hodge answered him curtly, quickly — almost too quickly. 'There were no vacancies.'

'So she couldn't get what she wanted?' Thane watched Mary Russo.

'Jane kept trying, everywhere she could. It was a waste of time.' The woman avoided Thane's eyes. 'Anyway, she got to like the Empire Lines job.'

Thane stayed silent, aware of a sudden strand of tension in the air, suddenly certain that both the man and woman facing him were lying, frustratingly unable to guess why. It would have to wait. He glanced at his watch, then at Hodge.

'I'll talk with your friend Spring, Mr Hodge. One of my people may want a statement from you later. But that's it for now.' He paused, giving a small smile which covered them both. 'Except I could use another minute with you, Mrs Russo. Alone might be easier.'

Hodge frowned, took a deep breath in a way that made his eagle beak flare, seemed ready to speak, then changed his mind. He gave Mary Russo's arm a reassuring squeeze, then rose and left. Deliberately, Thane waited until he heard the man go out past the constable at the front door.

'Formalities, Mrs Russo.' Again he used his smile on the widow. 'I need to see Jane's room.'

It was further down the corridor, a bright room with a single narrow window, still smelling of stale cigarette smoke. He looked at the make-up items scattered along a shelf, at a green silk kimono dressing-gown spread carelessly across the bottom of the dead woman's bed, at the clothes protruding from a half-opened wardrobe. Everything looked normal and natural — except that Jane Tamsin would never be back to use any of them again.

'Is this Andy?' Thane lifted a silver-framed colour photograph which was on the dressing-table. It showed a dark-haired little girl in a floral pattern dress. When Mary Russo nodded, he carefully put the photograph back again. 'I'll need to have this room searched, pure routine and done carefully.' He paused, looking around the room again, then surprised her. 'We talked a little about the men in Jane's life. Could any of them have been a biker?'

'None I knew about.' The woman's manner stiffened, for a moment that strand of tension was back in the air again. Then she slightly moistened her lips. 'Why?'

'We have to ask different things.' Thane led the way back out of the room. 'Here's another, Mrs Russo. You and Hodge — you said 'no ties'. But . . . ?'

'Do we sleep together?' She relaxed, unperturbed. 'We're adults, superintendent — would you expect us to spend our weekends watching television?'

'No.' Thane smiled, thinking of his own home life. 'The weekend programmes can get pretty awful. And that's all for now, Mrs Russo.'

Saying goodbye to the woman, nodding to the young constable on the door, he took the lift down to the ground floor. As he crossed the lobby with its wall-to-wall carpet and potted plants, Ernie Vass ambled over to join him but, as he'd expected, a purposeful Inspector Shaw appeared as if from nowhere and got there first.

'Sir?' The grey-haired woman officer made the word a total interrogation.

'I'm finished for now,' he confirmed. 'But

I need your help. I want to dump a few things on your lap.'

'There's a surprise,' she said stonily. 'Like what, sir?'

'Your constable on the door spoke with a Mrs Cowan — '

'He told me. I'll see the lady — and deal with him later.' She scowled in a way that boded ill for the luckless constable. 'That boy — God help him once his voice breaks! That's a promise!'

Thane sorted out the other details while Inspector Shaw resignedly hooked a thumb into the equipment belt around her waist and listened. Her divisional Scenes of Crime team should be asked to go over Jane Tamsin's room. Every resident in the eight-storey block should be asked if they'd seen the green Peugeot being torched — and as an apparent incidental they should also be quizzed on what they knew about the habits of Mary Russo and the late Jane Tamsin.

He glanced round. 'Ernie?'

Vass shook his head. 'Nothing to add, boss. That includes the old dear on the ground floor. She adds two and two and makes five.'

Inspector Shaw had already been busy in her own right. She had arranged for a two-man guard to be kept on Lamanda Quadrant overnight, with a duty car also checking now and again. If she could get more officers, she'd extend the door-to-door even further.

'I'm interested in any bikers seen hanging around,' mused Thane. 'That's something else. You've talked to the daughter . . . '

'Talked, nothing more — she's a child, and I was on my own.' The woman officer's manner cooled. 'I don't work that way, superintendent.'

'I didn't think you would,' murmured Thane. 'So — totally off the record, what did you get?'

She sighed. 'Her mother genuinely got along well with Jane Tamsin — and Andy liked her too. Liked her enough to be peeping out of a window at times when the child was supposed to be in bed.'

'And?'

'She saw Aunt Jane arriving back at night in any number of different cars — cars which stopped almost out of sight down the road.'

'What makes?'

'The child doesn't know one make from another.' The inspector paused, then sighed. 'I suppose this is what you want. Andy saw Aunt Jane being brought home by a biker. More than once, dropped off down the road, as usual.'

Thane whistled softly. 'Nobody ever came over the doorstep?'

'Nobody.' She shook her head. 'And Jane Tamsin didn't talk about them.'

'Thank you,' said Thane softly.

As he made to walk away, she stopped him. 'Superintendent, is Philip Moss still working with you?'

'Uh . . . ' Thane blinked. He seldom thought of Phil Moss as a Philip. 'Yes. He is.'

She gave a small, hard-to-read smile. 'I knew him years back, when we were constables. Will you tell him that Jinty Shaw said hello?'

'Jinty.' Thane nodded a promise. 'I will.'

Ernie Vass was at his heels as he walked over to where they'd left the Crime Squad car. The weather was changing. There was sullen grey cloud coming in from the west, a rising wind, and the temperature had fallen the way it always seemed to do around East Kilbride. This time he thumbed Vass behind the wheel and got into the passenger seat.

'Where now, boss?' asked Vass, starting the car and setting it moving. As he did, a thin speckle of fresh rain began to appear on the windshield.

Thane hesitated. One temptation was to stay around East Kilbride, and visit the

93

microchip firm where Jane Tamsin had suddenly been made redundant, then to explore around that connection. But the real priority had to be a visit to Empire Lines, where the dead woman had been employed.

Unless something else had turned up. He reached for the car's handset as they began travelling, calling in on the Squad's secure low-band radio to check. His timing was good. When the call was patched through to the duty room, he was speaking to a newly returned Sandra Craig. No, admitted his sergeant, she'd had little luck in her trawl around Paddy's Market.

'A few think they maybe — just maybe — saw two men and the Ducati bike.' Her voice crackled over the air. 'A few — just maybe again, super — saw a girl wearing jeans who was selling cloth. Of course, they didn't know her. That's it. End of story.'

'Surprise, surprise,' said Thane sarcastically, nursing the handset between chin and shoulder. Most people around Paddy's Market had memory problems. 'You spread the word?'

'Like I was scattering seed corn.' For a moment there was only a hum of static from the low-band set. Then she was back. 'The Broomstick Lady said to tell you there's no change at this end. And she wants to know if she can borrow Jock Dawson and his dogs again for tonight. The overtime would be on her budget.'

'Right.' Every now and again Sandra needed a small slap on the wrist. Thane grinned. A slap anywhere else, and he'd be on a discipline charge. Deliberately, he put some frost into his voice. 'Detective sergeant, advise Detective Chief Inspector Redder that she is welcome provided Jock agrees.' He winced as Ernie Vass made one of his favourite racing change-downs from top to second gear on the Ford's manual box, fed full throttle, and took them rocketing past a convoy of crawling garbage trucks. 'After that — and if I live so long — meet me in Paisley. We'll try tickling a Michael Spring, the boss of the firm who employed Jane Tamsin. Better check he's there.'

'Already done, sir. I got his name from an Eastern Division fax. He's expecting you.'

Thane blinked at his microphone. 'How the hell — ?'

'Female intuition, sir.' There was a chuckle in her voice.

He arranged a rendezvous and ended the call.

'Female intuition my backside, boss,' said

95

Ernie Vass grimly, scowling behind his steering wheel. 'She's just damned good at guesswork.'

Colin Thane didn't argue. Maybe it was the same thing.

3

It was past 5 p.m., into evening rush-hour time, when Thane's car reached a rain-soaked Paisley. Sandra Craig's white VW Golf slipped in ahead to act as a guide just as they cruised past the grey medieval stonework of Paisley Abbey. Ernie Vass gave a short double flash of his headlights, Sandra tapped her brake lights in a matching signal, and they travelled on through the drizzle as if tied together.

Paisley, about fifteen miles from East Kilbride, is the principal town of Renfrewshire and an historic burgh which through the sheer cruelties of time had eventually become a south-west satellite of Glasgow. But it was still different in every way possible compared with East Kilbride's new town concrete.

For a start, Paisley Abbey's proud provenance stretched back before the twelfth century, when the future city of Glasgow was little more than a fishing village. In the fourteenth century, Paisley Abbey was where a Scottish princess, a daughter of King Robert the Bruce, was brought to lie in state on the High Altar after being fatally injured in a hunting accident. Move on a few hundred years, and Paisley was a town where a steady stream of local women condemned as witches were regularly burned on bonfires — modern Paisley suggested a few more could still be dealt with that way.

A Paisley man had been one of the small group of Scottish settlers among the delegates who signed America's Declaration of Independence. Paisley's vast thread mills became known for their products throughout the world, its university had recently become at least equally famed for academic ability — while its citizens, the Paisley buddies, became a nationwide byword for their blend of doughty virtues and blind cussedness. Some declared that if a dog had the correct political label then Paisley would elect it to Parliament.

Others said that was a libel, that no sensible Paisley dog would want to be a Member of Parliament — then they would point to the way police were regularly summoned to local authority meetings to sort out open warfare among elected representatives.

Stir in outbreaks of political sleaze and alleged corruption, add a patchwork culture of drugs and armed violence, and the Paisley pattern could be awesomely unique.

'Crazy K,' murmured Thane as the two

cars crossed the busy centre of town.

Ernie Vass heard and grinned. Paisley was the hub of Strathclyde police force's K Division. The 'Crazy K' nickname which followed had stuck, no matter how much a Divisional Community Involvement team screamed.

'Heard what they call a Paisley man wearing a suit, boss?' asked Vass, wooden-faced.

'Tell me,' said Thane sadly.

'The accused,' reported Vass blandly. Then he was kept busy fighting off a new spate of traffic trying to get between him and the Volkswagen ahead.

Screenwipers still sweeping, they passed the clean white plinth of the town's war memorial and turned off on a network of oneway streets which led through a blend of shops and offices and bars. Sandra Craig tapped her brake lights again and they followed as she pulled off the road. Tyres crunched over a wide stretch of gravelled parking area and splashed through a deep pool of rainwater, then the cars stopped outside a red sandstone building. Once it had been a large parish church, complete with steeple, and had been the pride of its Presbyterian congregation. Now, with window gaps mostly bricked up and old gravestones from its churchyard propped along one wall, it had a strictly commercial role. A bright red neon sign announcing 'Empire Lines — Architectural Salvage' glowed above the ornate porch of the front doorway.

Sandra Craig waited beside her car in what had become a dying drizzle until Thane and Vass joined her. Thane greeted his red-haired sergeant with a nod, then glanced around. A thin scatter of other cars, one an elderly silver-grey Mercedes, the other a smart blue Toyota coupé, were parked on the other side of the entrance porch, and a large Volvo van and a smaller Leyland truck, both with 'Empire Lines' badging, were further along where a goods entrance was protected by large, closed metal doors.

'How do we play this, sir?' asked Sandra Craig. Something in her voice made Thane raise an eyebrow. She shrugged. 'I called Michael Spring, their managing director, and told him you were coming. Then — well, I ran his name through the CRO computer. Just in case.'

'And?'

'He seems clean enough now.' She gave a slight grimace. 'But go back about a decade and he was on the dodgy side of the blanket in the used car world. Two convictions listed for faking car mileages.'

'Don't they all do that?' asked Vass cynically.

'Shut up, Ernie!' Thane silenced the detective constable with a frown. Car clocking, reducing the mileage recorded for a vehicle, was the oldest and quickest way to make extra crooked money in the used car trade.

'He was fined first time, for clocking ten cars,' continued Sandra Craig, unruffled. 'A year later, the charge was clocking thirty cars. He got eighteen months.'

'Which didn't make him criminal of the year,' said Thane drily. 'We remember it, that's all.'

The main church door creaked open. A middle-aged man in faded white overalls came out of the building, closed the door again, mumbled a greeting as he passed, then climbed into the Leyland truck. He started it up with a dirty blue cloud of exhaust then drove out of the parking area in a new crunching of gravel.

'Damn him, that's a real crime.' Thane fought down a cough as the stinking diesel fumes caught at his throat. 'Anything else?'

'Maybe a lead on the murder bike, sir.' They had started walking towards the main door, with Vass trailing them. 'There's a late report on a Ducati stolen out of town, near

101

Helensburgh. It could have happened as long as a week ago — the owner has been away from home.' She wasn't finished. 'Another thing cleared is that Dougie Lennox says the two beat men at the High Court both remember the girl in blue jeans.'

'Good.' It helped. Anything that supported a story from two judges helped! They reached the outside porch, where the shelter took them out of the drizzle. 'Did Dougie have any luck with the crash helmets?'

'Not yet.' Sandra Craig wiped a few fine droplets of rain from her face. 'Plenty of outlets sell crash helmets for bikers, sir — all colours.' But none, it seemed, with double bands of white. Except that could easily be ordinary sticky tape added later.

Thane tried the large metal handle on the warehouse's heavy oak door and it turned easily, the door beginning to open. He had one thing more on his mind.

'Any more word from Phil Moss?'

'Just the same again. That he'll be in touch.' Sandra Craig shook her head. 'But nothing about when or where.'

It wasn't Phil Moss's usual style, but there was nothing Thane could do about it. He pushed the door open and led the way through, then let it close again once Vass and Sandra Craig had followed him in.

102

Narrow white fluorescent tube lamps threw a bright light on the time-scarred interior walls of the old church. But they also threw their light on long corridors formed from upright ranks of wooden doors, some polished mahogany, some oak, others teak or pine. Here and there were islands of dusty leaded glass windows, of art deco fireplaces, of decorative wood panelling and mouldings, even a complete oak stairway close to a small forest of lighting columns and lamp posts.

Thane's nostrils filled with the rich scents of seasoned wood. But he could also see Victorian cast iron baths and Edwardian high level lavatory cisterns, side by side with heavy old cast iron central heating radiators and piles of salvaged church pews. There were other scents he couldn't identify but which were all pleasing, so many of them stirring childhood memories.

Down near the end of one corridor a young couple were examining some old, brass-framed mirrors. A modest sprinkling of further potential customers were prowling around other areas. Any footsteps sounded oddly muffled, and when Thane looked down he discovered he was standing on thick squares of modern chipboard partly covered by scraps of old, painted canvas.

'It's like coming into a museum,' said

Sandra Craig, staring around.

'A museum, or a high-class junk yard,' muttered Ernie Vass. He brightened. 'Boss . . . '

Thane had alread seen. A broad-built man in his sixties was walking briskly down the length of the building, heading purposefully towards them. Medium height, with thick, iron grey hair clipped short, he had a small, neat moustache, and a round moon of a face. He was wearing a grey jacket and blue trousers with an open-necked green shirt, and brown ankle-length lacing boots.

'Police?' he asked cheerfully as he reached them. His bright brown eyes didn't waver as Thane nodded. 'I'm Michael Spring.' His gaze switched to Sandra Craig. 'And you're the female who talked me into staying on late?'

'Guilty,' admitted Sandra.

The man sighed. 'Do you realise I've a wife at home who'll give me hell if I'm late for another meal?'

'We appreciate it.' Thane took over the introductions, and Spring offered each of them a handshake. His grip was strong, his hand calloused and rough.

'You run Empire Lines, Mr Spring?' asked Thane mildly.

'With a little help from a couple of banks,' said Spring drily. 'They don't know about each other. Yes, I'm founder, managing director, general manager — and you're here about Jane Tamsin?'

Thane nodded. 'Where can we talk?'

'Give me a moment.' The man looked around. 'Danny — where the hell are you?'

'On my way!' A long, thin, watery-eyed man in a grey warehouse smock appeared from behind one of the high piles of mahogany panelling. 'Well?'

'Police about Jane.' Michael Spring thumbed at them. 'Take over on the floor, Danny. That pair of lovebirds at the bottom end will buy a mirror but need talking into that pretend Adam fireplace.'

'Right.' Danny gave a brief glance at Thane and Vass, considered Sandra Craig slightly longer, then stalked off towards his targets.

'You sometimes sell fakes?' queried Thane.

'And they're labelled that way. If that fireplace was for real, it would be worth a fortune,' declared Spring. 'That pair know it is a fake, but they like it, they can afford it, they'll buy.' He saw Ernie Vass was wandering off on his own, but didn't comment. 'So, superintendent — you and your sergeant follow me. Right?'

They followed the owner of Empire Lines across the width of the old church, and past

105

another pile of oak pews. Then they skirted a jumble of brass Victorian saloon bar fittings before he nimbly led the way up a narrow stairway to a high-set gallery level.

'Used to be the organ loft,' explained their guide. The gallery considerably widened a little way along, then was partitioned off.

'The office!' Michael Spring opened a plain glass door just ahead and waved them through into a comfortably furnished office area with large glass windows that looked down on the main floor below. The grey-haired man smiled at a plump, poker-faced brunette who had looked up from her desk-top computer. 'Police, Joan. The ones we expected. I'll see them alone — but you'd better hang around until they're finished.' Then he winked. 'Just in case they march me off in handcuffs, eh?'

Expression unchanged, Joan tapped a few more computer keys to store what she'd been working on. Then, not saying a word, she lifted her handbag from the floor and left.

'Not exactly talkative, our Joan. But she's damned good at her job.' Spring went over to his own desk which was positioned at one of the windows. Standing beside it, he took a brief glance at the main floor below, then turned. His expression sobered. 'All right, Jane Tamsin. I heard what happened. A mugging that went wrong. Correct?'

'Maybe. Maybe not.' Thane shook his head. 'It's too early.'

'Bloody hell,' said Spring softly. He considered Thane and Sandra as if seeing them properly for the first time. 'And that's why you're here?'

'Here — and going round a lot of other places,' agreed Thane. 'Either way, we're talking murder.'

'Sit down.' The grey-haired man frowned around, produced two chairs, and brought them over. He waited while his visitors settled, then perched himself on the edge of his desk. 'What do you want to know about her?'

'How has she seemed lately?' asked Sandra, taking a slight nod from Thane as her cue. 'Upset? Worried? Anything different about her behaviour from usual?'

'Nothing.' Spring chewed an edge of his moustache, his manner becoming wary. 'She'd only been with us a short time, and to be honest, I didn't know much about her. A good customer of mine asked me to give her a job — '

'Kenneth Hodge?'

Spring nodded. 'Ken said she'd been made redundant or something, and that she'd been working with some computer outfit. Anyway,

I gave her a try and she seemed reasonably good. That was all that mattered.'

The red-haired sergeant pursed her lips and frowned. 'Did she have references?'

'I didn't ask. Ken Hodge's word was good enough, and she was only scouting, on commission.' Spring shrugged. 'Anyway — computers? Here? Joan drives that thing on her desk, who else needs to know more? For the rest of it, I'd label Jane Tamsin as pretty much a loner — likeable enough, but not particularly close to anyone.'

'What about men?'

'Around this place?' Spring almost chuckled. 'I've a son, Dirk. He works with me, and if it wears a skirt, Dirk's interested — so he tried his luck and she chased him off. Anything else that is male around here is long past it.'

Thane leaned forward, taking over again. 'You say Jane Tamsin worked for you on commission. Commission for doing what?'

'She looked for things, followed up tips. Empire Lines is architectural salvage, right?' Spring eased round on his desk-top and thumbed at the view below. 'We've maybe half a million pounds' worth down there, brought in from all over. We're among the best, I've been in the trade a few years now — '

'Since you left used cars?' murmured Sandra Craig.

'How did you know about that, sergeant?' The grey-haired man showed mock surprise. 'Yes, since I left used cars. Once I'd learned enough about the architectural salvage game, I bought this old church. Do you know my first real sale? Two weeks after Empire Lines moved in, a crazy Dutchman visited. He looked around, then — ' he pointed down — 'you saw what you walked on when you came in? He bought the damned church floor, every last plank, and shipped it off to Holland!'

The way Michael Spring told the tale, it all came down to a blend of fashion and sound economics. More and more people throughout Europe and North America, sometimes further afield, wanted to restore properties to their original appearance, converting or refurbishing, ripping out black plastic and chrome and replacing them with materials better able to blend with Georgian or Victorian buildings. From ceilings or ceiling moulds to doors and door furnishings, even hinges and their original brass hinge screws, anything old was suddenly in demand. The supply came in from large country houses or city tenements, from closed-down bank branches or redundant government buildings. And it was often a race between the salvage specialists and the demolition teams.

'I was out in North Carolina last month,' said Spring, beaming at the memory. 'I told them what we had, showed them photographs, and they waved dollars at almost everything we offered.'

'That happens often?' asked Thane.

'Pretty regularly.' Spring nodded. 'Either I go or Dirk goes — we'll travel to wherever there's a market, sell on photographs. Lots of our stuff ends up abroad.' He paused, lifted a small bag of boiled sweets from among the confusion of paperwork on his desk, popped a sweet in his mouth, and offered the bag to Thane, who shook his head, then to Sandra Craig. He saw her reaction. 'Like them? Then take a couple!'

She did.

'Anyway — ' the grey-haired man chewed for a moment while Thane could only wait — 'these days the home trade is getting bigger. That's another reason I took on Jane. You saw that young couple downstairs?'

'The fake fireplace pair?' Thane nodded.

'I talked with them. They've bought an old wreck of a house on the west side of town. They're stripping it out and renovating, they're using salvage stuff whenever they can.' Spring slapped one hand on his desk-top. 'They'll save themselves a fortune, and they'll have quality fitments you can't buy any more.'

'So get back to Jane Tamsin,' suggested Thane patiently.

'Sorry.' Spring frowned apologetically and took another quick chew. 'Sometimes a demolition worker will tip us off that he's knocking down something interesting. Other times, we've a little string of pensioners and bag-ladies who rummage in builders' rubbish skips and contact us fast. Jane went out on jobs for a couple of weeks with one of us — could be me, could be Dirk or someone else — and learned the basics. Then she was on her own, with a cash float.'

Eyes narrowing, Colin Thane stiffened. 'Was she buying yesterday?'

'She told me a contact had found something good, but that she needed her cash float topped up. I'll show you.' Spring came down from his desk, opened a drawer, and brought out a cardboard box. Inside it, a delicately painted porcelain door handle rolled from one side to the other. 'I know people in Germany who'll pay a fortune for just a few of these. Jane said her contact had greased a demolition foreman the price of a few drinks, and could pick

111

up twenty handles. They sounded better than this one.'

'Who was the contact?'

'She didn't tell, I didn't ask. All I knew was she had a meeting set up somewhere.' Michael Spring shook his head. 'It works that way — the same way as your people get information, right?' He chewed again. 'If it helps, I think there was someone she regularly met around Paddy's Market.'

'And she wanted her float topped up.' Sandra Craig paused, using her tongue to move the sweets to one side of her mouth. Academically speaking, and not for the first time, Thane told himself that his sergeant had particularly attractive lips. He wiped the thought as Sandra asked, 'So how much did she get?'

'I can tell you.' The man rummaged around the littered desktop for a moment, muttering to himself, paused, then tried again. At last he gave a grunt of triumph and looked up, grinning, a small notebook in his hand. 'Got it! You know the saying, 'A tidy desk means a sick mind'? If that's true, I'm safe enough!'

Thane smiled a little, thinking of the very few tidy desks he knew, including the one used by a certain Crime Squad commander. He wondered if Jack Hart had ever thought of things that way — and yes, on reflection, the saying could be true. Patiently, he waited and Sandra Craig chewed while Michael Spring's stubby fingers flicked more pages.

At last Spring halted, checked an entry then cleared his throat. 'She signed for £300 in cash, superintendent.' He paused, then chose his words carefully. 'If — uh — the money turns up, or if you maybe even find those porcelain handles . . .'

'We'll let you know,' promised Thane woodenly.

'Good.' Michael Spring suddenly stopped and beamed in the direction of the glass door behind Thane. Silently mouthing a greeting, he beckoned. As his visitors looked round, they saw a man standing at the other side of the door, then the door clicked open and he came in.

'Hi, Dad.' The new arrival took a couple of loping steps into the room, letting the door swing shut behind him, and raised a questioning eyebrow. 'All right?'

'Fine.' Michael Spring gestured an introduction. 'My son Dirk — Detective Superintendent Thane, Sergeant Craig. Dirk's title is sales director.'

'Hi.' Dirk Spring gave the visitors a nod of greeting, but left it at that. He turned to his father again. 'I talked to Joan outside. She told me this was about Jane, so I thought I'd come up.'

'To keep me out of trouble?' His father gave a slight, appreciative smile. 'Reasonable thinking.'

Sitting back in his chair, Thane considered father and son for a moment. Dirk Spring had to be around thirty years of age. Add a few inches in height, substitute close-clipped chestnut hair for the close-clipped grey, accept the lack of a moustache, and Dirk was very much a younger version of his father in build and features. Even his voice had a similar resonance, but with an overlay of education. When Thane glanced at Sandra Craig, he saw his copper-haired sergeant was giving the younger Spring a lazy but similarly careful scrutiny, a mild glint in her large green eyes.

More important, she had stopped chewing.

'So what's going on?' Dirk Spring swept a glance between Thane and his father. 'Is there a problem?'

'They reckon Jane wasn't killed in any four-by-two bagsnatch,' said his father grimly. He nodded as a sudden frown clouded Dirk Spring's face. 'Something worse. So they want to hear anything we know about her.'

'That isn't a lot.' Dirk Spring joined his father on the edge of the same desk and scratched his head. 'Sorry, you won't get much here.'

'Your father says you invited Jane Tamsin out as your date on a couple of occasions,' mused Thane. Looking at Dirk Spring, he estimated that they were an equal match in height. 'Only twice?'

'Only twice, superintendent.' The man nodded. 'The second time, we were having a drink in a bar when Jane asked if dating me was part of her job. I said to think of me as an optional extra.' He gave a reminiscent chuckle. 'She said goodnight and walked out, but she was back at work next day.'

'Did she mention someone else in her life?' explored Sandra bluntly. 'Someone named Peter?'

'No.'

'Did you ever notice her wearing a gold chain with a good luck pendant at her throat?'

'No.' Dirk Spring grinned at Thane. 'And positively not when she was out with me, sergeant. That I can guarantee. I . . . uh . . .'

'Have wandering hands?' asked Sandra stonily.

'It's called exploring.' His grin widened.

'Leave it, Dirk,' growled his father, then took over. 'Look, superintendent, call off your dog. It was the way I said. Jane didn't tell anyone much about anything — and we didn't ask.'

'Did she have a desk of her own?' asked Thane.

'No.' Dirk Spring casually produced a comb and ran it through his hair, then glanced at his father. 'But didn't we give her a locker?'

'The old green one.' Michael Spring nodded, then glanced at his watch again. 'I'd like to finish off here and get home, superintendent. Maybe Dirk could show you her locker. There are spare keys to them all here, in the petty cash box.' He rummaged in a tin box lying open on his desk, then slid a key across to his son. 'All right by you, Dirk?'

'No problem.' Dirk Spring pocketed the key and got to his feet. 'Superintendent?'

They followed him out of his father's office and he took them back through the old organ loft, down the stairs to the main hall area, then along a side corridor. Empire Lines' sales director paused where another flight of steps led down into darkness. He flicked a wall switch, and more neon tube lights spat to life.

Spring was first down the steps into the basement of the old church. It had a bare

116

concrete floor, electric cables and rusty cast iron heating pipes snaked around the walls, and most of the area was filled with stacks of salvaged doors and piled-up heaps of old bathroom fitments.

'Careful now,' warned Spring, leading the way across it all. He ducked under a massive beam. 'Watch — ' he winced as Thane, following closely, ducked too late and one detective superintendent's skull hit the same beam with an audible thud — 'watch your heads!'

The pain almost blinded Thane for a moment, then he recovered enough to go on. A corner of the basement was a work area, with benches and carpentry tools. It also had a table with a battered electric kettle, some tea mugs and an opened carton of low-fat milk beside a couple of crumpled dog racing sheets. Some half a dozen battered wardrobe lockers formed a line close to the table, and one in worse condition than the rest was old and green.

Dirk Spring got to it first, bringing the key out from his pocket. Then he stared.

'Shit,' he said savagely. 'I don't believe this!'

They had been beaten to it. The locker was open, the green wood door ajar, the spring lock forced in a way that had splintered it

117

free and had left the metal barrel hanging at a drunken angle.

'What the hell is going on?' Spring reached for the locker door, blinked as Thane grabbed his wrist and stopped him, then understood. 'Fingerprints?'

Thane nodded, watching. Either Dirk Spring was a consummate actor — which he doubted — or the future heir to Empire Lines was both startled and genuinely angry at what they'd discovered. He asked, 'How many people can get access to down here?'

'Any number.' Spring looked down at his feet, eyes half closed, and sighed. 'In fact, think of a number then double it. I wouldn't even guess.'

Sandra Craig squeezed past then used the clip edge of her ball-point pen to pull the locker door fully open. A light fawn raincoat had partly fallen from its hanger and lay crumpled on the floor on top of a pair of shoes and a torn shopping bag. The locker shelf held a lipstick, a comb, some items of make-up, a clear plastic bag containing black tights and a spare pair of clean knickers, an unopened twenty pack of cigarettes, and an almost empty half-bottle of vodka. The raincoat pockets had been turned inside out.

'No house keys?' asked Thane.

She shook her head.

But someone had come looking ahead of them, looking hard for something.

What it had been, whether they'd found it, was another matter.

'How much of the time would this place be empty?' asked Thane.

'That would depend on what was going on.' Spring chewed his lip, his brown eyes still bleak. 'Totally? Not long. Only since the two porters who work from down here would knock off for the night. Say — say, during the last hour or so.' He peered at the broken lock. 'I reckon a minute with a half-decent screwdriver would be enough to force that.'

'But why?' Sandra Craig was puzzled and showed it.

'How the hell would I know?' The man's anger had come under control. Casually, he used his comb again. 'We buy from plenty of different punters, any number of them know what's down here.' He scowled. 'Maybe someone knew that my old man had topped up Jane's float, and maybe thought she'd maybe hidden some of the cash in her locker . . . '

'Because she was maybe taking her own private cut?' Thane heard a small scraping noise somewhere further back in

119

the basement. He ignored it. Old churches could have rats like anywhere else. 'Did you think that was happening?'

'Thought it? We knew it!' Dirk Spring nodded. 'And she wasn't the only one. But whatever she siphoned off, the old man just treated it like it came from the petty cash. That way, everyone stayed happy and Empire Lines got the best of any good stuff around.'

'That's business,' accepted Thane. 'You could get an invite to join Rotary.' His thought shifted. 'When you were with her, did she ever tell you anything about her time with computers?'

'Me?' The man gave a derisive snort. 'I'm like my old man — I wouldn't know a computer if one bit me! And could you imagine computers as any kind of chat-up line?'

'Probably not,' said Thane stonily. 'We'll send Scenes of Crime to check here, then we'll organise formal statements from you and from your father.' He heard the small scraping noise again, and from Sandra Craig's expression she had also heard it. His sergeant didn't like rats.

'Can we still use the basement?' asked Spring.

'Once Scenes of Crime are finished.' Thane

went on to qualify for a glare from Sandra Craig. 'It will save time if we take a look around while we're down here.'

Dirk Spring nodded, brought an incongruous roll of pink silk ribbon from a cupboard and quickly used it to mark a no-go area around the locker. As he finished, Thane and Sandra began a token prowl around the rest of the cluttered basement area. There was a patch of damp near its centre, otherwise the concrete floor seemed dry —

Suddenly, the rat-scrape noise sounded again, more loudly, became a clatter of disturbed lengths of wood. A despairing curse, then a figure had risen from behind a tall stack of salvaged wooden doors and was rushing for the stairway which led out. Thane had a fleeting impression of a thin man with dark, collar-length hair, blue denim trousers and a scuffed leather jacket.

'Stop! Police!' Sandra Craig was already chasing towards the fugitive as she yelled, with Thane also pounding in pursuit. Thudding footsteps from the rear told that Dirk Spring was galloping to join them.

Their quarry reached the foot of the stairway, went up a couple of steps, then stopped beside a mountain-like pile of Victorian bathroom fitments, and shoved at it desperately. The pile swayed, the thin man gave another desperate heave, and the entire pile of baths and sinks and lavatories toppled with a noise like thunder straight towards Sandra Craig.

There wasn't time to shout a warning. Thane catapulted forward in a rugby style charge which slammed into his copper-haired sergeant hard below the waist. The impact picked her up and they fell together on the concrete of the basement floor, clear of most of the rumbling, tumbling collection.

Most, but not all. A heavy wash-basin smashed beside Colin Thane, a large piece of something else crashed on his right knee, fragments of shattered white porcelain cistern spattered across Sandra Craig's chest and legs. Cursing, hauling himself to his feet, Thane saw their target heading on up the stairs and made to limp in pursuit. Another moment, and he crashed into Dirk Spring as they reached the stair together. Spring grabbed at Thane for support, and they went down in a tangle of arms and legs.

Within seconds the two men were disentangled and off again. But the delay had been enough. In the lead, Thane climbed suddenly empty stairs and emerged on the ground floor of the old church. There was no one in sight. Another moment, and Dirk Spring panted up to join him.

Thane peered back into the basement. Down there, Sandra Craig was sitting up, looked dazed, but signalled she was all right. He grabbed Spring, shoving him back towards the stairway.

'Stay with her,' he ordered, hearing a vehicle engine starting up outside.

Then the vehicle outside was accelerating and Thane, already clear of the basement, was limping towards the main door, which lay open. On the way, he lurched past a startled middle-aged couple who had been inspecting stained glass panels, then a gaping elderly woman. Another moment, and he reached the front porch of the building and was out in the open. The drizzling rain had stopped; it was a typically mild early summer evening. He could see traffic moving as normal.

'They're well away, boss. Sorry!' The broadly built figure of Detective Constable Ernie Vass hurried across from the far side of the parking area, reached him, and frowned as he registered that Thane was alone. 'Is Sandra all right?'

'Fine. Give or take.' Thane massaged his aching knee for a moment. 'What happened with you?'

'I was inside, at the far end. Then a character in a leather jacket appeared

123

midway down, scarpering for the door like a bat out of hell!' The Grampian man shrugged. 'I took off after him, same style, but he had a pal waiting outside with an old Commer work van. Pal had it moving while Leather jacket was still hauling himself aboard. The Commer was either dirty cream or fawn. Rusty. Registration plate too dirty to read — probably smeared that way. No distinguishing features. They made the road, turned left. Goodbye, Commer.'

Thane swore. But if it had been different, he'd have got it from Vass. 'The occupants?'

'Driver male, maybe early twenties, probably clean shaven, long hair. Leather jacket . . . ' Vass frowned. 'I wouldn't put money on it, boss. But he was maybe a known face.'

That was better. Any cop anywhere knew about known faces, remembered from somewhere, often pulled in as a usual suspect. Known faces had names — but names knitted with them later.

'We'll call it in.' He walked with Vass to the parked Crime Squad car. Once Vass had used the car's radio, reporting the van and adding a request for a Scenes of Crime team to attend at Empire Lines, Thane made a radio call of his own. It was a patch through, to speak with the Crime Squad night shift supervisor. The supervisor, a uniformed branch inspector, had newly started duty. But he'd been fully briefed at the shift handover, and there was still nothing new to report.

'Anything, boss?' Vass raised a hopeful eyebrow as Thane tossed the radio handset back on to its shelf.

'No luck, no miracles. Not yet.' Although there was never any harm in hoping — and any spare bodies on the night team would be working on various aspects of the Jane Tamsin case for most of their shift, whether that meant trying telephone numbers or knocking doors. Thane thumbed towards the building again. 'We'd better check on a certain sergeant.' Wryly, he rubbed his knee again. 'She may need a vet.'

They went back into the building, where all seemed peaceful again, and went down into the basement. Sandra Craig was sitting on an upturned bath. Dirk Spring stood near her, frowning, scratching his head in bewildered style.

'Any luck?' asked Spring quickly.

'No chance.' Thane shook his head. 'He had transport waiting.'

All in aid of raiding a single shabby locker in a basement workshop? Even the idea was almost ludicrous, Thane told himself. And yet it held its own puzzle. Almost certainly the dead woman's personal keys, including her locker key, would have been in her handbag when it was stolen. Whoever had them wouldn't have needed to force the locker. Nor would the Springs. And who the hell did that leave to work on?

He took another slow look around the basement then turned back to Dirk Spring. 'What about you? Any thoughts about who your visitor could have been?'

'Sorry.' Spring scowled and used his comb again. 'He probably just walked in. We encourage people to drop in.' He glanced towards the stairway. 'My father should be told. He'll know something has happened.' Thane nodded, and the man gave a faint smile towards Sandra then left them.

'Next time you decide to throw me across a cellar, leave me with a better nursemaid,' complained Sandra Craig once the sales director had gone. 'That character tried a hand up my leg while he said he wanted to take my pulse!'

'So what did you do, sarge?' asked Ernie Vass, grinning.

'Told him I'd tear his lungs out.' She glanced back at the tumbled heap of heavy iron bath tubs and almost equally heavy porcelain that she might have been under. Her clothes showed some small tears, she had small abrasions on one cheek, and porcelain fragments streaked her hair. But at that, she had been lucky. She shaped a wry grimace towards Thane. 'Thank you, sir. That lot could have flattened me.'

'I don't allow my sergeants to be hit by Victorian lavatory pans,' said Thane solemnly.

'And she's flushed with gratitude,' murmured Vass, then ducked as a fiercely aimed piece of broken porcelain hurtled towards him.

At that, Colin Thane decided to call it a day. He told Ernie Vass to speak with anyone still in the building, then hang on until Scenes of Crime arrived. Sandra was told she didn't have to wait.

His sergeant knew what that meant. 'What time tomorrow, sir?'

'7 a.m., and organise a full team conference for seven thirty.' Thane saw her expression. 'Here. Catch.'

She grabbed the half-pound block of raisin and nut chocolate that curved towards her. Diplomacy came in different ways when dealing with Detective Sergeant Sandra Craig. Like Thane having learned to always have some iron rations aboard his car for easing moments of stress.

She was munching when he left.

★ ★ ★

He wasn't quite sure why, but before Colin Thane went home he first drove across to their old headquarters building in its parkland setting and stopped briefly outside. The building was closed and empty. It was the first time he'd ever seen the parking area deserted, and as he drew up he saw an indignant fox lope away from the front door.

There were rival schemes already afoot for the building. Strathclyde's Mounted Branch, still in residence nearby, said they wanted it. So did those other old neighbours, the Dog Branch. So did Research and Development and other people. But the Crime Squad wouldn't be back. Thane set the car moving and saw the fox was sitting under a tree patiently waiting to take over again.

It was called progress. The new location was a major improvement, they'd get used to it. Eventually.

It was around 8 p.m. when he got home. Home was a small, comfortable, very ordinary bungalow in a south side suburban street where every house had been constructed by the same builder from the same plan about twenty years earlier. The only houses which had changed since were those where

128

a family had found the time and money for some kind of extension or garage or an added-on porch. Most new outside paint jobs were do-it-yourself projects. The gardens had had enough time to become either mature or overgrown and if his patch of front garden wasn't the fanciest in the line-up, it still escaped being the scruffiest. And some day, when he had time . . . .

Thane ran the Mondeo into his narrow driveway, which wasn't much longer than the car. He had a small garage round the back but there was so much junk stored inside its walls that it was never likely to know wheels again. If it did, Mary had already staked a priority claim for her own car, a Japanese-built station wagon which sheltered under a lean-to carport.

He left the Ford, locked it because three neighbours had lost car radios the previous week, then stopped for a moment to pull a token weed out of the driveway gravel and toss is to one side. He saw that as daylight began to fade a new band of heavy cloud was coming in from the west, and gave a sympathetic chuckle. It could be the kind of night he knew well, when a back-shift beat cop had to plod around pulling padlocks and rattling doors while rain hosed down the back of his neck.

One of the benefits of rank was that he could stay dry most of the time!

The house door opened as he reached it and Mary Thane greeted him with a slightly tired smile but a warm kiss.

'Long day?' he asked.

'One of my 'I'll blow up that damned health clinic' days.' Mary Thane was wearing a patterned yellow shirt-style blouse and a blue velvet skirt, the waist of the skirt emphasised by a narrow leather belt which had a large silver buckle. 'Everything would be fine if we didn't have patients.' Her brown eyes looked him over. 'I spoke with Maggie Fyffe. The way she told it, you had problems — and not just the move.'

'A few.' He followed her in and through to the rear kitchen, hung his jacket over a chair, then made his usual fuss over the brindle boxer dog who had ambled over and was enthusiastically wagging his stumpy tail. Clyde now ambled more often than he ran. That, and the zigzag white scar on his chest, were reminders of when Clyde had ferociously saved Mary from a knife-wielding burglar.

'Dutiful wife and faithful dog greet husband.' As he stopped fussing Clyde, Mary handed him a whisky. She had already poured one for herself. 'Water?'

'Thanks.' Gratefully, Thane lowered himself into a chair, sipped at the whisky. It was a good blend, not his favourite, treasured single malt. He massaged his aching knee again. The house was strangely quiet, meaning Tommy and Kate were out.

'Phil telephoned,' she reported. 'He'll look in later.'

'When he'll hope to be fed,' snorted Thane. 'Any hint why else he is coming?'

She shook her head. 'He didn't say, I didn't ask.'

Thane watched her as she finished preparing their evening meal. He still found it impossible to believe that this slim, dark-haired and attractive woman had become the mother of two early teens children, found it even harder to believe that her fortieth birthday would soon be rumbling round.

He knew she still took a size twelve, which had been her size when they'd married. He knew he was still in love with her, hoped she felt the same about him.

'In this house, as you tell our children, we usually wash before we eat,' she reminded with a mock solemnity.

He went upstairs, washed, changed into a grey cotton sports shirt and a pair

131

of comfortably old tweed trousers, then returned to the kitchen as Mary began serving. She was enforcing a weight control diet until he lost a couple of pounds, which meant a single glass of white wine, a fruit juice starter, thin sliced and broiled steak overkilled in vegetables, then black coffee, and he decided not to tell her about the second Sandra style quarter-pound block of chocolate which he'd eaten in the car on the way home.

'What happened to your knee?' asked Mary, seeing him rubbing it again.

'Someone almost flattened Sandra with a lavatory cistern.' He forestalled her question. 'She's fine. I took a thump.'

'How bad?' She gave him a quizzical glance.

'Horizontal mobility isn't affected,' he assured her.

'That's good,' she said demurely. 'Maybe we can check that aspect later?'

They were sharing the washing up when the kitchen door burst open and a noisy teenage invasion burst in, Clyde coming out of his basket and adding his barking to the din. Tommy and Kate found some left-over food in the refrigerator, then had a brief verbal skirmish about which TV show to watch.

'You two.' Thane made it a plea. 'Cool it!' As the noise level reduced, he considered them again. 'Whose home life did you wreck this evening?'

Brother and sister exchanged a grin, each waiting for the other to speak. Kate was growing more like her mother every day, decided Thane. Including the same hard-to-resist twinkle in her eyes. Tommy was different, Tommy was still at the stage of having days when he should be donated to a zoo.

It was Tommy who answered him. 'We were at Biffo Black's place. Both of us.'

'He's on the Internet,' confirmed Kate. 'It's awesome!'

Thane checked his mental filing system. Biffo Black's father was an accountant, Tommy was in Biffo's class at school, but Biffo's name didn't crop up often. Never till now, involving Kate.

'What happened to Duckbreath?' he asked Kate. Duckbreath was her current teen style idol.

'He's still around.' Kate dismissed the subject. 'Dad, if we were on the Internet — well, it would help at school.'

'Unbelievably,' declared Tommy earnestly. 'You can log into anything — '

'That's what worries me,' said Thane

grimly. They had a computer. He had bought the thing at a car boot sale and it lurked upstairs, where he tried to avoid it.

'At school — ' tried Tommy again.

'Another time. Not now.' He thumbed them on their way again.

Tommy left, glum. Kate hung back then came over, draped herself against Thane's shoulder, and her eyes twinkled up. 'Dad, about the Internet — '

'No.' He scowled. 'Let's talk about Duckbreath. Is he about to be dumped?' Duckbreath, who was so eager to please he sometimes washed Mary's car for free.

'For Biffo?' She blinked. 'Dad, don't be stupid. There were about ten of us there, doing Internet things. Anyway — ' she lowered her voice confidentially — 'Biffo isn't too interested in girls. You know what I mean?'

'I . . . ' Thane knew his mouth had fallen open.

'But Tommy likes girls. In case you wondered.' She grinned, kissed him lightly on the cheek, and headed after her brother.

Thane closed his mouth hard and swallowed. Children grew up too quickly for their parents' good.

★ ★ ★

Phil Moss arrived with a double ring on the doorbell at around 10 p.m. He came into the house with fresh rain spotting his grubby anorak, and a brief cheerfulness on his face as he greeted Clyde, Mary and the two young Thanes in that order. As usual, Mary Thane ushered him into the kitchen. She made him remove the damp anorak and dump the briefcase he was carrying, then inspected him carefully.

'Have you eaten?' she demanded.

'Uh . . . ' He hesitated, a wry look on his thin, lined face.

'Meaning no,' Mary translated. 'Phil, you're an idiot, and you're asking for trouble! Colin, sit the man down and give him a drink.'

While Thane obeyed, pouring their visitor his usual small whisky drowned in water then topping up his own glass, Mary did busy microwave things. Within minutes, she presented Phil Moss with scrambled eggs, hot buttered toast, and a pot of Moss's preferred light-coloured peppermint tea. 'Eat,' she commanded. 'Give that ulcer something to work on. Then I'll leave you in peace. I'm going through to watch the end of what sounds like a hellish video.'

She left, Clyde padding after her.

'Colin — ' began Moss.

'Eat,' said Thane stonily. He could read the signs among the tight lines on the man's thin face and the strain in his eyes. Quite apart from being tired, Phil Moss was having one of his bad gut days.

'Eat.' Moss gave a resigned nod and obeyed.

Scrawny, as always looking as if he'd slept in his suit for several nights running, Phil Moss was about ten years older than Thane and several inches smaller. They'd first come together when Thane had headed Millside Division CID, a dockside division which was one of Glasgow's roughest patches, with Moss as his number two. The team had to break up when Thane, promoted to Detective Superintendent, moved to the Scottish Crime Squad.

For his part, Moss first agreed to overdue surgery for his much renowned stomach ulcer then was invalided to a Strathclyde headquarters desk job. The operation wasn't a success — and Moss showed how smoothly he could play the police system. Within months he was out beside Thane again. Still allegedly in a desk job, except it never seemed to quite work out that way.

Colin Thane sipped his whisky and considered the older man closely. Moss had missed a patch of stubble on one check when he'd shaved that morning. There was a dried red spatter on his string-like tie which was probably tomato sauce. One of his shoes had been polished, but the other one —

'God, that was good!' Moss finished his meal, shoved away his plate, gave a long sigh and released a carefully restrained belch. A china cup on the draining board beside the kitchen sink responded with a gentle vibration. Sitting back, Moss shook his head at the offer of a refill from Thane's bottle. 'That'll do me.'

'Then do I get to hear what the hell you've got into?' Thane tried to appear patient.

'In a moment.' Moss gave a lop-sided attempt at a grin, which failed. 'You first. How's the High Court Killing?'

'Trudging.' Thane poured himself a final small measure from the bottle, sipped the glass once, then left it untouched. 'Sandra nearly got flattened by a flying lavatory.'

'Dangerous things, flying lavatories,' mused Moss. He stifled another gathering belch, reached into his pocket, and took out a small metal tobacco tin. Opening it, he took a pinch of the white powder inside. The powder was magnesium oxide, used as insulation inside some power cables. Sandra Craig had first suggested it — it had worked for her grandfather and it now worked for

Moss. 'She's all right?'

'Fine. You can catch up with the rest at tomorrow's morning conference — seven thirty, sharp.' The last of Thane's patience evaporated. 'So . . . ?'

'Right.' Moss carefully sucked his lips. 'My job for today was supervising moving out from the old headquarters building, sending everything on to the new. No problems, everything fine. Then, in the main duty room, Colin, we're moving out filing cabinets. This was behind one of them.' He reached for his briefcase, opened it, and pulled out a grubby, dog-eared cardboard folder. 'Hidden there for over three years.'

'Damn,' said Thane softly, his lips suddenly drying. 'What was in it?'

'What's still in it,' corrected Moss. 'Six items that a certain detective inspector should have dealt with or allocated out that morning. Some are trouble, Colin. Real trouble. Be glad they're before your time — and mine.'

'How the hell . . . ?'

'How did it happen?' Moss gave a thin-shouldered shrug. 'We're talking about Detective Inspector Tyndall Black, suddenly called out that morning to an airport hostage situation — '

'Which went pear-shaped. He was shot twice — one bullet in the head, one in

138

the chest. Pensioned out with a wheelchair and a bravery medal.' Thane looked at the drink in his hand and set it down slowly. The shooting had been long months before he was transferred to the Crime Squad. 'And the file got lost in the general chaos?'

'Probably left on top of the filing cabinet, then slipped down during what was going on — it must have been that way. At the moment, I know, Francey Dunbar knows, the removal man who found it knows — and now you know.'

'But not Jack Hart?'

'Not Commander Hart. Not even Maggie Fyffe. And it's no use trying Tyndall Black. I spoke with Black's wife, he still doesn't remember anything that happened that day, he's in no mental state to be harassed.' Unhappily, Moss scraped a thumb over the patch of unshaven stubble on his face. 'Want to see what we've got?'

Thane nodded, cleared space on the kitchen table, and waited while Moss opened the file and spread out its contents like an overgrown poker hand.

'These we can forget about. A detective constable's expenses sheet waiting to be signed, a memo about overtime payments, and a fax from Dublin thanking for help in a safe-blowing arrest.' Moss shoved the three items to one side. 'Three down, three to go.'

Thane nodded and picked up the remaining trio. The first, scrawled on prison notepaper, was a tirade alleging the writer had been beaten by a detective sergeant while under arrest and in the back of a police car.

'He's dead,' said Moss stonily. 'Got out on bail, OD'd on heroin. Found in a backyard with the needle still in his leg. No other trace of the complaint lodged anywhere else.'

'Dead man, dead complaint.' Thane gave a grim shrug and discarded the letter.

Which left two items that mattered, each several pages long, and he read them with a gathering frown. One was a draft report typed by Tyndall Black, who had been investigating a major fraud being worked by a Tayside solicitor and a Bank of Central Scotland assistant branch manager. They had been milking money from trust accounts held on behalf of some wealthy, very elderly women. The other, a clipped-together set of hand-written scribbles, amounted to Black asking himself if the solicitor and the assistant manager were the end of it all — and underlining his belief there could be someone else involved.

'Phil?' He glanced at Moss, the question unspoken.

'They were charged, they denied the lot, they were found guilty, they got seven years each,' said Moss stonily. 'Nothing suggested about anyone else being involved. But . . .'

But Tyndall Black had always had a reputation as a totally thorough cop. If he had come round to believing there might be a third party or that one of the arrested men might be innocent . . .

'Work on it, without making waves,' said Thane softly. He thought of the wheelchair-bound detective, a man he'd never met. 'We owe him that much.'

'I will.' Moss glanced towards the whisky bottle. 'Ach, to hell! I'll maybe change my mind about that drink. If it's still on offer.' He watched as Thane poured liquor into both glasses, with the video playing in the front room producing a new crescendo of screams and gunfire. Then he raised his glass in a token toast. 'Tell me something about this Jane Tamsin murder.'

Thane did, briefly and unemotionally, while his companion took an occasional sip of whisky but mostly nursed his glass.

'Early days,' mused Moss at the finish. 'Trudging, like you said. Anyone you've met you can trust?'

'Two judges — I think.' Thane grinned a little. 'We'll keep digging at her general background. There has to be something there, somewhere.'

Moss sniffed agreement. 'Including Edinburgh? Why did she suddenly move over from there to this side of the country and long-lost cousin?'

'Edinburgh.' Thane nodded. 'You're right — and it goes on the list. Along with things like tracing the mystery Peter. And whether he could be a biker.' He pointed a sudden finger, remembering. 'I met someone out at East Kilbride who knows you. A woman.'

'A woman?' Phil Moss made it sound unlikely.

'She asked me to say hello. Says you were both constables when you knew her. Jinty Shaw — she's a shift inspector now.'

'Jinty Shaw.' Moss stared, swallowed hard, then drained his glass and laid it down. 'Yes, I — uh — remember her.'

'Grey-haired, smart, still good-looking, nobody's fool.' Thane eyed him with a hidden amusement. For once, Phil Moss seemed caught totally off guard. 'She'll be doing local legwork, so you'll probably meet.'

'I — yes, I might recognise her.' Moss glanced at his wrist-watch and belched almost nervously. 'Time I was going.' He collected his things and got to his feet, frowning. 'Jinty Shaw . . .'

Colin Thane saw Moss out, heading back towards his bachelor lodgings.

But Jinty? Later, as they settled in bed for the night, Thane started to tell Mary. He didn't get to finish. Despite his knee, he found there was absolutely nothing wrong with his horizontal mobility.

4

The bedside alarm wakened Colin Thane at 6 a.m. He quickly killed the rasping buzz — but the noise still brought a moan of protest from Mary, buried deep under the blankets. Yawning, stretching, Thane peered round an edge of the curtains at an early morning sky clear of cloud. The local bird population was in noisy chorus, and something which sounded like a crow in hobnailed boots was parading across the roof. Add barely enough wind to rustle the apple trees in the next-door garden, and things seemed set for a warm day.

Warm in more ways than one. Thane sighed at the thought. He showered and shaved, dressed in a fresh white shirt, teamed it with a summer-weight suit of soft Donegal tweed, and added a silk necktie which had a pattern of blue and black diagonals. His regular slip-on brown moccasin shoes completed the process and he took a wry glance at the dark-haired, grey-eyed individual reflected in the mirror. He was beginning to collect a gathering crop of crows-foot wrinkles around his eyes.

Thane checked he had everything in his pockets that he needed, then tiptoed downstairs to the kitchen. As usual, Clyde was snoring in his basket but then heard him and half wakened. The dog opened one eye, glared indignantly, then the eye closed again. He chuckled, made himself a cup of coffee, and drank it while he checked the news headlines on BBC Teletext. At six thirty he quietly left the house, started the Ford Mondeo, and began driving.

Traffic was still light at that hour, mostly night shift workers heading for home or delivery van drivers making their first rounds of the new day. The police radio network was silent, and Thane switched to a Radio Clyde early morning news programme, which was a mix of international political gloom and Scottish sporting despair. After that, he felt something like relief when he reached the tall outer fence of the Crime Squad headquarters compound and the security gate slid open.

It was 7 a.m. as he parked the Ford in the nearly deserted inner courtyard area and got out. Sandra Craig's white VW was already there, lying a few spaces along. When he went into the headquarters building, the spread of CCTV surveillance screens above the reception area and showing the camera sweeps covering the external approaches were all live, but with little to show.

'Canteen's working, sir,' an early shift orderly greeted him.

'Give thanks for small mercies,' said Thane solemnly. 'Who called the cook a bastard?'

The orderly grinned and completed the ritual of the old music-hall routine. 'Who called the bastard a cook, sir?'

Overnight, more progress had been achieved in bringing a semblance of order in the Squad's new location. Carpeting was complete, most fitments had been screwed into place, more boxes of files and equipment had been stowed away. Even the smell of new paint had died down in scale from asphyxiating to merely overpowering. As Thane used the stairway up to operational territory there was another sign of approaching normality. Commander Hart's prized collection of framed prints of nineteenth-century sailing ships had been hung along the stairway walls. Jack Hart knew each of the tall ships and knew their histories — all had been used at one time to carry convicts to Australia.

After that particular export trade had died out, most of the tall ships had ended their days moored as prison hulks along Clydeside's docks. With the passage of years, that flow had reversed. Scots criminals not wanted in Australia were now deported back to the UK by air.

Business Class. What else?

At the top of the stairs, the operations floor was almost deserted. Most of the day shift couldn't be expected in until around eight, and an unusual peace ruled. Thane reached his office, hung his jacket on a black plastic hook which had appeared overnight, and settled at his desk. A small pile of faxes and other messages had already been sorted out and awaited attention.

'Good morning.' Sandra Craig came into his room looking bandbox fresh. His sergeant had brushed her rich copper hair until it glinted like burnished gold, then had used a Spanish silver comb to pin it back. Her wardrobe for the day was a green and blue plaid shirt with black bone buttons, a loose and sleeveless suede waistcoat, and crisply laundered jeans. Her feet were in short paratroop style leather boots. She gave a start-the-day smile. 'Everything's set, sir. Team conference in the duty room at seven thirty.'

'Good.' Thane looked at her suspiciously. His sergeant was carrying a large, steaming mug of coffee, her other hand clutched a paper bag. 'Been at the canteen, sergeant?'

'Here, it's a restaurant.' She grinned. 'Yes.

Collecting breakfast.'

'Restaurant, not canteen.' Thane eyed her stonily. 'Same rules?'

'Same rules, sir.' In Detective Sergeant Sandra Craig's book, sergeants didn't act as handmaidens. They summoned an orderly. A male orderly for preference.

She had a fried egg sandwich in the bag. Thane settled for the same and coffee, she telephoned the order, and with the kind of service at that hour it arrived within minutes. By then, they had gone through the messages on his desk, discarding some, splitting the others into two sets.

On the one side were the negatives. The Scenes of Crime team who examined Jane Tamsin's forced locker at Empire Lines had located a few smudged and partial prints. But none were even half-way good enough to help identify the man who had escaped from the cellar. Scenes of Crime at East Kilbride hadn't managed to achieve much. The only identifiable prints found in the murdered woman's room had been her own. Two bank books and the few other documents found in the room were being forwarded — and although the East Kilbride uniformed team were still knocking doors around Lamanda Quadrant and asking questions, they had nothing fresh. Thane's own team hadn't done much better. A report from Dougie Lennox said that the microchip used in Jane Tamsin's pendant necklace was a factory reject — and there was still no trace of the Ducati murder bike or its crew of two. Other tries had ended against blank walls.

But having some kind of a report was always better than having nothing. At very least it could eliminate a possibility. Thane had called a halt when breakfast arrived, they ate, and his fried egg sandwich, deceptively crisp at the edges, dripped yellow yolk across the fax messages. Opposite him, Sandra Craig bit busily and coped more tidily.

'Jane Tamsin.' Thane paused between mouthfuls. 'Did you get round to looking through the clothes she was wearing?'

She nodded, still chewing.

'Anything that mattered?'

'Yes.' She swallowed, and moistened her lips. 'The outer clothing was ordinary enough, everyday quality. But she had a damned expensive taste in lingerie, sir.'

'Lingerie as in underwear?'

'Yes, sir.' She nodded patiently. 'And as in knickers. They were silk, boutique quality. Inspector Shaw at East Kilbride says the same about Tamsin's clothes at the Russo flat. Most items in her wardrobe were chainstore quality, but not when it came to lingerie. Everything in that department was the best. She was one lady who knew what she wanted next her skin — and spent to get it!'

'Serious money?' asked Thane.

'Serious enough. The only things of that quality I own, I keep for weekends — special weekends!' Sandra Craig took another bite of fried egg sandwich, chewed, then carefully used a finger to wipe a trace of yolk from the corner of her mouth. 'So how did Jane Tamsin get that kind of money?'

Which made a very good question.

Thane went through the other reports. They didn't tell him much. Jinty Shaw's team at East Kilbride had found other neighbours who remembered a motor cycle occasionally making night-time journeys to and from the Lamanda Quadrant apartment block. Some had vague memories of unexplained cars that stopped near their homes, of a woman getting out and walking on — but it stopped there. A few tentative sightings of the bikers who had torched Mary Russo's car all ended with both machines vanishing towards the nearest main road.

There was nothing new in overnight from Eastern Division, not as much as a whisper so far from their often fruitful contacts in Paddy's Market. Nothing from anywhere

150

around the area around the High Court buildings. And nothing from anywhere else — including a total blank about what had happened to the Ducati and its two riders after it had been driven away from the murder scene.

His thoughts switched back again to East Kilbride, then to the microchip firm said to have made Jane Tamsin redundant. 'Did we get anywhere with Sonnet-Bytes?'

'I phoned late yesterday, before Paisley,' said his sergeant. She shook her head. 'The office had closed for the night, the production department had only a skeleton night shift working. I said we'd get back to them.'

'Do that.' Thane finished the last of his coffee and tossed the emptied plastic container into his waste basket. 'As soon as they open. Get hold of somebody called Abigail Carson, their local managing director. Tell her I'm coming over.' He paused, then remembered his own preaching. 'And tell her we need the name of the Edinburgh firm who employed Jane Tamsin before she moved here.'

There were details to sort out, some belonging to existing cases on his workload, the type of cases that automatically went on hold when the more urgent turned up. Thane marked two to be referred back where they'd come from, glad he wouldn't be around when they landed on the desks concerned. Others were non-urgent and there was one he decided to try and palm off on Customs and Excise. Then, at last, it was finished. It was almost seven thirty. Conference time.

★ ★ ★

After only a day, the Squad's big duty room was already showing the first signs of occupancy. A large Spanish holiday poster showing the full virility of a magnificent black bull had been pinned to the door of the women's rest room. In a counterattack, the door of the men's room now sported a cartoon drawing of Goofy. A first crop of notices had appeared on the walls, including one offering special rate domestic insurance to serving and retired officers and another from the Police Federation inviting views on the latest issue of knife and bullet resistant body armour.

There was a full turn-out of his team occupying one corner of the room. Thane took a seat facing them, and Sandra Craig slipped into the chair beside him. For a moment he said nothing, considering the little group.

First, there was a surprise. Jock Dawson,

their lanky dog handler, lounged against a windowsill. Dressed as usual in khaki work overalls and calf-length rubber boots, Dawson had brought his dogs along. A massive tan and black German shepherd, Rajah, was sound asleep at his feet, mouth half open and showing fang-like teeth. His other dog, a slim young yellow Labrador bitch named Goldie, sat beside Dawson's chair with her tail gently twitching and big, intelligent brown eyes darting everywhere.

'Jock.' Thane raised a quizzical eyebrow. 'I thought you were on loan again to Tina Redder.'

'Cancelled, super,' reported Dawson cheerfully. 'Chief Inspector Redder didn't need me after all.'

'I heard about it.' Sandra Craig's murmur was for Thane's benefit only, her amusement barely hidden. 'I don't know why — not yet, sir. But the Broomstick Lady's mega-raid went belly-up. She's — uh — not totally happy.'

Thane mentally cursed the growing feud between the two women, spared a moment's silent sympathy for Tina Redder, then his attention moved on. Next in line was Ernie Vass; the heavily built former patrol car driver slouched in his chair, sleepy-eyed, one of his small black cheroots smouldering gently

153

between his jaws. Inevitably, he was sitting beside the boyish-faced Dougie Lennox. Originally they had arrived in the Squad on the same day — and although it was hard to imagine two more dissimilar individuals than the big, slow-moving Vass and the slim, womanising Lennox, they somehow worked well together. Detective Inspector Phil Moss and Detective Inspector Francey Dunbar were also both there, something Thane hadn't totally expected. They were sitting behind Dawson and his dogs and trying hard to fade into the background.

But in addition they had an uninvited visitor from Glasgow Eastern Division. The fat and moon-faced Detective Sergeant Alex Paulson perched uncomfortably on the edge of a chair and gave a wary half-smile.

'A social call, Alex?' asked Thane drily.

'No super.' Paulson quickly shook his head. 'My people sent me round.'

'To find out what's going on?' suggested Francey Dunbar with a mild sarcasm. The others grinned. Goldie the Labrador yawned.

'No.' Paulson flushed but didn't budge. 'We've turned up a couple of things. Tom Radd, my DCI, thought you'd want to know about them.' He saw the way that captured their attention, and made an awkward, throat-clearing noise. 'One is about the way that

154

Ducati vanished — '

'Magic wand style,' murmured Dougie Lennox sourly.

'Maybe — just maybe — we've a witness!'

'Go on,' said Thane softly.

'Suppose the two on it had transport waiting just out of sight. A van or something, so they could shove the Ducati aboard and take off . . . '

'Possible.' Thane's eyes had narrowed.

'There's a bag-lady named Old Aggie who ends most nights getting drunk out of her mind, then sleeps it off next morning on the banks of the Clyde — her favourite spot is not far from the High Court building. Old Aggie was seen sleeping there two mornings ago. She's — well, she's been hinting to her pals like she could have seen something.'

'You've talked with her?' asked Thane.

'No. CID only heard about her on the night shift.' Paulson grimaced. 'She'll be snoring somewhere with an empty bottle beside her. We're keeping an eye open for her now. But — uh — DCI Radd thought you'd probably want to take over when she's found and needs to be wakened.'

'When we can do the dirty work?' suggested Sandra Craig acidly. 'Nice deal, Alex!'

'We'll take her.' Thane silenced the redhead, then considered the Eastern sergeant

155

again. 'She's one possibility. You said there were two.'

'Yes.' It came like a sigh from the moon-faced detective. 'Something everyone totally forgot about. Everyone, sir. Your people and our people alike.' He paused, drew a deep breath, then ploughed on. 'The High Court complex is fully protected by hidden CCTV security cameras. They give total coverage . . . '

'Total?' Thane stared.

'Total.' Paulson gave an uneasy nod. 'We're talking a full chain of time-lapse security cameras, controlled by the court's people. Most cover entrances, exits, and the interior, but there's also basic perimeter cover. I — well, I only thought about it when I woke up this morning. That's when I realised . . . ' He looked at Thane as if ready to be struck by lightning, then thankfully moistened his lips when it didn't happen. 'Anyway, right now the court security people have started checking all recorded camera footage for the last two days.'

For a long moment there was a total silence in their corner. A telephone rang somewhere else and was answered. At the other end of the duty room, where there was a fully lit theatrical make-up mirror, a black woman officer was skilfully adding an

156

extra twenty years to her appearance. She was being helped by a Sikh colleague who had a raucous laugh. Both were in the final stages of breaking an immigration racket case being headed by Jack Hart. There was big money, ruthless money, in immigration rackets.

'Give my regards to DCI Radd.' When Thane did speak, his voice was empty of emotion. 'When I've anything to tell him, he'll hear. Until then, I don't think any of us has won medals for this. You understand, sergeant?'

'Sir.' Paulson nodded. Although the day had still to warm, his plump face seemed damp with sweat. Getting to his feet, he gave a weak token grin at the others, then left.

'Bloody hell,' said Dougie Lennox softly as the muster room door closed behind the man. 'Want to know what I think — ?'

'Be quiet, boy!' Phil Moss made it a vicious snarl. 'You haven't been told to think yet, have you?' He gave a long thunder of a belch, loud enough to silence the couple over by the make-up mirror, painful enough to twist his lined face in a quick wince. Then he looked across at Thane. 'So who does what?'

That didn't take long to parcel out. Ernie Vass was despatched to Paisley, a return based again on Empire Lines. Thane promised him help as soon as possible, his task to be a continuing search for information about Jane Tamsin's work as a scout for Michael Spring's business operation — including the hunt for the 'known face' who had escaped from the Empire Lines basement.

Dougie Lennox blanched when he was paired with Jock Dawson and his dogs. First, because Lennox was no animal lover. Second, because their workload stretched from collecting the CCTV stills being prepared at the High Court to taking over on Old Aggie when the alcoholic bag-lady was found. Women like Old Aggie were a type of female Lennox would rather avoid.

'Dougie boy, in this job you learn to take the rough with the smooth,' said Francey Dunbar drily.

'And she sounds rough,' declared a delighted Ernie Vass.

'Sergeant Craig will be with me, concentrating on East Kilbride,' Thane told them. 'For now, Inspector Moss and Inspector Dunbar are working on a separate and unrelated case.' He saw puzzlement on Sandra Craig's face and remembered she didn't know about that other problem. 'They'll be with us again as soon as possible — and that's all you want to know. Understand?'

158

He ended it there and their meeting broke up. While the others headed for telephones or canteen, Moss and Dunbar hung back.

'We're being shut out, sir,' said Francey Dunbar unhappily. 'It doesn't have to be that way.' He looked at Moss, usually an unlikely ally, for support. 'This Tyndall Black file has been lying hidden long enough to gather its own dust. The only possible hassle is around this one fraud case. That's not exactly urgent.'

'It could wait.' Moss frowned his agreement. 'Hell, Colin, the Tyndall Black file isn't a murder — would a delay matter for a few days?'

'I'm tempted.' Would a few days make any difference to the crippled Tyndall Black, given the small gamble that they could keep the lid on things? Thane sucked his teeth, then made up his mind. 'All right, we do it your way. You're back on the team. Joint mobile reserve and paper-pushers, and you give the Tyndall Black fraud any time left over.'

Dunbar grinned. Moss gave a satisfied nod. For both, honour was satisfied.

Thane headed back for his office, but was waylaid in the corridor by Maggie Fyffe. Commander Hart wanted him.

'Like now,' said Hart's secretary sweetly.

159

'And he has a meeting coming up.'

'So move it?' Thane grinned and set off in a long-legged stride towards Jack Hart's office. He could hear the woman's high heels pattering furiously behind him, trying to keep up. 'Damn you, Colin,' she said breathlessly. 'I hope it's expenses trouble again!'

It wasn't. When Thane entered the Squad commander's office, he found Jack Hart was sitting behind his desk like an emaciated Bhudda, arms folded.

'This High Court murder,' began Hart without preliminaries. 'I've had a phone call from the Crown Office, asking what's happening — and you know something? I don't damned well know!'

'There's an update on its way,' Thane soothed, only lying a little. 'Phil Moss is working on it.'

Then, while Hart sat building a thoughtful steeple with his fingertips and listening, Thane gave the Squad commander a quick outline of how things had begun and how they were shaping. Along the way, Hart gave an occasional grunt which could have meant anything. At the finish he sat silent then swore resignedly as a sudden loud banging filled the room.

'Builders or giant mice, God knows which — or what they're doing,' he said sourly.

'But they claim we're getting there.' As the banging stopped as suddenly as it had begun, he stabbed a sudden forefinger. 'How about you, Colin? Where are you heading? Do you still have your hunch that computers are involved in this? Or are we talking damned Victorian door knobs — meaning we landed a murder we could have done without?'

'I don't know.' Thane said it slowly, reluctantly.

'Well, at least you're honest about it.' Hart scowled. 'Meantime, Tina Redder's counterfeit case collapsing gives me a separate problem to sort out — and it seems like your sergeant could cause another.'

'Sergeant Craig?' Thane was lost.

'She's our new Federation delegate, right?' The Squad commander didn't wait for an answer. 'The word is that the Federation aren't happy about the new style police body armour — the style we've just been issued with for operation use. It's a sensitive issue, budget variety. So — uh — sit on her hard if she tries to make waves, will you?'

'I can try,' said Thane warily.

'You're her boss, Colin. Do more than try!' Hart's leathery face shaped a quick on-and-off smile then he reached for his telephone, a sure sign their meeting was over.

This time, Thane reached his own room

without incident. As he walked in, Sandra Craig was putting down the telephone. His sergeant looked pleased.

'Success. That was Abigail Carson, the Sonnet-Bytes boss lady,' she reported. 'She'll expect us at East Kilbride any time this morning. But she says that Jane Tamsin wasn't made redundant — she was fired for thieving.'

Thane gave a soft whistle. 'Thieving what?'

'Microchips.' Sandra fought down a grin at the look of relief that came to Thane's face. 'From the Sonnet-Bytes production line — the boss lady says she'll tell us all about it.'

'Right.' Thane allowed himself a moment's self-congratulation that his hunch had paid off. Now anything might come next. 'Did you get the name of the Edinburgh firm who employed Jane Tamsin before East Kilbride?'

She nodded.

'Contact Kerr Munn.' Detective Inspector Kerr Munn, a dour-faced Presbyterian, headed the Crime Squad's satellite office in Edinburgh. 'Tell him I need everything he can get on Jane Tamsin's background before she moved here — including any men in her life.'

'Like one named Peter, don't worry too

much about Paul?' Sandra Craig chuckled and reached for the telephone.

Thane took a deep breath, then let it out slowly. This new day was starting to take on a better shape.

★ ★ ★

They left for East Kilbride a few minutes later, using Sandra Craig's white VW Golf and with his sergeant driving. As usual, she kept her small transistor radio propped against the wind-screen, tuned to a Country and Western show. Guitar-throb rhythms and voices like Wanda Jackon and Ferlin Husky seemed to wash around the car as they headed out towards the new town. But Thane knew that his sergeant, although humming gently to the music, would also pick up the slightest squeak coming on the low-band police radio located under the instrument panel.

Regular exposure to his sergeant's tastes meant he could blank the music out of his mind and simply think. When you were a cop, thinking time was too often in short supply. He gnawed at a rough edge of fingernail then grimaced at his reflection mirrored in the Golf's windscreen glass. He knew he was still at the stage where much alleged thinking still came down to guessing. But maybe that was going to start changing . . .

They reached East Kilbride around 9 a.m., headed north through a sunlit profusion of roundabouts at an industrial estate, took a left at a prominently signposted Sitka Road, and drove past a line of impressive factory buildings, some with Pacific Rim ownership names, few offering clues about what they made. Sonnet-Bytes was one of the last in the line — an oblong two storeys tall with glass and concrete walls and an aluminium sheet roof. The building was half the length of a football pitch and almost as broad, Sandra Craig left the white Golf in one of the visitor slots in the parking lot, then they went into the building by the main door.

The front concourse area was spacious and comfortably furnished, the floor carpeted around a fringe of plastic greenery and a pebbled fish pond with a miniature waterfall. There were posters of computing equipment on the walls and a glass display case held silver trophies awarded at sales exhibitions.

'Looks prosperous,' murmured Sandra Craig.

'And is,' said Thane softly. He'd taken time to run a quick file check on Sonnet-Bytes before they came out. As a company, they were multinational players in the computer world, with the Scottish plant a modest outpost. He saw a uniformed security man coming over. 'Here we go.'

The security man escorted them over to a reception area where the furniture included chairs and a coffee machine. A uniformed receptionist took their names, and checked a list.

'IDs, please?' She smiled her thanks when they obliged. 'Then if you'll take a seat, and look this way . . . '

They did. There were two quiet clicks from a camera shutter. Two minutes later, they each had a clip-on security pass carrying a head and shoulders photograph. With it came a small advice sheet covering a list of Dos and Don'ts while in the Sonnet-Bytes building. It ended with a warning that any property not left at reception on the way in could possibly be searched on the way out. Then the receptionist used her internal telephone, spoke to someone at the other end, and beckoned the security man over again.

'Ms Carson says both of you can come on through,' she declared brightly. 'Now have a good visit!'

They followed as the security man set off. The carpeted reception area ended at a rubber-lined door which had a glass window and a warning notice which said 'Pressurised Beyond Here.'

On the other side, they found total change. First, as the door closed, there was a faint sighing of air movement and a sense of an increase in pressure. Then they were following the security man again, down a long corridor where the floor was a smooth green composition material and the walls and ceiling were of white tile. Every few feet, they passed large glass porthole style windows which gave glimpses into clinically clean laboratory-like areas.

Everything was strangely quiet. Behind the glass, they glimpsed workers dressed in one-piece white overalls and wearing white caps and face masks, their feet in moon style plastic boots. Suddenly, Thane realised that almost the only noises they could hear were the sounds of their own feet on the composition floor. His nostrils sensed the neutral feel of heavily filtered air.

'First time here?' Their security guide grinned at their reaction. 'Like visiting a hospital it is, coming to this place.' He thumbed at the latest window, where more overalled workers moved unhurriedly around equipment. 'And hygiene? It's cleaner through there than in any flaming operating

166

theatre. If I tried to stick my nose inside they'd throw me straight out again!'

They turned a corner, passed some larger windows and side corridors, then went through another air-seal door. On the far side, there were office doors. Their guide stopped at the third along, knocked and a green light flashed on. The man opened the door, waved them through, then closed the door again behind them.

It was a big room, bright with sunlight coming through a large picture window which also gave glimpses of a strip of garden divider before more of the factory began. The room was simply furnished with a large desk, filing cabinets and, in front of the desk, a circular glass-topped coffee table with a surround of upholstered chairs. A man and a woman rose to greet them from the chairs, the picture window behind them.

'Superintendent Thane?' The woman smiled and was first to speak, her voice outwardly easygoing, with a light North American drawl. 'I'm Abbie Carson, plant managing director.' She gestured towards her companion. 'Frank Alder is our European sales director, and I'd like him in on this. Any problem with that?'

'None.' Thane introduced Sandra Craig, and they exchanged handshakes with the two Sonnet-Bytes executives.

'Sit down,' invited Alder. 'Don't worry about me, superintendent. It's not that we expect you'll drag Abbie off to a cell, but when police are involved, then head office policy is to have a company witness any time possible!'

They took seats around the coffee table, Thane directly across from Abbie Carson. The Sonnet-Bytes managing director was a tall, big-boned Saxon princess of a woman, almost matching Colin Thane in height, her curly, corn-silk hair cut shoulder-length. She had regular features, a strong mouth and large, sea blue eyes, and she was wearing a tailored grey jacket and skirt, power-dressed style.

'Can we offer you coffee or anything, superintendent?' she asked crisply.

'No, thank you.' Thane dragged his attention away from the woman's long muscular legs, so near to his own under the glass-topped table. 'And this shouldn't take too long.'

He wondered. For once, he wasn't sure he wanted to hurry things.

Strong in personality, magnetically female, probably in her late thirties, Abbie Carson seemed a woman who expected to achieve her own way — quite simply because that was the way it should be. Their eyes met, and her mouth twitched in a slight smile, as if well aware of his under-the-table interest. By comparison, Frank Alder was older, around fifty, with a North of England accent. He had pepper-and-salt brown hair and a small, tight mouth that twisted a carefully controlled smile. Medium height and with the makings of a future pot belly, his shrewd eyes and large, protruding ears left him looking like a garden gnome who had gone wrong. He was in a thin-striped blue business suit a dark blue shirt with a button-down collar, and a red silk tie.

Where Abbie Carson radiated confidence, the signal that came from Alder was something different, definitely cooler, more calculating. Meaning, decided Thane, that both Sonnet-Bytes executives could be problems.

'So can we get straight into whatever this is, Superintendent Thane?' suggested Abbie Carson. She nodded to the diary display on the computer monitor screen to one side of her desk. 'I've a quality control meeting coming up. But I gave you priority because your sergeant more or less threatened me.' Her grin quelled Sandra Craig's murmur of protest. 'I'll take that from another woman, and good luck to her. But if you'd had a male sergeant . . .'

'Abbie would have put him through a blender,' suggested Alder stonily. 'Her personal microchip-controlled kind.'

'What else?' agreed Thane. He moved his gaze away from Abbie Carson's long legs, a chance to note that the woman's only jewellery was a small silver signet ring on one forefinger and a dangling pair of luckenbooth silver ear-rings. 'All right, we're talking Jane Tamsin.'

'As in murder of same,' murmured Alder. He blinked almost apologetically. 'This isn't a big plant, superintendent. We may employ something like eighteen thousand people world-wide, but here we're less than two hundred and fifty — and even when she's an ex-employee we can listen, we can read, and a murder is a murder.'

'And your sergeant was putting out signals,' mused Abbie Carson. She pursed her lips. 'You know we fired the woman for theft?'

'I was told.' Thane nodded. 'Exactly what happened?'

'She was a production line operator, good at it — and they don't grow on trees.' Sonnet-Bytes' managing director pursed her lips. 'When she applied for a job, we had vacancies and she sailed through our induction training course. She completed

170

our eight-week production operator course in four weeks — which didn't totally surprise us, coming from another computer firm. Then she joined the production team, and everything seemed fine.'

'For a few months,' said Frank Alder. He scowled. 'Except we have a Paris plant, working at the mass production low-cost end of the market — we're up at the other end, small and specialised, into a lot of research and development or into expensive early prototype runs. And we thought we had security nicely buttoned up.'

'No thefts?'

'Nothing recent that we knew about. Then suddenly Sonnet-Bytes Paris tell us a couple of our East Kilbride microprocessors — you call them microchips — have surfaced in one of their sales territories.' Alder gave a sour growl. 'Prototypes! Paris asked what the hell was going on.'

'A surprise?'

'One we didn't like,' snapped Abbie Carson. 'We've always clamped down on thieving every way we can — if necessary, we'll even strip-search workers on a random basis. That's in everyone's employment contract.' She saw the question coming. 'Including mine.'

'But you caught Jane Tamsin,' reminded

Sandra Craig unemotionally. 'How?'

'Mainly because we had to, sergeant.' Frank Alder didn't look totally comfortable. 'Look, we specialise in advanced generation microchip production.' He looked at their two visitors. 'Do you know what that involves?'

They shook their heads.

'Right. Then I'm going to tell you — because unless someone does, you won't know what the hell we're talking about.' He turned to Abbie Carson. 'Any demonstration stuff here?'

'Yes. From the last study course.' She nodded at a filing cabinet. 'Bottom drawer — help yourself.'

Alder rose, went over, opened the filing cabinet, and came back with a long shoebox-size plastic container. He placed the box on the table and opened it.

'I said that as far as Sonnet-Bytes is concerned we're a small and specialised outpost of their empire. I meant very small. We maybe turn out a few thousand microchips a week.' He shrugged. 'Two miles from here there's a multinational production plant that cost £40 million to build and makes ten million chips a week — I mean every week — then exports them world-wide. They go into everything from cars to washing

172

machines, from domestic equipment to cheap watches.

'But here's how they all begin. Hold out your hand, superintendent.'

Out of the box came a fat, sausage-like shape, silver in colour. The Sonnet-Bytes executive dumped the sausage in Colin Thane's outstretched hand. It was thick enough and heavy enough to have been an artillery shell.

'Thirty inches long, weight thirty pounds.' Alder grinned. 'That's a single silicon ingot, the computer world's basic raw material.'

A raw material made from ordinary beach sand, one of the most inexpensive items on earth. Until it moved on. Purified, melted in giant crucibles at almost fifteen hundred degrees Centigrade, each ingot was shaved into thin wafers, each wafer about one twenty-thousandth of an inch thick and cut to the size of a small coin. One side was polished, where the vital integrated circuits would be photo-engraved.

Integrated circuits started out as patterns on a drawing board then were shrunk down and down in size until they were camera-ready. The wafers, specially coated, automatically etched and re-etched, their backs gold-coated for good electrical contact, then came together in layers — and each wafer in this world of the infinitesimally small could contain up to several times one thousand circuits.

Alder had returned the silicon ingot to the box. Reaching in again, he brought out and scattered half a dozen tiny, spiderlike shapes on the coffee table glass.

'Miss out a hell of a lot of technology you don't need to know about, and this is our final product. Microchips, with protective lids and circuit leads.' He thumbed at the spider shapes. 'If these were real, they'd be worth around £5000 each.'

'You said research and development,' mused Thane, considering the little shapes. 'Any special development programme in progress?' He saw the quick, questioning glance that passed between Abbie Carson and Alder for a moment, then was gone again. 'I mean right here and now?'

'Nothing that is going to make anyone's Hall of Fame.' Alder gave a humourless grin. 'Like always, we've some commercial development work under way. My job is to sell to Europe, and the computer world is a cut-throat place.' The man drew a deep breath. 'You exist on new ideas, you take them around the market place, you stay on top — or you die. And that's the end of the lecture, folks. Feel happier?'

'It helps,' agreed Thane woodenly. Helped. Except that he had the feeling that even if Alder was telling the truth he was still holding something back — and, from the tight look on Abbie Carson's face, she knew it. He gave Sandra Craig a sideways glance, and her dead-pan expression showed she felt the same. He looked down at Abbie Carson's legs again, then returned to Alder. 'So you travel a lot?'

'A hell of a lot.' The man swept the dummy microchips into one hand and dropped them back in the box. 'Have passport, will travel — that's me.'

'Get back to Jane Tamsin,' suggested Sandra Craig. 'Jane Tamsin and how she was caught . . . '

'Our people just worked through possibilities,' said Alder cagily.

'Frank's shy about it. I'm not.' Abbie Carson chuckled, leaned over, and gave Alder a mocking pat on the arm. 'Superintendent, we just covered a traditional blind spot. We put a CCTV camera in the women's changing room, with a female security officer at the other end. She saw Jane Tamsin come through alone in mid-shift for a comfort break, and the chips came with her. Our security officer saw how the little bitch hid them. A woman's way, right?'

'Then we grabbed her at the end of her shift,' shrugged Alder. 'The plant nurse searched her. She was carrying three microchips.'

'Value?' queried Thane.

'To her?' Alder frowned. 'Depends who would buy locally. Maybe £100 each. To a crooked end buyer, maybe £2000 each. Factory selling value, around £6000 each. They were part of a run we were producing for a German banking group.'

'Surprised, superintendent?' Abbie Carson smiled wryly. 'Don't be. Sonnet-Bytes Corporation aren't major league ball-park players, but on a world-wide basis we take an annual loss by theft of around £4 million sterling — God knows what that is in European Ecu funny money.' She sighed. 'Until now our East Kilbride operation literally had a crime-free record — and losing that really did annoy us!'

Jane Tamsin hadn't been arrested or charged. Sonnet-Bytes had a rigid international policy of avoiding publicity. Yes, she had been questioned — by Abbie Carson — but had refused to say anything. She simply accepted dismissal on the spot and had signed an agreement to it so there could be no legal comebacks. Then she had left the plant within the hour, and hadn't been back.

'When you hired her, did she have a reference from her last firm?' queried Thane.

'Yes.' Abbie Carson nodded at a file on her desk. 'I looked it out again when I knew you were coming — and it was good.' She lifted the reference letter from her file, swung away, and made a copy of the sheet on the printer beside her desk. Handing it to Thane, she made an apologetic gesture. 'I should get to that production meeting, superintendent. Anything more that can't wait?'

'One thing maybe matters.' Thane tucked the copy sheet in his pocket. 'She had some kind of relationship with a man named Peter. We're trying to trace him — or any other men in her life. There seem to have been a few.'

'You're welcome to look, but you won't find them here.' Abbie Carson shook her head and that corn-silk hair swept her shoulders. 'This Peter or anyone else — we checked that out at the time we fired her, in case there was more than one rat in our nest. But all we found was that she had a reputation as a loner around the plant.'

'And no more thefts since she was fired?' queried Sandra Craig.

'No more we know about, sergeant,' said the Saxon princess.

She made a telephone call which brought

177

the same security man along to escort them out.

'Superintendent — ' Abbie Carson placed a hand on Thane's arm as he made to leave — 'one news report said Jane Tamsin was stabbed.'

He nodded.

'Was the fact she was killed anything to do with what happened here? As managing director, I think I've a kind of right to know.'

Thane was careful. 'It's possible, Ms Carson.'

'Abbie,' she corrected with a grimace of protest. 'Only the taxman calls me Ms.' Then the grimace vanished, the sea blue eyes were suddenly sober. 'If we can give more help, call me. I'll make whatever time you need. That's a promise.'

The two Crime Squad officers were politely shepherded out of Abbie Carson's office then back along the corridor with its tiled, portholed walls and echoing floor. At the far end, they went through the rubber door again, left the pressurised area, and had to check out at reception. Their security passes had to be returned, then the security man, who had stayed hovering in the background, went with them to the main exit door.

'You don't exactly let people wander,' Thane told him.

'Orders, sir.' The security man made it an apology. 'I was Military Police for twelve years, and this outfit hasn't much to learn from anyone.'

'Even about Jane Tamsin?' reminded Sandra Craig.

'We can't win them all.' The man's face reddened. He went with them out through the main door and into the open air, looked around, then gave a satisfied grunt. 'No sign of him. Maybe we've done better here.'

'Meaning?' asked Thane.

'We've had a prowler around the parking area,' explained their escort. 'Male, white, probably mid-thirties. Not much more than that, superintendent — appears medium height and medium build, just hangs about, then the moment he knows we've spotted him, he's off!'

Thane swung to face him. 'How long has he been around?'

'A week or so.' The security guard eyed him warily. 'Whoever he is, there's been no problem, sir. He hangs around under cover for a spell most mornings, then he's back for another spell in the afternoon.' The man grinned. 'For his sake, I hope he's not fool enough to be stalking our production girls.

They could eat him for breakfast!'

'Have you advised the local police?'

'We can cope,' declared the security guard firmly. 'If I get near him, he'll get my boot up his backside for starters!'

Thane left it at that. Back in the Crime Squad's VW Golf, with Sandra Craig driving them out of the factory parking area, he glanced across at her.

'A prowler, sergeant?' he asked.

'I wouldn't put money on it, sir.' She changed gear and fed the car more accelerator as they joined the main road again. 'Too much coincidence. Do we let the local troops know?'

'Better.' Thane nodded, then looked back down the road. The Sonnet-Bytes plant was almost out of sight. 'What did you make of things back there?'

Sandra Craig muttered under her breath, her eyes staying with the road.

'Try again.' Thane waited.

'I said that damned Carson woman had legs up to her armpits. And knew it!' Sandra scowled in his direction. 'Don't tell me you didn't notice?'

'Don't tell me you didn't notice — sir,' corrected Thane. 'There's no crime in looking.'

'Whatever you say — sir.' She sighed.

'And Alder?'

'Knows his job, but I wouldn't trust him,' said Sandra Craig bluntly. She nursed the steering wheel. 'Where now?'

'Lamanda Quadrant — Jane Tamsin's cousin.'

It was only a few minutes' drive. When they got to Lamanda Quadrant the burned-out car of the previous day had gone and there was only a solitary police car with a solitary constable aboard to show that anything out of the usual had happened.

They left the VW in an empty parking space and walked towards the apartment block with the sun now warm on their backs and a low murmur of bees coming from the flowering shrubs that flanked the entrance. When they took the elevator up, they heard a TV programme coming from inside Mary Russo's apartment but it was switched off when Thane rang the doorbell. A few moments later, Mary Russo opened the door.

'You again!' The raven-haired schoolteacher was wearing a loosely tied pastel pink dressing-gown, her feet were bare, and although her hair was brushed she hadn't reached the stage of putting on make-up. She sighed. 'More questions?'

'Just a few,' promised Thane.

'You'd better come in,' said the woman resignedly. She let them in, closed the door again, and tightened the dressing-gown more. 'I'm taking today off work — and Andy's here too.'

They followed her through to the kitchen. Her daughter, hair in short pigtails and wearing pyjamas, was sitting on the floor beside the TV set, eating toast and with a mug of coffee beside her. The child looked up, smiled, then the smile faded.

'No Inspector Shaw this time,' agreed her mother, and gave Thane a sardonic glance. 'Friendly, your Inspector Shaw. Likes chatting with children — when the mother isn't around.'

'Sometimes it's easier that way,' countered Thane warily.

'Maybe. There won't be a next time.' Mary Russo bent, lifted her child off the floor, and placed her on her feet. 'Andy, take your breakfast through to the front room. Watch telly in there — I won't be long.'

The youngster gathered up her toast and coffee mug, grinned as Sandra winked at her, and left them. They heard the front room door open and close, then the television set switch on to a children's cartoon channel.

'Well?' Mary Russo had her own mug of coffee on the kitchen table. She lifted it and sipped, watching them. 'Has something happened? Have you got the two brutes who killed Jane?'

'No.' Thane shook his head. 'We've come from talking with management at Sonnet-Bytes.'

'And?' Mary Russo saw Sandra starting to move towards the door. 'You! Don't even think of going to Andy!'

'I wasn't.' Sandra waited.

'Mrs Russo.' Thane spoke her name quietly. 'Your cousin wasn't made redundant, whatever she told you. She was fired — for thieving.' He watched the woman's face. It had paled, but what he saw wasn't total shock. 'Did you know?'

The schoolteacher bit hard on her lip, and her grip on the pottery mug tightened in a way which made coffee slop unheeded down her dressing-gown. Then, reluctantly, she nodded. 'I heard gossip.'

'Did you ask her?'

'Yes.' Mary Russo almost whispered the words. 'She said it was malicious rubbish. She didn't get a reference from Sonnet-Bytes because she made trouble when she was paid off.' She paused and shrugged. 'I — well, I decided to believe her.'

'It was easier?' suggested Sandra Craig.

'We were living under the same roof.'

183

Mary Russo shrugged. 'She was almost the only blood relation I had.'

'Tell me about that, Mary.' Thane rested the tips of his fingers on the edge of the kitchen table, beside a rack of toast and the coffee pot. 'How well did you know her? Had you always kept in touch?'

'No.' Mary Russo shook her head. 'She — well, just appeared when I said, about a year ago. I hadn't seen her since we were both about Andy's age, but she'd found an old address and tracked me down because she was moving west.' Then her expression froze as if she read his mind. 'Jane was my cousin, superintendent. She had photographs, we still shared too many memories . . . '

'I understand.' Thane thought of the man in Mary Russo's life. 'Did you ever talk with Ken Hodge about this?'

She nodded. 'Ken said he believed her. That's — well, that's why he got her the job with Empire Lines.'

Thane didn't want to push it further — not yet. He signalled his sergeant and they thanked the woman and made to leave. On the way out, they passed the front room door. It was closed, and the TV cartoon noise was in full flow. They left things that way and left the building.

'Ken Hodge next?' asked Sandra Craig when they were back aboard the Crime Squad pool VW Golf. She had a street map guide to East Kilbride lying beside her.

'Might as well,' agreed Thane. Once again, he was left feeling there were too many gaps in the background they were building around Jane Tamsin, too many coincidences, too many mysteries.

'She seems all right.' His sergeant glanced over towards the apartment block. 'Nice daughter.'

Thane sucked on his teeth but said nothing. He wasn't going to — not yet.

The constable in the police car watching Lamanda Quadrant gave a mild nod when they drove past.

It was the kind of nod that meant he'd run a PNC check on the white Golf. All Crime Squad pool cars changed their number plates every few weeks, a system which confused the enemy whom Francey Dunbar called the Black Hats, but all — well, most — of the changes were immediately updated to the Police National Computer. The system provided steady employment for a certain minor-league Glasgow criminal, who kept busy updating and photocopying his own weekly list of Squad number plates. The list sold around a regular circuit of bars

185

and clubs in Central Scotland, and as a courtesy he tried to make sure his visits didn't clash with those of punters buying or selling stolen jewellery, nicked car radios or similar goodies.

Again it was a short journey for the VW Golf. Kenneth Hodge's office in the Plaza Centre was right in the heart of town, and Sandra Craig solved an obvious parking problem by leaving their car on a double yellow line — then immediately engaged in a snarling match with an overweight traffic warden who thundered towards them. Having won the snarl, she arm-twisted the traffic warden into pointing them towards the architect's office.

Hodge's office was on the third floor of one of the Plaza Centre's business blocks. It had a heavy multicoloured glass door, and the small but modern outer office was under the charge of a solitary secretary-receptionist in her early twenties. The girl had a kettle boiling and had been making tea when they arrived. She considered Thane's warrant card open-mouthed, and then she gave a nervous giggle.

'He's on the phone.' The girl nodded towards a closed inner door of vintage, richly oiled mahogany. 'In there — he won't be long.'

She saw them settled in chairs beside a well-lit, well-filled aquarium, then went back to her tea-making. Thane had time to note the framed array of panels and certificates around the walls, realised that his sergeant had somehow talked the secretary-receptionist into giving her a couple of the small sweet biscuits lying in a saucer ready for Hodge, then a buzz signalled the end of Hodge's call. The girl used her internal link and the oiled mahogany swung open a moment later.

'Superintendent, you're a surprise!' The tall, thin architect, his bald head glowing pink under the main office lights, shaped a greeting. 'Here with good news?'

'Not yet,' said Thane mildly. 'I need to ask you about a couple of things.'

'Oh.' The man's small eyes flickered briefly towards Sandra Craig, her mouth still full of biscuit, then he ignored her. 'You'd better come through.'

Thane signalled Sandra Craig to stay then followed the bald, beak-nosed man into his office, Hodge closing the door once they'd entered. It was a big, well-lit room, the centre dominated by a large drawing board mounted on a stand. A pencil sketch plan pinned to the board was elaborate in detail.

'Work in progress.' Hodge forced what

was meant to be a smile. 'I've a client who wants to knock down a ruin of a country house and build a new hotel.' He gave a conspiratorial wink. 'So I make the drawings look super-good for the planning committee. Draw in trees and things around the edges, maybe even a horse or two at a hedge — damn all to do with the planning application, but it helps.'

'And Empire Lines at Paisley would love to get in on the salvage side?'

'Probably. Why not?' The man's long beak nose twitched, as if scenting the spoils, and he crossed over to the board. 'It's a sizeable job superintendent.' He broke off and frowned. 'This isn't why you're here. You said you wanted to ask me things — ask, man.'

'All right.' Thane nodded. 'It's fairly simple — '

'What you call routine?' Hodge raised a sarcastic eyebrow.

Thane ignored the interruption. 'I've come from talking with Mary Russo again, about Jane Tamsin. Did you know Jane was fired by Sonnet-Bytes because she was caught thieving?'

'Mary told me there was gossip, but that Jane denied it.' The man shrugged his thin shoulders. 'It didn't worry me.'

'Not even when you fixed that job for Jane over at Empire Lines — when she didn't have any kind of reference?'

'Who believes a reference?' The man tried a bluster. 'I told Michael Spring I thought she'd be all right. He knows me, that was good enough!'

'Nice to have friends,' murmured Thane woodenly. 'They can come in useful in the strangest ways.' He ignored the man's angry scowl and switched to something else. 'You first met Mary Russo at a dance, correct?'

Ken Hodge moistened his lips but nodded.

'Good.' Thane sprang his mousetrap, a trap built on what had been a growing hunch. 'She says Jane was with her. But when did you first meet Jane, Mr Hodge?'

'None of your damned business.' Hodge was suddenly hoarse. For the first time, too, an odd blend of panic and fear showed in his eyes.

'Do you really want me burrowing around?' Thane gave a faint, warning grin. 'You wouldn't like it.'

The man paled and hesitated. 'All right, I knew Jane before I met Mary.' He swallowed. 'Does it matter?'

'How long before?'

'A couple of months or so.' Hodge swallowed again and stared down at the plan drawing. 'I picked Jane up in a bar one evening. I saw her another couple of times, then — well, she told me she was living with this widow cousin who needed company, male company.' He shrugged. 'Jane never had any problems that way.'

'And Mary Russo didn't know how the way you met was fixed?'

'Still doesn't know.' The man avoided Thane's eyes. 'Look, what harm did it do? Damn — I like her. We get along. Even her kid likes me. And now she has lost Jane — ' he took a deep, hopeful breath — 'does Mary need to know?'

Thane considered him in silence for a long moment.

'We'll see,' he said grimly. 'But no promises. We're talking murder, Mr Hodge.'

And no, he told himself, he still didn't trust Kenneth Hodge.

He spent another few minutes going back over the rest of Hodge's story and found it still didn't vary in any other detail from the original version. Then he thanked Hodge, ignored the outstretched hand he was offered, and left. On the way out, he collected Sandra Craig. His sergeant had been gossiping with Hodge's secretary — at least, his secretary would consider it gossiping.

Sandra didn't. She told Thane why when

they were back down from the third floor and had left the building.

'Her name is Irene, and she's not a total bimbo. She has Hodge's card marked as an almost over-the-hill womaniser — '

'There are a few of them about,' mused Thane.

'I know.' The redhead threw him a glare. 'Anyway, she knows all about Mary Russo, and she also knew Jane Tamsin. Mary was flavour of the month, but he didn't totally drop Jane.'

'She's sure?'

His sergeant nodded. 'Sometimes Jane would ring him and they'd talk by phone. Sometimes she'd come to the office and they'd leave together. Now and again Irene had to do a juggling act to make sure the cousins didn't trip over each other — '

'Why did she tell you?' Thane was puzzled.

'She was talking about men, sir,' she explained patiently.

'Of course,' accepted Thane stonily.

Then he had no more time to digest that. The metal buttons of her inspector's uniform glinting, the sunlight picking highlights in her carefully styled grey hair, Jinty Shaw was walking towards them along the busy pavement.

'Inspector.' Thane greeted her with a dry

smile, remembering the man on duty outside Mary Russo's block. East Kilbride's jungle drums were efficient. 'You'd better meet my sergeant.'

He introduced the two women, who for a moment considered one another with a single scanning glance which seemed to satisfy. Then Jinty Shaw looked past him, a slight disappointment on her face.

'Just the two of you, superintendent?' she asked.

He nodded. 'How did you know we'd be here?'

'Mainly guesswork.' The woman inspector shrugged. 'How did you find our Mr Hodge?'

'Worried.' Thane told her why, which was also the first time Sandra Craig had heard. He added his sergeant's bonus item, then asked, 'How much do you know about him?'

'Not much more than we know about any of them yet.' Jinty Shaw made it sound personally unacceptable. 'Hodge lives in a converted barn over in the Old Village, he has been there for a few years, and he keeps his head down locally. On the business side, he doesn't seem any kind of high-flyer. We're working on the rest of it, superintendent.' She paused, letting a bustle of shoppers pass by on the pavement. 'Anything special we should know about?'

Thane told her about Sonnet-Bytes' apparent parking lot prowler, and she winced, reacting as if it was a personal insult.

'I'll take care of it,' she promised. 'I'll be in touch.'

'Inspector — ' Thane stopped her as she turned to leave. 'Phil Moss sends his regards.'

'Does he?' She smiled in a way which crinkled the faint lines around her eyes. 'That's kind. Maybe we'll meet.' Then she had gone.

'She knows Phil Moss?' Sandra Craig frowned after her. 'How?'

'How would I know?' murmured Thane. 'Ask her.'

'She'd set my tail alight,' scowled the redhead.

'Then don't,' agreed Thane. 'Just get me back to Glasgow.'

They walked to where they'd left the white Golf. Another prowling traffic warden had given it a parking ticket, which Sandra Craig bleakly tucked away in a waistcoat pocket before they got aboard. Another couple of telephone calls had just been added to her workload.

Thane used the Golf's low-band Squad radio as they began driving towards the city. He had the call patched through to Phil Moss, who sounded sourly pleased to hear from him.

'Different things happening, Colin,' he reported. 'Top of the list is Edinburgh.' He spoke in the shorthand style favoured by most cops, no matter how secure a radio system was claimed to be. 'That Edinburgh factory and your query. Kerr Munn says the woman did work for them for a spell. But if she had a reference, it was a fake. She left one step ahead of being charged with theft.'

'Microchips?' asked Thane.

'That's probable,' grunted Moss. 'But mainly because she was caught after hours, photocopying technical documents in the production office. Kerr Munn says he'll keep digging.'

'Thank him.' Thane knew that the Edinburgh detective inspector, his Calvinistic curiosity roused, would need no urging. 'What else?'

'Nothing new from Paisley. Our people are gathering those pics at the High Court and playing Find the Lady.' Moss allowed a low, rumbling belch to escape on the airwaves for a long echoing moment. 'On the — uh — other matter, Francey and I think we're maybe getting somewhere useful. But that can probably keep.'

As it had for a long time already. Thane told Moss to pass the word that he was on his way back towards the city, heading for the High Court area, then signed off and put the handset away.

'I heard most of it, sir.' Sandra Craig kept her eyes on the road and accelerated past a line of fast-travelling articulated trailer trucks, a convoy belonging to a firm notorious for their tight delivery schedules. 'Would you say our Jane had a busy little life?'

'It looks that way.' Thane sat back and listened to the car's engine note while he added the latest pieces to the jigsaw jumble being gathered, a jumble which had to fit a pattern. Whatever kind of pattern that might be. Then he remembered something totally different.

'Sandra — ' He stopped his sergeant as she lifted one hand from the Golf's wheel and reached to switch on the personal transistor, still clipped on the dashboard. 'Let's talk Federation. Just you and me, off the record.'

'Sir?' Suspicious, her voice chilled several degrees. 'About what?'

'Body armour and the Federation.' He raised a mild eyebrow. 'What's going on?'

The redhead shrugged. 'The Squad are being used as guinea pigs to test a new

195

body armour issue. Have you seen what the gear is like?'

'Seen, yes.' He knew the new armour was lighter in weight, made of the latest synthetic fibre, was claimed to absorb the impact of a bullet or knife with equal efficiency, was even machine washable — which was useful after a cop had worn one of the vests for a full, perspiring summer-weather operation.

'Did you try wearing it?' she demanded.

'No,' he admitted. 'But I've heard it is comfortable enough.'

'Designed by men, for men.' Sandra Craig took the white Golf through a roundabout in an indignant squeal of rubber, then scowled. 'I'm a woman, sir!'

'Yes, sergeant.' Thane fought down a grin. When she was angry, Sandra Craig could look at her most attractive. 'I'd noticed.'

'Women are built differently from men.' She pursed her lips. 'We have different shapes. You've — uh — noticed that too, sir?'

'Yes, sergeant.' For his own safety, he gave a sympathetic nod.

'And that's what it is all about. This new issue is awkward, impossible to wear for any length of time. They give women problems that no man could imagine. Every policewoman I know — even the dreaded

Broomstick Lady — wants the old issue back.'

'And if that can't happen?'

'Try us!'

She switched on the dashboard transistor set, and Tammy Wynette took over for the next part of the journey. Detective Sergeant Sandra Craig was content to peel and eat a banana. By midday the Golf was travelling through the centre of Glasgow with the sun still sending the temperature soaring, the streets bright with summer dresses and sports shirts as the city's office workers and shoppers took advantage of a kind of day that didn't come too often.

The High Court complex was first on their list, and Sandra Craig managed to squeeze the Squad car into a vacant parking slot outside the next-door City Mortuary and just across from the usual open-air bustle of Paddy's Market. As they stopped, Dougie Lennox emerged from another Squad vehicle parked on ahead, came towards them with a large, well-filled brown paper envelope nursed under one arm, and climbed into the Golf's rear seat.

'Got them, boss.' The baby-faced detective constable gave the envelope a happy tap. 'External security video camera prints. All time-lapse still frames, more than a hundred of them from two days ago — '

Thane cut him short. 'Covering the murder?'

'Before, during, and after,' confirmed Lennox. 'Some good, some very good, some just God-awful. I selected — '

'You what?' Thane swallowed.

'Selected, super.' Lennox was pleased with himself. 'To cut down on the work load. I told them we wanted only the relevant murder locus not the rest of Paddy's Market . . . ' His voice died away under Thane's gathering scowl.

'Wrong. We want the lot. We don't know what we expect to find.' Thane glanced around. 'Where's Jock Dawson?'

'Down beside the river, super.' Lennox was wary. 'Keeping an eye on Old Aggie.'

'Has she moved?'

'Not since she was spotted, sir.'

'Anything at all about the girl in blue denims?'

'No, super.' Lennox was learning. He said nothing more.

Thane decided to alter his plans a little. For the moment, the envelope with the security stills could stay in Sandra Craig's Golf. His sergeant's new chore was to speak nicely to the court CCTV staff and have them process as many more time-lapse prints as they could. After that, she was to make another tour around the Paddy's Market stalls, trying yet again for some lead to solve the mystery of the young girl in blue jeans.

'Which leaves you and me,' he told Lennox. 'We'll join Jock Dawson — then I'll give you a small treat. You can get to wake Old Aggie!'

The Crime Squad's curly-haired Romeo gave Sandra Craig a despairing glance which was almost a plea for help, but drew an amused grin.

Sighing, Lennox followed Thane's example, got out of the car, then together they walked the short distance to the busy Saltmarket and crossed over to the other side. From there, they strode the rest of the way towards the river. The battered Land-Rover dog van was parked near the river bank, nearside wheels up on the pavement, and Dawson was leaning against the vehicle's scarred radiator grille, smoking a cigarette. His yellow Labrador was quietly panting in the shade under the front wheels. There was no sign of Rajah — the giant German Shepherd had reached the age when he was wise enough to snooze in the dog van until needed.

'Boss.' Dawson made a lazy attempt at a salute, but gave up half-way through and pointed instead. 'Over there. We've left her alone.'

About fifty yards away from them, partly hidden by a small straggle of scrub, what could have been a bundle of rags lay slumped full-length on the grass only a stone's throw from the edge of the river bank.

'Has she moved?' asked Thane.

Dawson shook his head. 'She's out like a log, sir. Could have been that way for long enough.'

'Let's move her.'

'You mean in my van, sir?' The big dog handler was horrified.

'Should I get a taxi?' asked Thane sarcastically.

Dawson shrugged, turned, gave a soft whistle, and Goldie came out with her tail thrashing. The pair started off towards the river bank and Dougie Lennox followed. Except Goldie had come to a complete halt and was looking round at Dawson.

'Goldie, what the hell?' asked Dawson, frowning. 'Shift!'

The Labrador bitch kept looking up at him, making a whimpering noise.

'Jesus!' exclaimed Dawson. He hand-signalled Goldie to stay, then was running forward. Not certain why, but knowing it was expected, Lennox followed. With a sick realisation, Thane did the same. The Labrador didn't move.

Thin, with a straggle of grey hair and a wrinkled prune of a face, Old Aggie lay on her back with a crumpled grocery bag of possessions still clutched in one hand and the inevitable empty bottle lying on the grass nearby. She smelled, liquor apart. Her clothes were old and dirty, flies were already crawling across that raddled face and those dulled, staring eyes.

Feeling icily cold despite the sun on his back, Thane squatted down beside the dead woman. Two small, close together puddles of congealing blood had formed on the grubby shirt covering her chest. Puddles marking where she had been stabbed by something which must have been very thin and very pointed.

Like a sharpened metal spoke from a motor-cycle wheel?

He looked across at Jock Dawson, who knelt opposite him.

'Poor old wifie,' said Dawson sadly. His rugged face shaped an almost gentle smile. 'Och, bless her, the soul was probably too drunk to feel anything.'

Thane nodded. A slightly green-faced Detective Constable Lennox was hovering in the background, and he beckoned him over.

201

'Dougie, we need a full murder team and the mortuary van,' he ordered, then drew a deep breath. 'Tell Eastern Division. This is their patch.'

Lennox hurried off.

Within ten minutes the troops had arrived — and with them came Sandra Craig. By then, Colin Thane had something else on his plate. To settle Goldie down, Jock Dawson had taken both dogs for a walk along the river bank. When they reached the water's edge at a point almost due south from where Old Aggie had died, Rajah began growling and then Goldie yapped.

Jock Dawson found the cause. A black plastic tote bag, open and empty, floated against the bank. A few feet away under the water, at first no more than a glint of chrome showing under the lapping river, lay a Ducati motor cycle.

All they lacked were a pair of crash helmets.

5

Jack Hart always labelled it Crisis Management Time. Meaning that when an investigation appeared ready to go totally pear-shaped then the Scottish Crime Squad commander would arrive on the scene unannounced, making a few mainly encouraging noises to the troops, then vanish again.

He'd been, he'd seen. What he really thought about things and precise instructions about what he wanted done to haul the situation back under control would later be spelled out to the senior officer handling the case. Usually in the privacy of Jack Hart's office. Abrasively.

Hart was in a strangely reasonable humour when he finally arrived, hauled away from a golf course where he'd been hosting a politician who might be persuaded to vote against any fresh cut in the Crime Squad's annual budget. By then, the summoned technical team had finished their immediate chores, photographing the murder scene in an electronic snowstorm. Old Aggie's body, decently deposited in a black plastic body bag, had long since gone round to the

City Mortuary. A shirt-sleeved squad of uniformed constables, men and women, had made a fruitless fingertip search of the river bank area.

Now, standing just a few feet from the water's edge with Colin Thane beside him, Hart watched the same search squad get ready to do it again — this time for the benefit of a gaggle of press photographers and a couple of TV cameras. It was a quiet day for news, and a rerun for the cameras would guarantee a 'support our gallant police' mention of the bag-lady murder on local evening bulletins.

'Strathclyde's press office are issuing the usual kind of handout. 'Well liked old woman done to death in apparently senseless, motiveless killing.' That will keep the media Mafia happy enough.' A grimace crossed Jack Hart's lined, leathery face. 'What they don't know about the rest, hell mend them. We'll keep it that way. Nobody gives them even a hint of a link with Jane Tamsin's murder. You understand, Colin?'

Thane nodded. A modest distance away, a small media circus were being shepherded by a Strathclyde police press spokesman. Police press spokespeople were notoriously selected — and promoted — on their ability to say as much as possible about as little as possible. For the rest of it, Jack Hart had arrived in company with Strathclyde's Assistant Chief Constable (Crime) and an escort which included the Glasgow Eastern Division chief superintendent. An unhappy-looking DCI Tom Radd represented the Eastern's CID squad. There had been a brief meeting, as short as it was formal, with Radd, who sported another of his Technicolor neckties, scowling at Thane but saying little.

The mutual aid arrangement that already covered Jane Tamsin's murder had been extended to cover Old Aggie — at least for the time being. That decided, the meeting had broken up at the same time as an incident unit caravan had arrived and been found a priority place with its promise of coffee for the VIP visitors.

'You know your job, keep at it.' Hart glanced at his watch, a signal he was leaving. 'Then we'll have a meet of our own, in my office, when you get back.' He pursed his lips. 'I'll be honest, Colin. So far, I'm underwhelmed at the way things are going.'

'I know the feeling.' Thane nodded wryly, then tried to change the subject. 'Uh — how was the golf?'

'That?' Hart brightened. 'Word about your body caught up with me on the fifteenth fairway. I played out, sank a ten-yard putt which made me three up and three to go, then I pulled out and called it a draw.'

'Bad luck,' said Thane absently.

'No. Solved a problem.' The Squad commander twinkled a smile. 'You know me, Colin. When it comes to something as sacred as golf, I only play to win. Not always too clever. Not if you should be thinking budget thoughts and your opponent is an evil politician! But a draw? Pure magic!'

Once Hart had gone, Thane made a quick check around his own people. The Ducati bike quietly recovered and removed, Jock Dawson and Dougie Lennox were checking their way further down the river bank on the off-chance of any other finds. Sandra Craig had gone back to the High Court complex and its security cameras.

That left Tom Radd. Thane found the divisional chief inspector standing behind a fold-down counter in the incident caravan and using a radio phone link. His visitors had gone, leaving only a cluster of dirty coffee cups.

'Tom.' Thane laid a hand on Radd's shoulder. 'Spare me a moment?'

'Wait.' Radd brought his call to an abrupt end, put down the handset, and faced Thane. His face was stony. When he spoke, there was a rasping edge to his voice. 'What can I do for you, superintendent?'

'Give over, Tom,' said Thane wearily. 'I've enough problems.'

'That makes two of us,' snapped Radd. 'And mine now include an Assistant Chief who doesn't totally believe the Crime Squad should have as much as their nose in the High Court murder. He's ready to hold me personally responsible for any other death on my patch — then transfer me back on school crossings duty!'

'The way I hear it, school crossings duty these days should earn danger money,' mused Thane. Hands resting on the counter-top, he held the man's gaze. He knew he might well need Radd's willing help. 'Look, Tom, forget mutual aid. Suppose we do a personal deal? I'll keep off your back, you keep off mine — but we both know exactly what the other is doing and give what help we need? That way, maybe we can both end up smelling of roses!'

'With my luck, I'd give you better odds on a smell of horse manure,' suggested Radd grimly.

'Roses love horse manure,' reminded Thane neutrally. 'Will we give it a try? Hell, man — I've seen happier faces than yours peeping out of second-hand coffins!'

'At that, you could be right.' Tom Radd took a deep breath, sighed, then finally allowed himself a faint grin and nodded. 'I'll give it a try — Colin.'

* * *

At least temporarily, one problem had been put on hold. Relieved at even a small success, Thane left the incident caravan and went back out into the sunlight of the river bank. A fish jumped in the middle of the sparkling Clyde, splashing heavily into the water. The ripples it left were big enough to be caused by a leaping salmon — after more than a century, salmon were beginning to return to Glasgow's river as industry died down and industrial pollution went with it. There was even a new, bitter joke that the city's unemployed could soon be reduced to eating salmon — unless the seals got there first. Seals were the latest promise of tomorrow returning up-river.

Suddenly he realised that it was already mid-afternoon, that he hadn't eaten since breakfast, and that maybe he could kill at least two birds with one useful stone.

For a start, he made the short walk from the Green and up Saltmarket to the High Court complex then went straight on past the City Mortuary without slowing. He'd been told that Doc Williams had dumped a

208

lecture to a university pathology class so that he could carry out the autopsy on Old Aggie, but the police surgeon would still need time. Instead, Thane entered the court building at the main door and crossed through into the cool space of its atrium area.

He was spotted by an ex-policewoman who was on reception duty. She smiled, dumb-showed sergeant's stripes on the sleeve of her dress, then thumbed towards the main stairway. Nodding his thanks, Thane went up the broad steps of grey-flecked marble then along to the restaurant area. At that time of the afternoon only the public facility, a cafeteria layout fronted by a long counter, was still serving. Most of the tables were empty, but Sandra Craig was sitting alone near a potted plant. She smiled a greeting, but continued working on the mountain of pink ice-cream on the plate in front of her.

'What's left?' Thane asked the counter hand who appeared.

'Meat pie, some chips, no veg — you're late.' She relented and thumbed towards Sandra Craig. 'If you know that one, she got the last of the stew. But I could maybe find you some apple sponge for afters.'

He took a tray, settled for a wedge of pie and chips, saw the sad remnants of apple sponge lying in a glass cabinet, decided to let it stay there, collected a cup of coffee, paid, then took his tray across to join his sergeant.

'That's all they had left, sir, is it?' She considered his tray with a mild sympathy. 'I got — '

'The last of the stew,' said Thane grimly. 'I was told.' He laid out his meal on the table-top, vaguely aware of movements and a mutter of voices from a half-hidden corner table. He tried a first bite-sized sample of meat pie, and either it was better than it looked or he was hungrier than he'd realised. Then he chewed for a moment, looking across at the redhead, who had gone back to demolishing the pink ice-cream. When he'd seen her last, Sandra had been returning again to the High Court CCTV control room. 'How did you make out, sergeant?'

'Not bad, sir.' She tapped a fat new envelope on a chair beside her. 'Second instalment, and they're working on more now.'

'What have we got?' He ignored more noises from the voices at the corner table.

'It's good.' Sandra Craig looked pleased. 'All time-lapse stuff. But I think we're going to have most of what you want.' Opening the envelope, she fished out the top video print sample from the bundle inside. 'Here's a sample.'

Thane looked and gave a silent, appreciative whistle. The CCTV picture was next best thing to pin-sharp, an exterior of the High Court complex with a broad view of the Paddy's Market scene in the background. He peered more closely and this time whistled softly aloud. It was better than he'd dared hope possible — and all on one video print. The security camera lens had caught Jane Tamsin as she collapsed, stabbed and dying. Her killer was no longer a vague description but a firm reality who wore black motor-cycle leathers and who had been captured on time-lapse tape. He appeared well built, no more than average height, his face masked by that crash helmet, a crash helmet with two white horizontal bands. There was a general mid-morning market background — and that included another crash-helmeted figure in leathers coasting his motor cycle through the crowded area to join his killer companion.

'We've more, but that's the best,' said Sandra Craig.

'And it's a winner.' Thane scrutinised the print again as if he was afraid the thing might disappear. Then he laid it down. 'What about the girl in blue jeans?'

'The CCTV team found her, but more on the edge of the camera frame. Now they know what we want, they're looking again. I'll show you what they've got as a starter.' Sandra Craig slid the first photograph back into its envelope, started to produce another then stopped and looked past Thane. Suddenly, there was a warning in her eyes. 'Sir — company!'

There was no time to say more. A peroxide blonde of a woman, tall, beanpole thin, of uncertain age, was marching over from that corner table. She had a gaunt, lived-in face, and caked make-up. But her wafting perfume had to be expensive and her tailored dark suit hadn't come cheaply. Her fingers were a sparkle of oversized diamond rings, and an industrial-size gold chain hung around her veined neck. She stopped, considered Thane closely for a moment, then gave a satisfied nod.

'Aye, it's you all right!' She gave a pleased twist of a smile. 'Hello, Mr Thane. Remember me?'

It took a moment, then something about the glint in her eyes and the set of her mouth brought a memory back. Thane nodded wryly and got to his feet. 'How are you, Babs?'

'Surviving.' The smile widened, her hands

gripped the back of the nearest of the heavy cafeteria chairs. 'I've heard you've done all right too, Mr Thane. Even made superintendent, God help us!' She winked. 'Sit down, man. Having a cop treat me like a lady would be bad for my reputation.'

He sat. About eight years had passed since the last time he'd seen Babs Riley. By then, she had been on her third husband and he'd arrested each of them at different times for burglary. It was that kind of a family. Her uncle and her brother had been well-known safe-blowers. That last time, he'd arrested her son for armed robbery.

'What brings you here?' asked Thane warily. Babs Riley had sometimes carried a knife. At least he didn't have to worry about the way she was gripping the chair. Tables and chairs in the High Court public restaurant were all firmly bolted to the floor, a reasonable precaution in such a location. Even architects sometimes learned sense. 'Family again, Babs?'

'You could put it that way, Mr Thane.' The dyed blonde nodded. 'I found myself a new man a couple of years ago — Numero Four, right? Fine, until the stupid bampot gets himself caught raiding a post office. Then with enough witnesses against him to fill a church hall he still tries for not guilty.'

Her face showed disgust. 'The man's a real numptie! Anyway, I came along to watch wi' a couple of friends. The jury's out, so we took a break of our own.' She glanced at Sandra. 'Who's this — uh — person you're with?'

'My sergeant,' said Thane solemnly.

'Dear God, you catch them young these days!' The woman shook her head in near-disbelief then faced Thane again. 'Well, Mr Thane, I came over because for long enough I've wanted to thank you for something.'

'Thank me for what, Babs?' Thane raised an eyebrow.

'Remember how you jailed my son Fergie?'

'The payroll job — he got five years.' Thane nodded.

'If you'd really gone for him, he could have been handed serious time.' The woman's mouth tightened. 'But, thank God, at least he got the five — and five was long enough.' Her hands tightened knuckle-white on the chair. 'Three of Fergie's best pals all overdosed dead on drugs in the first six months he wasn't around them. Fergie would have gone the same way — if you hadn't landed him inside.'

'It happens,' said Thane softly.

'It happens.' She brightened. 'But now I've seen you, Mr Thane, remember that if you need a favour some time — any kind, even your kind . . . '

'I'll let you know,' he promised.

'Good.' Babs Riley smiled and flashed the diamond rings. 'And I'm doing all right, no complaints. I talked Numero Four into buying me a wee used car sales business. Totally in my name, over on the north side, Springburn way. It's like a licence to print money — and even legit!' She winked. 'Now I'll get back to my friends. The big fellow there could be in line as Numero Five.'

'Take care of yourself, Babs,' said Thane almost affectionately.

'I'll try.' Suddenly, the woman laid a hand on Sandra Craig's shoulder and beamed. 'Here's a wee tip for you, sergeant — though maybe more for when you get older. Always try an' keep a spare man on your back burner. You never know when he could be useful!' Her gaze considered the meat pie in front of Thane with disdain. 'But feed them better than that, girl!'

She beamed, left them, and walked back towards her table.

'Interesting lady, sir,' said Sandra Craig with a studied innocence. 'And she likes you.'

'Most women do,' Thane told her blandly, then had the grace to grin.

He ate on while his sergeant continued to show him more of the security stills. The pie was good, and Thane finished it. But the chips were wet and greasy, and the coffee had gone cold, and he left them untouched. After the stills, he gave Sandra Craig a new list of things he wanted organised, then they parted — he saw Babs Riley give a wave as he left the restaurant.

The quickest way to reach the CCTV monitoring room was through the most tightly sensitive area of the High Court complex. Thane took a restricted use elevator down to the building's basement level and had to show his warrant card to get through two guarded metal doors. From there, a uniformed man walked with him the rest of the way.

This was the holding cells area, an underground corridor which had a blank wall to one side and a long, brightly lit row of cells on the other. Each cell was divided from the next by a baffle wall. A couple at one end offered limited privacy for women prisoners. The rest were individual cages fronted floor to ceiling by gleaming metal bars, each cage furnished with a concrete bench and open-to-view, vandal-proof toilet. Some of the cells held prisoners waiting their turn to be taken up to one of the courts for trial. Someone was singing in one cell,

216

someone was weeping in another. Graffiti had been scrawled on a few of the walls.

'Hellish spelling, sir,' said Thane's escort. He grinned as a sudden torrent of abuse greeted them from behind one set of bars. 'Sounds like he knows you. But I don't think he wants your autograph.'

The torrent of obscenities followed them down the corridor. At the far end of the holding cells facility Thane was admitted through two more locked and guarded doors, then at last reached the modest cellar-like room which was his goal. Two uniformed officers, a sergeant and an inspector, both long-service and grey-haired, were operating the controls of a bank of electronic equipment which fronted a row of monitor screens.

'Cup of tea, sir?' The inspector indicated a steaming kettle.

'Why not?' Thane waited while the sergeant performed the necessary ritual. The milk came from a plastic carton, the sugar straight from a paper sack. The result was stirred with a chewed HB pencil. When he sipped, the brew tasted like it would have stripped paint. He saw they were waiting for a verdict, and nodded. 'That's fine.'

'Good.' The inspector beamed. 'Well, we haven't gone through all of the time-lapse tapes in full — we'll need more time.

But — uh — ' he dealt out a selection of still-frame prints on a shelf in front of their visitor as if they'd been a pack of cards — 'will these help?'

They did. Thane stared at one particular group of prints, all taken by a time-lapse security camera which had focused towards the boundary fence between the court complex and the next-door market area. In the background, customers clustered around market stalls. There was the teenage girl in denim jeans, squatting on the ground exactly as she'd been described, that single sales stock length of cheap cotton cloth spread in front of her. In two of the prints she was talking to a heavily built middle-aged man, then he vanished between time-lapses.

In his place, Jane Tamsin was suddenly there, walking slowly past the girl. The woman about to be killed seemed to be looking around, frowning. Putting a small strip of the time-lapse prints together, Thane read it as if Jane Tamsin had expected to meet someone who hadn't turned up. But then another figure appeared at her side between time lapses — a man on foot, wearing biker's leathers and the red crash helmet. Into the background in that frame came the second biker, straddling the Ducati, using his feet to keep it moving, still keeping his distance.

The camera had captured one more potentially vital fact. As the first biker walked past her, the sequence of prints showed the girl in jeans mouthing what had to be some kind of a greeting.

Then, two time-lapse stills on, as the Ducati trundled past her, the action had moved away.

'Happy, sir?' asked the sergeant. The service medal ribbon on his uniform showed he was near enough his pension not to have to care.

'Happy,' confirmed Thane.

'More tea, superintendent?' asked the inspector. Thane knew not to say no.

When he left a few minutes later, he had the latest collection of stills in a new envelope under his arm and a promise that the CCTV team would guard the time-lapse tapes as if they were bars of gold. He made his way back up to the court complex's main reception area, managed to locate the same black-gowned court officer who had been his escort on his previous visit to judicial territory, told the small, round-faced man what he wanted, then had to wait.

A full ten minutes passed, then the

court officer returned, nodded success, and beckoned.

'One jury are about to get a surprise comfort break. The other team are already out of court, considering a verdict,' he told Thane, and grinned. 'You'd be amazed to know how much Their Lordships seem to be enjoying all this. They say they'll give you ten minutes. But do me a favour — don't let them feel too important, superintendent. They can be enough damned trouble as they are!'

Once again, Thane was taken aboard the small private elevator with the keypad controls and was carried up to the carpeting and polished wood of judicial territory. This time, he was taken straight along to the long, narrow, judicial library room. It was empty, and for a few minutes he was left alone with the shelves of law books and their new-age computer facility companions. He had gone over to a window and was looking down at the back-to-normal market bustle when the door behind him clicked open. He turned as the two law lords came into the room, both still wearing their red velvet judicial robes with that white ermine trimming.

'Back again, superintendent?' Lord Lewis, the Lord Justice General, made it part statement, part question. Removing his heavy wig of once-white horsehair, he tossed it on one of the library tables. 'Well, as long as you've something good to tell us, fine. But on a day like this, dressed like this, it would be wise not to try my patience too much. I could use personal air-conditioning!'

Behind him, the smaller, sharp-faced Lord Kirk closed the library door again, loosened his robes, unfastened his stiff-winged white shirt collar, gave a happy grunt, and dropped into a chair.

'Make that two of us glad of a break, superintendent,' he confessed. 'I'm working in an oven, not a courtroom. Just keeping the jury awake is a full-time job.' He eyed Thane. 'The clerks said this was urgent.'

'So, superintendent?' The Lord Justice General produced a gold cigarette case from a deep pocket under his robes, opened it, and lit a cigarette with an ordinary book match. 'How urgent? We heard you'd found another body, but — '

'Take a look at these.' Thane brought the bundle of security video prints out of their envelope and spread a small, selected group on the polished wood top of one of the library tables. 'Look, then tell me what you think.'

The two law lords came nearer, produced spectacles, and peered at the prints. Frowning,

Lord Lewis took a long draw on his cigarette then let the smoke out in a long, slow breath.

'I'll be damned,' he said softly. 'That's what we saw.' He tapped one of the prints which showed the two bikers. 'Can you identify them?'

'Not yet.' Thane shook his head.

'And here's the girl we told you about — the girl wearing jeans.' Lord Kirk pointed at another print, his small nostrils flaring. 'This is what we meant, superintendent. She definitely seems to be saying something to those killers.'

'Alleged killers,' murmured his fellow judge with an acid edge of humour. He paused, lips pursed, his cigarette burning almost forgotten between his lips, then tapped one of the prints again. 'There's maybe something else that might help you.'

'My Lord?' Thane raised an encouraging eyebrow.

The two men exchanged a glance, their scarlet and white judicial robes bright splashes of colour in the sunlight streaming in through the library windows.

'John?' Lord Lewis made it a question to the junior judge.

'I'll tell him.' Lord Kirk nodded. 'More recalled memories, superintendent. Did you notice that two of the photographs show a heavily built man standing near the girl?'

Thane nodded.

'His next appearance was immediately after the murder, and it would be off camera,' said Lord Kirk carefully. 'The last we saw of him, he had returned and he was urging the girl to leave. Which — ah — might make him useful, I imagine.'

'Damned useful, as a potential Crown witness,' agreed Lord Lewis grimly. 'I'd think so, if it was a case that came to my court.'

'Which, as we told you, can't happen to either of us.' Lord Kirk produced a handkerchief and loudly blew his nose, taking a moment to examine the results. 'Is your other body linked to all this, Thane?'

'Probably.' Thane nodded.

'A suitably cautious word, Superintendent Thane.' Lord Lewis drew on his cigarette again. 'You're wise to use it, given the brainstorms that seem to affect some of today's juries.' He flicked ash in the general direction of a spotless ashtray. 'Right now I've a jury deciding their verdict on a man who carried out a remarkably stupid armed robbery at a post office. Provided they possess even a modicum of sense, their verdict must be guilty. Unless defence

223

counsel makes some particularly tearful plea in mitigation, I'll give the idiot in the dock six years. Then what? Most likely he'll come out, most likely he'll do it again, then you people will catch him again.' He frowned. 'I try to be fair and impartial. Otherwise, I'd be tempted to make it eight years!'

Thane said nothing, but felt glad that Babs Riley had Numero Five in reserve.

'The whole process of so-called justice is becoming more and more complex,' mused Lord Kirk. 'People elect politicians to make laws. Then the court's role is to administer their laws and deliver justice — justice without concern about reactions from said politicians. With suitable compassion when required. Yet every time a court exercises compassion some judge gets it hard in the neck!'

'There used to be a popular song that 'things ain't what they used to be'. It's true.' Lord Lewis used a hand to gently massage his bald head. 'You know, two hundred years or so ago a senior Scottish judge named Braxfield won his place in the historical hall of judicial fame by describing an accused as 'a fellow who'd be none the worse of a good hanging'. But I prefer his more general view. That if you hang a thief when he's young, then — '

'Then he'll no' steal when he's old,' completed Lord Kirk with a cackle. 'We've all known the temptation. How do you feel about that view, superintendent?'

'The civil liberties mob wouldn't like it.' Thane chuckled and gathered up the photographs. 'Thank you. I'm finished.'

'Where's your young sergeant today?' asked Lord Lewis conversationally.

'Handling another part of the inquiry.' Thane put the photographs back in their envelope and closed it. 'You know her family, sir?'

'I've known her father most of my life. We went to the same village school.' The Lord Justice General crinkled a smile. 'Angus Craig was a hooligan, superintendent. But totally reliable. How would you describe his daughter?'

'The same, My Lord.' Thane grinned. 'It must run in the family.'

Lord Kirk pressed a buzzer, and the black-gowned court officer returned.

'Keep in touch, superintendent,' reminded Lord Lewis. He turned to Lord Kirk who had now removed his wig. 'Coffee, John? That's if you think your jury can wait . . . '

'What they don't know won't hurt them,' said his fellow judge blandly.

They nodded a polite goodbye and Thane was guided out.

* * *

The way he'd expected, he found Sandra Craig when he walked round to Glasgow Green and the grassy spot where the Strathclyde force incident caravan was located. She was inside, and the Eastern Division CID was there in the form of the moonfaced Detective Sergeant Paulson.

'Sir!' Alex Paulson sprang up from his seat and somehow managed to slam his head against the caravan roof with an almighty crash. For a moment the man looked dazed, then he recovered. 'I'm — uh — minding the store until Detective Chief Inspector Radd gets back, superintendent. It's that damned gang war again — '

'You mean that damned group disorder, sergeant,' corrected Thane cynically. 'Got a name for your rocket scientist yet?'

Paulson scowled. 'It's no joke, sir. There was another homemade rocket launched in the same area last night. This one didn't explode — if it had, it would have demolished a betting shop.'

'Then they're serious,' sympathised Thane drily. 'But what about here? Any luck?'

'Yes and no.' Paulson shrugged. 'Scenes of Crime are still prowling — nothing there for certain. But we've found a local 'who sort of thinks he remembers' seeing a grey van parked near here for a spell a couple of mornings ago.'

'Mid-morning? Around the time Jane Tamsin was murdered?' guessed Thane.

The Eastern detective nodded. 'Then when he looked again later, it was gone.'

'Getaway wheels once they'd dumped the Ducati?' Sandra Craig made the suggestion, but frowned. 'Taking a chance, weren't they?'

Thane shrugged and looked out of the incident caravan window. This part of the river bank was quiet enough. There was plenty of through traffic on the nearby Albert Bridge, but the average driver's attention was usually on other moving vehicles. Ask beyond that, and most could have been wearing blinkers.

'They empty Jane Tamsin's handbag and get rid of it, dump the bike in the river — then they escape in the van.' Paulson scowled. 'Hell, it wouldn't take much more than a minute. Take off those damned crash helmets and they'd look like real people again — who'd think of stopping them?'

'Nobody,' agreed Thane.

Except they couldn't have anticipated that a drunken old woman would be lying there among the grass and shrubs, dozing her way out of a hangover. Had she wakened enough to see them after they'd removed their crash helmets? Enough to maybe recognise them again — and had killing her been the easy way to remove that chance?

'We checked anything she had on her — which was probably everything she owned. Apart from a gold wedding ring, there was nothing even worth pawning. She'd no permanent home. Just the occasional Salvation Army billet,' volunteered Paulson. 'More important, we're trying to verify that story our night shift picked up. If Old Aggie was doing a local hero act, telling her story to anyone for the price of another drink — '

'Then it was the next best thing to suicide,' Sandra Craig was sadly realistic. 'Poor daft old wifie.'

Thane nodded, saying nothing. But this had been a poor daft old wifie who, whatever else, hadn't parted with her gold wedding ring. Gold? Police Speak would describe it as 'yellow metal' in the official report. But that wedding ring had probably been her last, treasured link with another time.

Further along the river bank, the same squad of uniforms were lining up to carry out yet another fingertip search pattern along a slightly different stretch of ground. He could see the Scenes of Crime team continuing to do patient things around the taped-off area where Old Aggie's body had been found.

It was only too familiar, yet it was all part of a routine which could never be allowed to become boring. A high percentage of all serious crime, including murder, only ended in arrests because of that same repetitive, plodding routine.

Police officers who forgot that did so at their peril.

★ ★ ★

Colin Thane headed back for Crime Squad headquarters a little later, aboard Sandra Craig's white VW Golf. His sergeant was driving. Before they left, he had made sure that Tom Radd would see duplicates of the key CCTV prints from the High Court cameras and would also know the latest contributions from their two law lords.

He shook his head in mild amusement. Any more from that judicial pair, and he'd have to think about enrolling them in a witness protection programme.

Dougie Lennox was still out with Jock Dawson and the dogs, making yet another check along the water's edge. As soon as that was over, they would also return to base. The whole investigation into Jane Tamsin's murder was becoming more and more of a tangle, and it was time to sort things out, decide new priorities . . . and make suitable soothing noises to Jack Hart as Squad commander.

'I had another trawl around the Market,' said Sandra Craig as they drove along. The redhead paused for a moment, narrowing her eyes then flipping down the visor as the sun hit their windscreen at a blinding angle. 'But it's still the same — nobody's talking.'

'Because they're scared?'

'I don't know, sir.' Sandra Craig shook her head. 'Let's say nobody wants to make waves. Not even my best girls. And now, when word gets around about Old Aggie . . . ' She left it there and shrugged. 'Anybody who knows anything is keeping a very tight mouth.'

Leaving only one question, decided Thane. Why?

It all came back to Jane Tamsin, caught photocopying technical documents in one microchip manufacturer's office and fired caught stealing actual microchips from another firm — where she'd used a fake reference to obtain employment.

The woman he'd first seen as a body on

a mortuary slab was the key factor in almost everything they knew to date. But there had to be more — there had to be very much more behind the murder.

Jane Tamsin couldn't have been an amateur thief. She had to have been both spying then stealing for a buyers' market. In the background, her mysterious friend Peter had probably manipulated most of what she did — and it was an easy mental step from there to conclude that the raven-haired woman might have been killed to keep her silent.

But why only now, after a gap of weeks?

That was another good question.

Thane heard an odd muttering noise from Sandra Craig, and gave his sergeant a sideways glance. Her driving was as smooth as ever, but her lips were moving and for the moment, from the occasional word he caught and the expression on her face, her thoughts were far away. Probably she was rehearsing a new Federation delegate argument about that damned body armour. But what he'd said to the Lord Justice General had been accurate enough. If her father had been a reliable hooligan, then it was a case of like father, like daughter.

He saw a new glint in her green eyes, wondered what new possible twist of argument had crossed her mind, and was glad he wasn't directly involved in this particular little war. Then he turned away, looked out of the passenger window, and was content to just watch the way sunlight glinted on the other traffic.

★ ★ ★

They reached the new Crime Squad building a little before 5 p.m., parked in the inner courtyard, and diplomatically avoided going anywhere near another parked pool vehicle, a bright red Volvo. It lay with its front end expensively shoved in, being balefully examined by the transport pool sergeant.

'Not one of ours,' growled Thane. 'Keep going.'

'Spook wheels,' murmured Sandra Craig. 'I know it. A white settler detective inspector from London.'

They exchanged a grin. Nose-in-the-air Special Branch spooks, particularly the so-called white settler variety, could sort out their own problems. There were old scores to settle.

Inside the building, the settling-in process had obviously continued. Business looked almost back to normal, and they went directly up to Thane's office, where an inevitable pile

232

of faxes and telephone message slips again lay on his desk. He draped his jacket over the back of his chair, then they got to work on what was waiting.

'This first,' he decided, making a quick selection. 'Edinburgh.' Kerr Munn wanted words, and the capital-based detective inspector seldom wasted anyone's time. 'Let's find out what he's got.'

There was a direct line through to the Squad's Edinburgh satellite office. Sandra Craig used it, got through, then handed Thane the instrument as soon as she had DI Munn on the line.

'You were looking for me,' said Thane without preliminaries. 'Something new, Kerr?'

'It's Jane Tamsin again, sir. Nothing about that damned woman was simple.' By Kerr Munn's dark gloom of Calvinistic standards, he sounded almost pleased with life. 'I told you how she did a runner from Ardee Concepts over here?'

'I remember,' said Thane patiently. 'And?'

'And now they admit that just a little earlier a male technician did the same.'

'A technician named Peter?' asked Thane softly.

'Peter Sonas.' The Edinburgh man's voice frosted. 'You mean you knew about him, sir?'

233

'That someone called Peter existed some-where,' said Thane flatly. 'Nothing more. So — Peter Sonas. What have you got on him?'

'Not as much as I'd like, and no positive link known between them.' Munn's snarl of disgust travelled loudly over the forty-mile telephone link between the two cities. 'Ardee Concepts say Sonas was caught attempting to steal technical information and fired. Jane Tamsin had another try at something similar after he'd gone. Neither case reported to the police.'

'Why not?' snarled Thane.

'Not enough court of law style proof, bad publicity they don't need — the usual,' said Munn resignedly.

They'd both heard it all before. Thane grunted and used a fingertip to shape a vague doodle on the fine coating of white builder's dust that had gathered on his desk. 'Personal backgrounds?'

'Not a lot. Tamsin and Sonas were both regarded as loners. Separate addresses, rented rooms.' Munn sighed at the inevitability of it all. 'Nobody knew much about either of them and they just vanished — no forwarding addresses. The woman claimed her last employer had been a London travel agency that went bust — so there was no chance of her getting a reference from them.'

'And Sonas?'

'Different,' admitted Kerr almost grudgingly.

'How?'

'He's English, but he'd spent some time in South Africa — '

'You're sure?' Thane gripped his receiver.

'That's what he told people — and that he'd left because he didn't like the way things had changed. I suppose plenty of people feel that way.' Munn stopped, puzzled. 'Does South Africa tie in with something?'

'It does.' With the stiletto style murder of Jane Tamsin, probably caused by a sharpened spoke from a motor-cycle wheel. A minor variation on a South African gang weapon. 'You've a description for Peter Sonas?'

'Late thirties, thin build, height around five ten, dark hair, brown eyes,' recited Munn. 'Women like him, and he likes women.'

It would do as a beginning. Enough, too, to see if SCRO's records could come up with anything. Thane told the Edinburgh-based detective inspector to keep trying for more, then ended the call.

Plenty of others wanted to speak with him. There was a message from Ernie Vass over in Paisley, another from the grey-haired Jinty Shaw in East Kilbride, and yet another from the Scenes of Crime team at Strathclyde's Eastern Division. Thane took the last of them first, spoke to a civilian assistant at Eastern Division, and was a further step forward when he finished. Scenes of Crime had found faint but identifiable boot prints on the grass beside Old Aggie's body and matching boot prints on the hard earth from the street leading to where the Ducati motor cycle had been dumped into the river.

Most important of all, they had one spanning boot print which began with its sole on the same earth and the heel on the strap of Jane Tamsin's abandoned tote bag.

At last, Colin Thane had his first unbreakable evidential link between the two murders.

He tried Jinty Shaw next and was patched through by radio link from East Kilbride to her car. She was returning from separate visits to the Sonnet-Bytes plant and to Mary Russo in the new town's Lamanda Quadrant.

'It's more an update than anything, superintendent.' The woman inspector made her report the way he'd expected, without frills. 'Security at Sonnet-Bytes say they've had no further sighting of their car-park prowler. If he's a flasher, maybe seeing some extra police around made him nervous.' She paused. For a moment there was only static over the radio link. Then she was back. 'I talked with some of the women who worked beside Jane Tamsin on the production line. A few had heard her talk of 'her Peter', the mystery boyfriend, but nobody ever saw him. Jane told them he'd got a big-money job out on the Celtic Sea oil rigs, and that as soon as they'd saved enough they'd buy a bar in Spain and move out.'

'Any mention of South Africa?' demanded Thane.

'No, sir. At least not here. Hold, please.' The link was good enough for him to hear a rustle of pages. 'No, I've double checked. But I talked Cousin Mary through the whole subject of men again — and for certain she doesn't know that Jane set her up with Ken Hodge or that she was still seeing Hodge.'

'You didn't — ' began Thane.

'No, I didn't tell her, sir.' Jinty Shaw coldly dismissed the possibility. 'Did you imagine I might?'

Thane winced. 'No, inspector. My apologies.'

'But you said South Africa.' She moved him on. 'Her daughter Andy was with her — and Andy said Aunt Jane told her about this special friend named Peter, who knew about lions and giraffes. Because Peter had lived in South Africa.'

237

That was it. That was enough.

Thane told her to keep in touch, added that Phil Moss sent greetings, and ended the call. The moment he had replaced the receiver, the telephone rang again and he nodded to Sandra Craig to answer it. She did, spoke, listened briefly, murmured an acknowledgement, then put down the receiver again.

'Commander Hart,' she told Thane. 'You've to go through.'

Thane mouthed a silent curse. 'When?'

'Like now — or sooner.' She grimaced. 'The way he sounds, sir, I wouldn't keep him waiting.'

'I won't.' Thane rose and pulled on his jacket. 'Get hold of Ernie Vass. Find out if anything's worrying him.' His telephone was ringing again, but he left it to Sandra Craig and was heading for the door as she answered the new call.

'Wait!' Urgently, his sergeant beckoned him back. 'Doc Williams for you.'

Thane spun back on his heel, returned, and grabbed the receiver. 'Doc — '

'Good!' The police surgeon made it a growl. 'This is my third try at getting through. How much time do you spend on the damned phone?'

'Sorry.' Thane grimaced at the mouthpiece.

'Sometimes I'm popular.'

'And sometimes you're a liar,' grunted Williams, unimpressed. 'Call this special delivery. Can you use a preliminary on the post-mortem on your bag-lady — no extra charge?'

'Yes — and you win a guaranteed gold star, Doc!' Thane took the pen and notepad Sandra Craig slid towards him. 'Go.'

'The same type of weapon and basically the same technique as in Jane Tamsin's killing. Something very narrow, fairly long, sharply pointed — '

'Your sharpened spoke from a motor-cycle wheel?'

'Or similar.' The police surgeon was professionally cautious. 'Two deep and distinct stiletto type stab wounds. Both delivered when your bag-lady was lying on her back, almost certainly on the ground where she was found, her attacker probably kneeling beside her, at her right side.'

'Doc — ' Thane stopped writing and didn't hide his scepticism — 'how sure are you?'

'I've had my crystal ball refurbished,' snapped Doc Williams sarcastically. 'Colin, do you want it step by step?'

Thane assented.

'Angle of wounds, position of wounds — both

on the left side of her chest,' rapped Williams. 'To achieve the angle of both wounds, either her attacker was kneeling over her, from her right side, or he was a double-jointed circus acrobat. I'm reliably told that circus acrobats are generally in short supply around Glasgow Green around 3 a.m. — which, give or take a little, is your estimated time of death. Are you with me so far?'

'Very much.' Thane gave a suitably apologetic noise. 'Go on. Please.'

'Right.' Doc Williams was satisfied. 'Then to how your Old Aggie died. I can't say which came first, but one stabbing blow was slightly deflected by a rib and gashed her left lung. The other blow caused an unimpeded and fatal penetration wound into the same lung.'

'Fatal, but not immediate?' hazarded Thane catching up with his notes.

'Exactly. Dying would have taken several minutes — while she literally drowned in her own blood.' The police surgeon gave a humourless growl. 'But I suppose the good news is that I'd wager she knew nothing about it. Her blood alcohol level was near record-breaking, she must have been in a drunken, unconscious stupor while it happened. And when we opened her up, the autopsy room reeked of cheap wine.'

'So no cries for help, no kind of struggle?'

'A moan or two at most.' Doc Williams made a tooth-sucking, almost consoling noise over the line. 'I can think of worse ways to die, Colin. And whether she knew it or not, she had advanced stomach cancer. It would have killed her in another six months.'

He was finished. Promising his formal and full autopsy report later in the day, the police surgeon said goodbye and ended the call.

Thane replaced his receiver and drew a deep breath. Now it was beyond any reasonable doubt. The same killer had struck for a second time.

'I heard enough, sir.' Sandra Craig spoke before he could say anything, then cleared her throat. 'I'll — uh — pass the word about how it was. A few cops will feel happier — they've wondered if she could have been saved if we'd gone in earlier.' She glanced towards the door, and reminded, 'Commander Hart.'

'Thank you, sergeant.' Thane gave her a resigned twist of a grin. 'Believe me, I hadn't forgotten.'

When he went along the corridor to Jack Hart's territory, he found Maggie Fyffe frowning over her computer terminal. But she saw him out of the corner of her eye, stopped, looked up and nodded.

'Go on in.' The Squad commander's secretary thumbed towards Hart's closed inner door. 'He's waiting.' She scowled. 'Patiently, of course. As always.'

Thane crossed over, knocked on the door, and a green overhead bulb spat an immediate Enter. He went in, then closed the door again. Hart was sitting behind his desk, arms folded, his thin, lined face in one of its scowling modes.

'Thank you for coming, superintendent.' Sarcastically, Hart glanced at his wrist-watch, then raised an eyebrow. 'Lose your way, then, Colin?'

'Doc Williams,' explained Thane. 'The PM on the bag-lady.'

'Oh.' Hart's manner changed to interest as if he'd thrown a switch. 'Sit down and tell me. That, and the rest.'

The solitary chair facing Hart's desk had been very deliberately placed so that the occupant sat in full sunlight, facing the commander's shaded area. Thane moved the chair out of the glare, saw Hart's small grin of amusement as he settled in it, then began talking. He kept the report factual and compact but with enough detail to bring any salient points to life. For his part, Jack Hart mostly listened in silence and made occasional notes on his desk pad using a slim gold ball-point. Any questions he asked were sharply relevant.

'Good.' He tapped the notepad absently with the gold ball-point when Thane had finished. 'Even better when I get some of this as a formal written report. Understand me?'

'Sir.' Thane's face stayed wooden.

Hart scowled. 'And don't 'sir'. Hell, Colin, we brought in Phil Moss to try and keep this Squad's paperwork in order — particularly yours! What happens?' The scowl deepened. 'He and Francey Dunbar — both detective inspectors, damn them — are still padding around on some half-baked inquiry they won't tell me about. What's going on?'

'Moss had a tip from one of his contacts,' said Thane carefully. 'It maybe gives us a new lead in a robbery case we thought was dead.' The half-lie encouraged him on. 'But we need time to be sure, and there's a small mountain of old statements to be rechecked. Phil Moss reckoned you've enough on your plate, that we shouldn't involve you until there's a clearer picture. I agreed.'

'Did you?' Jack Hart's eyes narrowed. 'Colin, I've been a cop long enough to smell a rat at fifty paces. Like now! But I'll let it ride — for now.' His thoughts moved on. 'Anyway, I've had to move Dunbar to join DCI Redder's team for a couple of days.

Tina needs help to sort out that self-destruct shambles her team caused last night.'

The Broomstick Lady wouldn't have appreciated the description. Thane stayed wooden-faced, watching Hart rise and go over to the window.

'You were right about one thing.' Hart looked out gloomily at the drab featureless landscape below. 'Jane Tamsin's murder has to have its roots in the microchip world. But — ' he turned, shaking his head — 'you've still no motive for the way she was butchered. That's what you need, Colin. A genuine motive.'

Commander Hart would have made a good military general. In his own kind of war, he was already there. In the next few minutes he proved it, setting down possible priorities for Thane to follow, acting as a sounding board for his second-in-command's own ideas.

'You need one other thing,' he said softly at the finish. 'Some luck. We can do damn all about that. How are you getting on with your pair of judges?'

'So far, no problems,' said Thane easily, getting ready to leave.

'Good.' Hart shaped a careful smile. 'Ah — have you spoken to Sandra about her body armour crusade?'

'So far, she's not for budging,' admitted Thane.

'Another stubborn damned female woman,' scowled Hart. 'The one I've got at home is just the same. My Gloria is — ' he glared — 'and your one is as bad, so don't grin like that! You know what's wrong? The bloody fool who first won those women the vote should have been horsewhipped until he saw more sense!'

Thane escaped. On the way out, he passed Maggie Fyffe. She winked, mouthed the one word 'dinosaur' and made a cheerful two-fingered gesture towards Hart's inner sanctum.

Maggie liked her boss.

★ ★ ★

Detective Inspector Phil Moss was draped around a chair when Thane returned to his office. Moss was nursing a mug of coffee, and Sandra Craig, perched on the edge of Thane's desk, also had one. Moss was the only officer Thane had ever seen his sergeant bring coffee — but one of the apparent benefits of having all the appearance of a social work case was that women suddenly became motherly. Even Sandra, who in the beginning had fought a war with him . . .

245

'How was Jack Hart?' asked Moss.

'Ready to bite.' Thane didn't expect to find a third mug of coffee waiting, and there wasn't. 'Your name came up. And we don't get Francey back for a day or so.'

'A pity.' Moss slipped a hand under his crumpled shirt front, which was held together by one remaining button, and scratched. 'We're starting to get somewhere with Tyndall Black's file.' He shook his head at Sandra Craig, who was looking blank. 'Need to know stuff, girl. Close your ears.'

'And up yours,' she said sweetly.

'Phil . . . ' Thane scowled him on.

'Tyndall Black goes after a lawyer and an assistant bank manager, right? Both are charged, both are found guilty, both are doing time. Now it seems the spotless bank manager who was left untouched has taken early retirement.' Moss gave an acid snort. 'Nice being a bank manager — seems he's been on two holidays already this year, has a new Top People car, and was out in Spain looking at Costa del Sol villas.'

'So we've maybe a naughty bank manager — Tyndall Black's third man?' Thane whistled.

'We'll need more,' warned Moss, sipping his coffee.

'We'll keep trying.' He saw Moss's

expression and knew there was more. 'What else, Phil? Don't mess about.'

'East Kilbride.' Moss shrugged. 'I checked the personal papers sent in to us from Jane Tamsin's room.' He paused long enough to give a polite low burp. 'The two bank books were interesting. Both were more than healthy — yet from the amount of cash she drew out she didn't exactly skimp herself.'

'Any regular pattern?'

'In one book, yes. Her Sonnet-Bytes wages, paid in direct.' Moss's thin, badly shaven face shaped a scowl. 'Her petty cash, Colin. Look through her credit card slips, and she knew how to spend her way around. The other book, very different. Mainly large lumps of money — cash money — deposited in no particular pattern.'

'It figures.' Thane couldn't even pretend to be surprised. 'Sandra . . .'

'Sir?' His sergeant looked at him over the top of her coffee mug.

'Did you raise Ernie Vass at Paisley?'

She nodded. 'He's calling back.'

'Flushed with success.' Moss made it a cackle.

'Meaning?' asked Thane wearily.

'Flushed — lavatories — oh, to hell with it!' Scowling, Moss gave up.

'Meaning that Ernie may have labelled

247

the ned who forced Jane Tamsin's locker,' explained Sandra Craig, those green eyes focusing icily on Moss. 'He's Wilson Bramble, age around thirty, single, fits our description. Unemployed, lives in Paisley, sometimes scouts for Empire Lines. Out walkabout at the moment, but somewhere around.'

'So we wait.' Thane considered his desk for a moment, thinking, deciding. 'Phil, I'm packing you out to East Kilbride.' He saw Moss's startled surprise. 'And don't glare at me like a horse in a huff! I'm not in the mood.'

'I thought Inspector Shaw was taking care of things,' protested Moss, colouring.

'You're a Crime Squad nasty, she isn't.' Thane wasn't looking for arguments, even from Moss. 'Take her with you, go to the Sonnet-Bytes plant, get to Abbie Carson, the plant managing director, and to Frank Alder, their sales boss. Break the happy news about Jane Tamsin's funny habits, and see how they react. Then tell them I'll come out again tomorrow, with more questions.'

'And I play it heavy?' frowned Moss.

'Just use your natural charm,' growled Thane. 'That should do it.' His expression changed. 'Afterwards call in on Mary Russo — but to make sure things are all right there. Go easy with her. The woman has had her share of trouble, and it hasn't ended.' He waited until Moss laid down his coffee mug and started to leave. 'Oh, and Phil — you won't forget to give my regards to Jinty, will you?'

Moss seemed to swallow. He took another step, stopped, released an explosive, echoing belch, then grimly walked on again.

For Colin Thane, the next couple of hours and more were spent with the hot afternoon sun pouring into his room while he and Sandra Craig shuffled endless paperwork or microphone-dictated the hard disk reports for the copies that more departments seemed to need every week that passed. Sweat made his shirt cling to his back, his head was gradually distilling a king-sized headache.

His copper-haired sergeant wasn't in much better shape. Eventually she surrendered, left him, came back with two soft drink cans, and dumped one in front of him. Thane ripped the tab open, drank, and felt the cool liquid trickle down his throat like nectar.

'Thanks.' He gave his sergeant a grateful nod. 'Breaking your rule?'

'You can collect the next one, sir.' She took a swallow from her own can, then moistened her lips with the tip of her tongue in a way that was hard to ignore. 'Fair?'

'Very fair.' Thane took a deep breath,

returned to the microphone, and began dictating again.

Other telephone calls came in. One was at a little after 4 p.m. Ernie Vass, still out at Paisley, was using his pocket mobile.

'Still waiting about, boss,' Vass reported. 'I'm at a friendly house in a high-rise block in Glencoma Park estate. It looks down at the four-tenant cottage block where this Wilson Bramble lives.'

'You think he's our man?' queried Thane.

'I'm certain, boss. But there's nothing happening around here. I've seen busier cemeteries.' Paisley traffic murmured briefly in his telephone's background. 'Want me to stay or move?'

'Stay,' Thane told him. 'Give me the address.' He took a quick note as Vass gave details, and his mouth tightened. If Paisley's K Division was known as Crazy K, then Glencoma Park municipal estate was its wildest, craziest slice. One of a long list of rent collectors who had tried working there had given up after a heart-felt plea that he wanted an armoured car escort. 'I'll send Dougie Lennox out as your relief. When Bramble does show, he could have company, Glencoma style. So sit tight, call in for back-up, and wait until it reaches you.'

'Will do,' agreed Vass cheerfully. 'Uh — could

Dougie maybe bring me some cheroots, boss? I'm down to my last two.'

'He'll call. Tell him yourself.' Thane hung up.

Outside his window, he could see that Jock Dawson's dog van was back. That meant that Dougie Lennox must have also returned. He sent Sandra to locate Lennox, initialled some overtime claims, tossed them into his out-tray, then groaned as an orderly arrived and carefully deposited another batch of paperwork in front of him.

That did it. He shoved everything aside, sat back, dialled his home number, and by a rare miracle got through on the first go. He'd hoped Mary would be home from work, and she answered on the third ring.

'Me,' he said, surprised. 'Why aren't the enemy blocking the line?'

'Tommy and Kate?' She chuckled. 'They're back from school. Dumped their stuff, then went out with Duckbreath the boyfriend.'

'Duckbreath? Fine. Out where?' Grinning, he slouched back in his chair, swung his feet up on his desk, and saw Sandra Craig returning with Lennox. As they hung back, he beckoned them in.

'Back to the new flavour of the month,' reported Mary cheerfully. 'Biffo Black's for another session.'

'Internet surfing — again?' Thane groaned, ignoring the way Lennox cocked his ears. 'That'll have to cool down. And Biffo with it.'

This time, she laughed. 'Colin, forget Biffo. We're going to have an Internet campaign on our hands from these kids!'

'Damn the Internet,' he complained. 'Look, I'm sorry — '

'I'll guess. You're going to be late home. Maybe very late.' A frantic boxer dog barking drowned her voice for a moment, then she tried again. 'Look, there's someone at the door. If you're late, don't wake me up.' She dropped her voice to a purr. 'Well, not unless you mean it!'

She hung up and the line went dead. Thane shook his head, replaced his receiver, then switched his attention to the curly haired, baby-faced Detective Constable Lennox.

'Dougie, I've a loaf-around job for you,' he began. 'Over at Paisley.'

'Sergeant Craig told me.' Lennox nodded. 'No problem.' Then he raised a questioning eyebrow. 'Did I hear you're interested in the Internet, boss?'

'No,' said Thane stonily.

'It could help your kids with their schooling — '

'Would you like to foot the bill, detective

constable?' he asked bleakly.

'Everybody's getting involved.' Lennox, the Squad's IT fan when he wasn't more occupied keeping his various romantic interests apart, stuck to his guns. 'We've got it here, into our own communications system. I've got it at home. Even Ye Olde Antique Empire Lines are into it — '

'Say that again!' Thane swung his feet crashing down to the floor and stared.

'True, boss.' Lennox grinned at him. 'I've an Interlink connection on my own home PC. I was surfing last night, showing — uh — a friend how it works, and I went searching.'

'Empire Lines,' reminded Thane.

'We'd tried the listings for airlines and for air taxis — she's long-haul cabin staff. Then I wanted to try something different but international, and I was curious about this architectural salvage thing. So we went searching — and there are plenty of firms like it listed, world-wide. Empire Lines was there, with a website page all its own.'

'You're sure?' Sandra Craig was also staring. 'Our Empire Lines, the one in Paisley?'

'Illustrations, descriptions and prices of special lines, the lot.' Dougie Lennox was vaguely uneasy, without knowing why. 'It's a

253

good idea, boss. Low-price global advertising. Someone there is really up and running into IT.'

'Dougie.' Thane stopped him. 'Explain one thing. I spoke to Michael Spring, the owner. I spoke to Dirk Spring, his son. They say they know slightly less than nothing about your damned computers.'

'Boss, if they do, there's only one answer.' Dougie Lennox flushed, but stuck to his guns. 'They're liars.'

Thane drew a deep breath, laid his hands on his desk, spread his fingers, and looked down at them in silence.

'Just this once, Dougie,' he said at last. 'Just this once — you might be right!'

6

Another twenty minutes, and Detective Constable Dougie Lennox was on his way to Paisley. His first stop would be at the Empire Lines warehouse, where he was to be an amiable potential customer having a look around the vast stock of salvaged fitments. In other words, he was to see what he was getting into. From there, he would go on to relieve Ernie Vass at the viewpoint.

But before he left, Lennox found himself centre stage in a demonstration to an audience which included Commander Hart, eager to know what was going on, and Maggie Fyffe, who didn't want to be left out. Thane and Sandra Craig were also there. They met in the headquarters communications room on the ground floor, where they were joined by Tina Redder, who brought along a couple of her team to improve their education.

'Any time you're ready, boss.' Lennox switched on a communications room terminal, watched it for a moment, then glanced at Thane. 'Yes, ready. Booted up.'

'I'm glad,' Thane said stonily. 'Go.'

'Starting now.' Lennox's young, smooth-cheeked face furrowed in concentration as he tapped instructions on the terminal's keyboard, then the computer mouse was moving its on-screen cursor in a smooth curve beneath his fingers. 'Clicking on search engine — now.' The monitor screen in front of his audience quivered and jerked almost in a life of its own, then steadied. Looking around again, Lennox grinned at Sandra Craig. 'Here we go, sarge.'

He tapped a few more keys. Words came and went across the monitor screen at bewildering pace, faded altogether to an angry, flickering black, then came back and steadied.

'Got it!' reported Lennox cheerfully. As it settled, the Internet website page of words and pictures was headed 'Hello From Scotland's Empire Lines'. Illustrated columns of 'bargain offers' ranged from stained glass and cornice moulds to a special offer of seventy feet of oak balustrade described simply as 'the property of a Highland gentleman' and priced at offers over $150,000. Most prices were in dollars. He looked around, gauged his audience's interest, and was satisfied. 'Now I'll download.'

More taps on the keyboard and the printer beside it gave a brief mechanical grunt before a paper copy of the page rolled into view. Jack Hart lifted the copy, considered it with some interest, then passed it to Thane.

'Interesting,' commented Hart.

'Any schoolkid knows how, sir.' Lennox started off with a grin then had second thoughts and flushed. 'That's — uh — ' he swallowed at Thane's expression but bravely decided to finish — 'that's presuming they come from a computer literate family.'

Thane gave him a glare, then studied the Empire Lines website page in more detail. The contact address was Paisley, listed under the names of Michael Spring, proprietor, and Dirk Spring, sales director.

'Available internationally in five languages. Changing content weekly,' added Lennox, reaching for the keyboard. 'I'll locate the rest if you want.'

'Later.' Thane shook his head. 'Would the page originate at Empire Lines?'

'Not directly, boss.' Lennox shook his head. 'They'll use a service provider. The way it works, Empire Lines supply raw copy, like in any other kind of media advertising. Their provider does the rest.' He beamed. 'First chance I get, I'll do some digging.'

They sent him on his way. Only Jack Hart hung back as the other spectators faded.

'What do you think, Colin?' He looked at

Thane and gave a long sigh. 'It's like the world keeps going faster every day — and I've already fallen off. Hell, at least you have kids to keep you organised! But I haven't. When I need to alter the setting on a digital clock, I bribe a ten-year-old!'

Thane knew what he meant. Rather than ask his pair for help, he had once spent six months of a year living with a car clock which wasn't changed between summer and winter time.

'Interesting,' said Hart again. 'Worth remembering.' His leathery face shaped a frown. 'But it doesn't prove anything, does it?'

Except that they couldn't totally rely on whatever either Michael or Dirk Spring might choose to tell them. In the background, too, Jack Hart might still give reasonable support to his second-in-command's way of investigating what was now two murders. But the Crime Squad commander was also serving notice that he preferred facts to hunches or theories.

Hart made a final encouraging noise, then strode back to his own territory. Once he'd gone, Thane saw Sandra Craig give a surreptitious glance at her wrist-watch, then heard his copper-haired sergeant give a sigh.

'Something wrong?' he asked.

'No, sir.' She shook her head. 'Nothing to worry about.'

That meant there was something. But he knew better than to ask more.

★ ★ ★

Half an hour later, it was their own turn to leave and Thane drove out of the sun-filled headquarters yard at the wheel of his regular black two-litre Ford with Sandra Craig curled in the passenger seat.

Her face was expressionless. But as they left she gave another glance at her watch and the faintest of shrugs — nothing more. She settled down to demolishing a thick bar of raisin and nut chocolate and Thane smiled to himself. As long as his sergeant was eating, there couldn't be too much to worry about.

Half-way to Paisley, travelling through a short stretch where reception was always at best a crackle, the Ford's low-band radio came to life with a call from headquarters. Phil Moss had returned intact from his East Kilbride mission, and Detective Chief Inspector Tom Radd had telephoned. Both would like to talk with Thane. But neither situation sounded a priority. Thane deliberately turned the volume down to a background murmur then used the Mondeo's regular factory-fitted set. He found a news channel, gave up on its mix of world-wide woes, and punched another button. That gave him a sports programme with an almost equal blend of track and field disasters and miseries, but he let it take him on through the early evening rush-hour traffic.

There was no sign of Dougie Lennox's car when they reached the Empire Lines building — which had to mean Lennox had already been and gone. Thane parked the Ford outside the former church, then Sandra joined him in the crunch across the gravel of the one-time churchyard to the main door, which was open. They entered, back into where the clear white overhead tube lamps shone down on the dusty array of salvaged architectural offerings. Once again, customers were wandering around the long treasure-house aisles. At one spot, two men in brown overalls were unloading a large trolley filled with carved stone garden figures. Everywhere, the redolent scent of old wood filled the air.

'Just pretend to look around,' murmured Thane. 'Leave it for them to find us.'

They began strolling. Within minutes they saw a salesman hurrying up the stairway to the gallery level office. Moments later, a smiling Dirk Spring came down the same stairway, fastening his jacket as he came towards them.

'Superintendent Thane — ' his brown eyes moved on — 'and the delightful Sergeant Craig! Back again.' He shaped a slight frown. 'On your kind of business, I suppose?'

'More questions, Mr Spring. Sorry.' Thane gave an easy nod. 'Just details to tidy. It shouldn't take long.'

'No problem.' Dirk Spring gave a resigned grimace. 'One of your people was here earlier, Detective Constable Vass. But that was personal — he was interested in pricing a load of cedar flooring.'

'Ernie Vass is working on some home DIY renovating,' lied Thane. 'He must have liked what he saw.'

'And I'll bet he tried for a good price.' Sandra Craig grinned on cue.

'He certainly tried.' Spring chuckled. 'We did our best. He said he'd be back.'

'Then he probably will.' For a moment, Thane considered the sales director son. Dirk Spring wore a blue linen sports jacket and dark grey trousers, teamed with black suede shoes, a blue shirt, and a darker blue tie. The close-cropped chestnut hair added to the businesslike air that was part of Spring's stock-in-trade. 'This is still about

Jane Tamsin's death. But now we've got a second murder.'

'Related?' Spring blinked his surprise as Thane nodded. 'Dear God! Who was it?'

'An old woman who might have identified Jane's killers.' Thane shrugged. 'The media aren't being told there's any link.'

'Hell!' Spring kept his frown in place, vigorously scratched his head, then made a sympathetic noise. 'You had enough on your plate without that! So how can I help?'

'We could start with another look at your basement,' suggested Thane smoothly.

'Let's do it!' Nodding, Spring led them over to the basement stairway. Then he paused and gave a dry chuckle. 'I don't think anyone should throw wash-basins at you this time!'

They went down the bare wooden steps and past the same piled-up bathroom fitments. The basement lights were on, and two elderly men wearing grey warehouse coats were stripping surrounds from some carved wooden panels. The men nodded a minimal greeting, then kept on with their work.

'Are they the pair who were here yesterday?' asked Thane.

'Our Arnie and Bob.' For a moment, Dirk Spring sounded almost affectionate. 'They've worked for us since Empire Lines started. Like I told you, they had gone home before anything happened. The reason they're still here tonight is because this is our late opening.'

Sandra Craig left to talk with Arnie and Bob. While she did, Thane walked across the basement and took another look at the row of employee lockers. All, including the one which had been Jane Tamsin's, were now liberally covered in fine grey fingerprint powder. After that, Thane spent more time prowling the basement without really learning anything new, then went back to where Spring was waiting.

'Any fresh ideas about who would want to break into her locker?' he asked Spring.

'None.' The dark-haired man shook his head. 'I talked the whole thing through with my father. But we can't help.'

'Any ideas from Arnie and Bob?'

'No.' Spring shrugged. 'I asked — and we've double checked with every employee we've got. Still nothing.'

'How about your freelance salvage scouts?' asked Thane. He had a feeling he was close to scraping the bottom of that barrel.

'Their kind come and go,' admitted Spring wryly. 'I made out a list of some names for you — at least, the names and addresses they give us. No guarantee that any of them are kosher.'

'At this stage, we'll try anything,' said Thane bluntly.

'While you're pursuing inquiries, right?' The man was sardonic.

'Pursuing inquiries means what it says — nothing more.' Thane wondered how often he used that magic formula in a year. 'We want some kind of a hint at a possible motive for killing Jane Tamsin.'

He kicked at a fragment of wood lying near his feet and watched as it went spinning. What he'd said was basic to everything. Had the woman been stabbed to death because of her past in the computer world — or had it been because of something since then?

'You're the detective, but I reckon she was caught up in something.' Spring's attitude was distinctly neutral. He could have been discussing a TV show they'd both seen. 'How about the drugs scene?'

'Anything's possible.' Except that the Crime Squad's contacts into the drugs world were better than good. Something like a murder would usually convey at least a scent of fear through from their regular informers. Thane rubbed a hand along the dusty top of a decorative table, carved from ebony and inset with mother-of-pearl. 'While I'm here,

I'd like to talk to your father again.'

'Be my guest, but you'll have to wait.' The Empire Lines sales director gestured vaguely, brought out his comb from an inside pocket, played with its close-set teeth, then ran it carefully, almost foppishly through his close-cut hair. 'He went off to sniff around some old mansion being demolished near Barrhead. We want the fireplaces — and maybe some of the roof tiles.'

They left it there as Sandra Craig returned from talking with the two carpenters and shook her head in a way that didn't need elaboration.

'Finished here?' Spring smiled at Thane's nod of agreement and led the way back up from the basement's cobweb gloom to the main floor then on from there up to the gallery office.

In the office, the same plump brunette secretary was using a telephone and making notes. Her conversation seemed to be with a customer who wanted to order some salvaged church pews. Dirk Spring went past her, opened a drawer in his father's desk, and brought out a single sheet of paper.

'That list of scouts, superintendent.' He handed over the list. 'It's not complete. Plenty of them are in the 'here today, gone tomorrow' category. And try not to frighten too many of them off — we need them!' While Thane glanced at the list then tucked it away in a pocket, Spring parked himself on the edge of the girl's desk. 'Anything else, superintendent?'

'The name Peter — Peter Sonas — still doesn't mean anything? To anyone?'

'No. And we've asked.' Dirk Spring turned to the typist, who had just finished her call. 'No reaction. Right, Joan?'

'Just that Jane Tamsin once told me the only man who had ever mattered in her life was a Peter but that they'd drifted apart.' The brunette gave a shrug. 'She laughed about it once when she heard I was dating someone named Peter. But when I made a simple, ordinary joke that I hoped it wasn't the same man . . . ' She grimaced at the memory

'Jane didn't think it funny?' Sandra Craig injected sympathy into her voice.

'Funny? She called me a fat, stupid cow, for starters!' The girl was indignant. 'I don't even know if her Peter really existed! But mine does!'

'Best forget it,' soothed Thane, then turned to Spring again. 'I'm mopping up. Your father told me Jane Tamsin probably went to Paddy's Market to complete some deal about antique door knobs. Correct?'

'That's what we think.' A touch of impatience in his voice, Spring nodded.

'Have you been offered them again?'

'No.' The man shook his head then glanced at his typist, who was listening. 'If they ever existed.'

'Then we're finished for now,' said Thane. 'We'll move on. But if anything else should turn up here . . . '

'Then I'll be in touch.' Dirk Spring came down off the desk. 'But do me a small favour, superintendent. Tell Detective Vass that if he finds a better deal for cedar flooring I'll match it.' He winked at Sandra. 'It never does any harm to keep a cop happy, does it, sergeant?'

'I wouldn't know,' she said tartly. 'I'm not into floorboards.'

Thane had already taken a first casual step towards the office door when he stopped. 'Something I don't understand.' He gave Dirk Spring a puzzled frown. 'You and your father both say you're not computer minded?'

'True. No need.' Spring nodded. But suddenly his mood seemed more cautious. 'It's just not our scene.'

'Yet Empire Lines sells through the Internet, doesn't it?' Thane smiled blandly and waited. 'Have I got that right?'

'Ye-s.' For a long moment Dirk Spring said nothing more. His eyes had blanked out, his face was impossible to read. Then just as suddenly he grinned again. 'True. Guilty, superintendent — and well done! We have an advertising agent who thought it would be good, low-cost idea. I write the words, he takes care of the rest. We win the occasional export order.'

'Thank you — and a small puzzle solved,' agreed Thane.

They were leaving the building by the main door when the old silver-grey Mercedes that had been there on their first visit drove into the parking lot and stopped.

'Wait,' said Thane softly, touching his sergeant's arm.

They stayed in the shade of the former church's entrance porch while two occupants got out of the silver-grey car. The grey-haired driver was Michael Spring, and his surprise passenger was Ken Hodge. Spring and the thin, bald East Kilbride architect were deep in conversation as they crossed the gravel and had almost reached the porch before Thane stepped out.

'Warm day,' he said laconically.

Both men froze. Hodge stared, his mouth fallen open.

'You're a surprise, superintendent!' declared

Michael Spring, recovering first. 'We've been talking about you!' The Empire Lines owner turned to his companion. 'True, Ken?'

'Yes. We — we were.' Hodge looked from Thane to Sandra Craig, then back again, and managed a nod. 'We were wondering — well, about what's happening in the case.'

'So what's new?' asked Michael Spring. 'Making progress, Thane?'

'Some — but slowly.' Thane shrugged. 'I had a few things more to ask. Your son helped with most of them.'

'Anything left for me?' asked Spring earnestly. 'Superintendent, I've kept my nose clean for a long time. I like it that way. So if there is any help I can give . . . '

'Not right now.' Thane shook his head. 'Dirk can tell you the rest — there was nothing really important.' He glanced at Hodge. 'How are things at East Kilbride?'

'You mean with Mary Russo?' The man reddened. 'She's more settled. Of course, I'm helping any way I can . . . '

'I heard.' Thane nodded gravely. 'What brings you over here?'

'Trying to make amends to Empire Lines.' Hodge forced a weak smile. 'When I brought them Jane, I brought them trouble.' He ignored a murmur of protest from his

269

companion. 'But I heard about a demolition job that might interest them . . . '

'The old mansion house?' Sandra Craig showed her interest to Spring. 'Dirk told us.'

'It's a real find.' The Empire Lines boss chuckled. 'We'll go for the fireplaces, for a start. I've a buyer in Normandy who'll drool for them.' He slapped Ken Hodge on the back. 'Architect gossip wins again, Ken. Believe me, we're more than square!'

The two men went on into the building while Thane and his sergeant returned to where the Ford lay in the sunlight. Once they were aboard, he set the fan churning in cool air, then they drove out of the yard and headed in the direction of Glencoma Park.

'Well?' Thane spared a sideways glance at his sergeant as they travelled. 'What did you think, Sandra?'

'Back there, sir?' Sandra Craig chewed lightly on her lower lip. 'Part of the time, we were given the treatment.'

'Like?'

'The Internet thing. Dirk's version surprised their secretary.' The redhead chuckled. 'She almost wet herself.'

'Putting it crudely, sergeant?' Thane blinked in mock horror.

'It's the company I keep, sir,' said his

sergeant mildly. 'But she nearly did.'

Thane nodded. It was probably good guesswork.

Dougie Lennox had been given a rendezvous point to pass to Vass. It was on the southern edge of the Glencoma housing estate, a row of small shops where the brave opened their steel shutters in daylight but where most — particularly the sub-post office and any others who handled substantial cash — lived in perpetual gloom. Only Glencoma's street glinted brightly, the result of broken glass being powdered down.

When they saw Ernie Vass he was smoking a cheroot and reading a newspaper while he loafed outside the sub-post office. As they pulled in, the big Aberdonian folded his paper, tossed away what was left of his cheroot, then came over and climbed into the rear seat.

'I was getting worried, boss.' He closed his passenger door. 'I was beginning to get some peculiar looks. One character told me that if I was planning to hold up the post office I'd need an appointment.' He settled back as Thane set the Ford moving again. 'Better drive around slowly for a bit. Dougie's taken over as lookout okay, but we may have a problem. I'll tell you about it.'

Mostly, what had happened to Ernie

Vass was typical of any number of Crime Squad target surveillances. He'd started off by walking openly into the Empire Lines warehouse and deliberately letting himself be recognised by the staff. Then he had made hopeful noises about being back in search of a bargain in salvaged wood.

Ernie Vass could tell a story well, and everyone knew that any cop offered a bargain was a happy cop. He'd been passed to a middle-aged salesman who had shown him samples and prices. By the time Vass had left, saying he'd have to think about it, he was on first-name terms with the salesman. He knew the nearby bar where the salesman went for a beer most lunchtimes.

And when lunchtime came, the said salesman didn't look totally surprised to find Vass leaning on the bar counter. Vass had paid for a couple of large whiskies, then had made a heavy play for a back-door deal in wood which the Empire Lines management didn't have to know about. Another large whisky, and they'd started talking about Jane Tamsin.

And then about two other freelance salvage scouts who used an old grey Commer van and were believed to go thieving when the salvage market was slack. One of them, Wilson Bramble, owned a motor cycle. Very little was known about his partner, vaguely the same build and general appearance. His name equally vague, Bramble's friend was labelled The Man. Neither had appeared at Empire Lines that morning. It happened often enough, at other times it wouldn't have been unusual.

But now it might matter.

'You're sure about the house?' asked Thane.

'My wife's cousin is the ex of a K Division cop. So I'm sure, boss.' Vass saw no need to elaborate, but gave a soft chuckle. 'He knows this friendly widow with a friendly window.' He wasn't finished. 'Remember how I got a glimpse of that locker bandit at Empire Lines, and said I had a hunch? Well, I checked with K Division, and Wilson Bramble is Bushy Bramble — a known face.'

'Your known face?' asked Sandra.

'A four-by-two ned, sarge,' agreed Vass. 'I've seen his SCRO pic, checked his form — one previous conviction for attempted murder with an axe. Two for armed hold-ups, shotgun style. Known to have worked for a spell as a casual on Glasgow Underground, but that wasn't yesterday.'

'Anything on his friend The Man?' she asked.

273

'No. Probably just another ned,' said Vass dispassionately. 'There are plenty of them about.'

'But these two might be what we're after.' Thane kept driving while he fished Dirk Spring's list of Empire Lines casuals from his pocket. 'Take a look, Sandra.'

She took the list, checked, then shook her head. 'No Bramble, sir.'

Somehow, Colin Thane would have been surprised at any other answer. But it was another fragment — potentially it could be a very important fragment, no matter if it was incomplete. However it was wrapped, anything to do with Jane Tamsin seemed to come incomplete.

There were so many apparently unrelated fragments of fact and suspicion, when what he needed more than anything was even a hint at a possible motive which could tie even some of them together. Put together everything he had so far, try to do anything without that motive as an anchor, even reach the stage of dreaming about arresting anyone, and tribes of lawyers would give happy cries as they lodged compensation claims for their clients.

Still thinking, Thane kept the Ford crawling along at the kind of pace which suddenly brought a warning grunt from

Ernie Vass. Vass thumbed at the rear window, and the suspicious traffic patrol car which had fastened on their tail. The traffic car stayed there until its crew completed an obvious PNC check, then it took off with an apologetic wave from the driver.

'You said a problem, Ernie,' reminded Thane once it had gone. 'What kind?'

'Fairly simple, boss.' Vass fished a cheroot out of his top pocket, remembered, and tucked it away again. Reformed smokers like this boss were always the worst, he knew. He called it jealousy. 'Bramble was at home — I saw him. Nobody came to the place and nobody left — until about half an hour ago.' He leaned forward, his thick arms draped over from the back of the front passenger seat. 'Then — well, it was the way that sales character from Empire Lines warned me. Bramble is a mad keen football fan who thinks God plays striker for Glasgow Rangers.' He snorted. 'That's daft. God keeps goal for Aberdeen.'

'What about Celtic?' queried Sandra Craig innocently.

'Them? Heathens.' Vass dismissed the possibility. 'Anyway, what matters is that Rangers are playing a European Cup tie tonight in Edinburgh.'

'Against Hearts.' Thane remembered. 'Bramble is going?'

'He's gone. Like on a crusade, boss.' Vass shrugged. 'I watched him collected by a minibus full of Rangers bears with supporters' scarves. Now I'll put money on him not being home this side of midnight — stone-drunk if Rangers win.'

'And worse drunk if they lose,' muttered Sandra Craig. She gave a sudden, thoughtful intake of breath and glanced across at Thane. 'Either way, it puts things here back until morning — and there's nothing else immediate. Is there, sir?'

'No.' Thane said it slowly, already suspicious. 'Although we leave Dougie Lennox on watch until the night shift can take over. And . . . ?'

Sandra Craig gave a hopeful grin. 'Maybe some of us could stand down until morning, sir?'

'Some of us?' Thane scowled and heard Ernie Vass chuckle from the rear. He made an educated guess. 'And the Royal Navy is in port yet again?'

'Flying in from London in about an hour — sir.' She nodded almost meekly.

'Usual start time tomorrow, sergeant,' he said resignedly. 'Anything else?'

'Well . . . ' She looked pointedly at the

speedometer. The Ford was still loafing.

'Damn you, sergeant,' sighed Thane, and they began moving.

★ ★ ★

As soon as they drew in at Crime Squad headquarters Sandra Craig had gone from the Ford. Seconds later, she sent her white VW Golf scalding out of the compound heading for home, a shower, a change of clothing, and then whatever.

For Thane, what was left wasn't so simple. The good news was that Phil Moss had already been back long enough to collate most of the new pile of message slips and faxes that had gathered on his desk. The bad was that none of the special search inquiries that were now in place had come up with anything that constituted a breakthrough.

But it was a phase that Colin Thane knew and accepted, a stop along the line in any investigation — except for the very few when a suspect threw up his hands and confessed. Even then, there was always a smart smarm of a lawyer lurking who would twist that round and shout about police brutality.

The real world of detective work was an unglamorous spider's web of SCRO records, of whispers picked up by Criminal

Intelligence, of dredging through MO computer files, of calling in old favours from the past or offering new favours for the future. It was a world which used trial and error to attempt a beginning, build from that shaky start, then use a blend of hope and guesswork to try to flesh out a possible result.

It was very much Moss's world. Being Moss, he had obtained the loan of two young civilian computer operators. Both girls were now assembling separate files on every individual even remotely involved in the deaths of Jane Tamsin and Old Aggie. Any time a gap was spotted, an immediate priority attempt was made to fill it.

Whatever else happened, Old Aggie could now have a death certificate which properly described her as Mrs Agnes Williams, widow, aged eighty, of no fixed abode, relatives unknown. They had the Salvation Army to thank for that.

The manager of the East Kilbride branch of the Bank of Central Scotland, where Jane Tamsin had kept her bank accounts, had produced a Last Will and Testament held in his safe. Jane Tamsin had left everything to her cousin Mary Russo. The document was several years old. It was immaculate in its clarity and brevity — but it said damn all about anything else.

The name of Wilson 'Bushy' Bramble and his nicknamed friend The Man had already joined the priority computer search list. Fragments surfacing about other names included an SCRO listing for Ken Hodge. He had an English conviction for theft, several years old and minor enough to have only warranted a six-month jail sentence. There was nothing to add to Michael Spring's known record, and the only entry found relating to Dirk Spring said that he had once held a police permit for a .22 rifle 'used for vermin control'.

Other Crime Squad officers were becoming involved. Some, like Francey Dunbar, still mainly working for Tina Redder, were contributing when they could. Commander Hart might be staying in the background, but his personal input helped keep things moving and made him a useful target for muttered curses. Both of which he knew and banked on.

At last things settled a little and Thane found time to return Tom Radd's call. But by then, inevitably, the Strathclyde detective chief inspector was out again in the hunt for the Rocket Scientist. The home-made rockets being used by his people in drugs turf clashes had stopped being funny. The latest, fired at a rival crack dealer's car, had totally missed the car but had punched a neat hole in the middle of a cashier's booth at a filling station.

Thane left a message that he'd called, then got down to yet another mental check list. Ernie Vass was on another tour around the Paddy's Market area, just in case something new might surface. In Paisley, Dougie Lennox was at his window in Glencoma Park, waiting to be relieved by the night shift team. That left Jock Dawson as the Thane team's total mobile reserve. The lanky dog handler and his dogs were snoozing together in a corner in the basement restaurant, where the dogs were assured of a supply of fried bacon sandwiches and buttered buns. But the restaurant staff said they didn't particularly give a damn about the handler's welfare.

There was only Phil Moss around when Thane made a grim return from a visit to Jack Hart's office. Thane scowled at Moss's welcoming grunt, and dropped down into his chair. He'd given Hart his best shot in an up-to-date briefing, then had been made to suffer an acid series of sceptical questions from an increasingly unhappy Squad commander.

'Ach, forget him, Colin,' advised Moss, a sour disgust wisping across his thin, lined, lived-in face. 'You know how it goes. If our brave commander gets some real worry now and again, then it can do him no harm at all.' He gave a gentle burp for emphasis. 'Maybe it will even help him remember what it was like when he had a real job!'

A little later, at 8 p.m., they were seated in Thane's room with the door closed against the outside world. An orderly had brought a pot of fresh coffee and a near-new plate of egg and tomato sandwiches only just starting to curl in the heat. The sun was still the same orange globe in the northern sky, an orange globe which wouldn't set for some time.

'The sane half of the world is out on a golf course somewhere,' said Thane suddenly. 'Not just waiting around the way we are!'

Moss scowled. 'Golf is a damned stupid game.'

'I play golf,' reminded Thane.

'Proves my point,' snapped Moss.

'Thanks for your support.' Thane sighed, wondered why he hadn't settled for an easier occupation like coal mining, and bit into another sandwich. He chewed for a moment. 'So how was it at East Kilbride?'

'Eh?' Moss gave a surprised blink. 'My report is on your desk.'

'And I've read it,' agreed Thane drily. 'Now tell me.'

'If that's what you want.' Moss grumbled

to himself then took a gulp of coffee and succeeded in splashing some down his jacket front. But his stained and faded shirt had mysteriously acquired buttons again and for once the scrawny detective inspector looked marginally tidier. 'For a start, Jane Tamsin's bank situation was the way we expected. Apart from her salary cheque, money deposited came in as lumps of cash. Then the will document wasn't any real surprise.' He sucked his teeth and moved on. 'Things seem peaceful enough for Mrs Russo. But, like you wanted, there will be a uniformed cop on duty outside Lamanda Quadrant for the next night or two.'

'And Sonnet-Bytes?' Thane reached for another sandwich.

'Not very happy campers.' Moss gave an evil grin and happily swirled the coffee in his mug. 'Shock horror stuff when they heard our Edinburgh version of Jane Tamsin's background. Somebody in Sonnet-Bytes will go head-on-a-block for not checking that reference.'

But now, at least, they had a face for the previously vague Peter Sonas, the man who had given Jane Tamsin the homemade microchip pendant when both had worked at Ardee Concepts — the pendant she had been wearing when she was murdered. The photograph had arrived by a police despatch rider from Edinburgh while Thane was being blistered by Jack Hart. Kerr Munn and his Crime Squad satellite team in Edinburgh had tracked down a print of a photograph taken at an Ardee Concepts staff party.

Peter Sonas had been on the edge of a group of grinning faces, probably not even realising he was included. The print had been grainy and slightly out of focus, most of the faces suffering from camera flash red-eye. Someone else who might have been Jane Tamsin was vaguely in the background. But a Scenes of Crime laboratory had concentrated on Sonas, carefully enlarging that section of the print.

Before, any description of the man had been vague — memories of someone in his late thirties and around five foot ten, thin, with dark hair and brown eyes. Now, the enlarged section of the party snapshot showed a man who had brooding dark eyes and a firm beak of a nose. His high cheekbones added to the overall impression of someone whom it wouldn't pay to cross.

Yet Thane remembered the Edinburgh verdict on the man. Women liked Sonas and he liked women. How much of the reason for Jane Tamsin's killing could lie within that simple statement?

More copies of the print were being made.

Moss wasn't finished with Sonnet-Bytes. 'The meeting you want out at the plant will have to wait. They've a group of Very Very VIP visitors visiting there tomorrow morning. They leave after an early lunch, and by then Frank Alder will be off by air to a London meeting.' He paused and gave a residual shrug. 'Still, the Carson woman says you should come out in the early afternoon. She'll keep her diary free.'

'And Abbie Carson is still the one who matters.' Thane leaned back in his chair, then enjoyed the small luxury of letting himself relax for a moment. 'She knows her computers, Phil.'

'Do I ask if you noticed her legs?' Moss released a cynical belch which vibrated around the room.

'I noticed.' Thane nodded. 'You'll see them again tomorrow.'

'Me?' Moss was instantly on guard. 'Why?'

'You'll be with me.' He shrugged at Moss's surprise. 'There are too many loose ends out there, Phil. I want things shaken up.'

'What about the baby sergeant?' Moss's eyes narrowed. 'What's she doing?'

'By then, she may have plenty to do — depending on Paisley. This way, you'll also have some time for the Tyndall Black inquiry. Your other happy bank manager.' Thane let Phil Moss catch up with what he'd said, then gave an innocent smile. 'Be happy. There's a bonus. You'll get to see your Inspector Shaw again.'

Moss scowled and threw a telephone directory at his head.

★ ★ ★

It was eight forty-five when Colin Thane's telephone rang again.

When he answered, Tom Radd was on the line.

'I tried to raise you earlier,' said Radd without preliminaries. 'Don't worry about it. They're at home.'

'They?' Thane was lost.

'Your High Court girl and her uncle,' said Radd grimly. 'The uncle is an old customer of mine — I knew him from those security camera stills. That way, we tagged the girl. Ready for a collect?'

'Whenever you are,' agreed Thane gratefully.

'Make it twenty minutes from now. Rendezvous at the lane in Lodge Street — the far side of Glasgow Green.' Radd broke off for a moment. There were other voices at his end, then the Strathclyde man was back on the line. 'We're ready now. It's on my patch, superintendent. So I'd suggest we do it my way.'

'I can live with that.' Thane thanked him, hung up, and gave Moss a triumphant victory sign. 'Our blue jeans girl. Now.' Then he punched telephone numbers, raised Jock Dawson in the basement restaurant, and told him to move.

Two minutes later they had left the Crime Squad building and were aboard Thane's Mondeo. As it started, Jock Dawson finished loading Rajah and Goldie into the rear of his battered Land-Rover. They left the compound in a joint roar of exhausts and a squealing of tyres.

'Nice night for it,' said Moss unemotionally, squinting against the glare of the sun until he remembered to flick down the passenger visor. They were joining the city-bound M8, traffic was growing, and he clung to his seat as the vehicle swayed on a curve. 'How do we play this?'

'We go along with Radd — at least until we see what happens. We owe him that much.' Thane made a racing double-declutch gear change, one of the few things about his driving that Sandra Craig genuinely envied. Responding, the Ford stormed past a pair of ambling maroon-coloured Rolls Royce limousines, both with uniformed government chauffeurs and flying ministerial standards up front. He heard a chuckle from Moss, took a quick sideways glance, and groaned. 'Phil, act your age!'

Settled back, Moss was giving the limousiness' occupants his own version of a regal wave.

All the way, Jock Dawson clung to their tail as if his dog van was on the end of a tow rope. The traffic thickened. Using blue lights and sirens, Ford and Land-Rover carved their way on, came near the heart of the city, then left the motorway before the River Clyde and the long span of the Kingston Bridge over the river. Lights and sirens off, they drove through the new build greenery of the modern Gorbals then crossed the Clyde higher upriver at the quieter King's Bridge.

From there, they were on the north side of the city — and only separated by the open parkland width of Glasgow Green from the High Court building and where it had all begun those very few days ago. In a few minutes more, they were cruising through a mixture of old sandstone tenements and three-in-block local authority housing. It was Lodge Street, where packs of children and marauding dogs seemed to outnumber the visible adult population.

Thane spotted Tom Radd's lane near the far end of Lodge Street, signalled for Jock Dawson's benefit, and both vehicles swung in. The lane was not for tourists. Fly-infested garbage littered its potholed surface and they had to steer a chicane-like course round obstacles from abandoned supermarket trolleys and old mattresses to a refrigerator and a mysterious pile of smashed television sets. Half-way along, an unmarked Strathclyde CID car was parked and waiting, and they stopped behind it.

Sporting another of his hideous hand-painted ties, Tom Radd emerged from the Strathclyde car, and came over as Thane and Moss emerged. Detective Sergeant Paulson nodded at them from the driver's seat.

'You made good time,' greeted Radd, then thumbed towards the Land-Rover. 'Dogs? Good! They could be useful.'

'Depends what we've got,' said Thane neutrally. Jock Dawson hadn't shifted from behind the Land-Rover's wheel. The handler was considering the state of the lane with a dour expression which probably meant he was worried about exposing his dogs to health risks. 'Where from here?'

'Down there.' Radd pointed to an alleyway off the lane. 'Then just round the corner — Atbara Street, upper floor. Name on the door is Laird. Everyone knows our man as Slider, his niece is Angela — and she's no angel. Enough?'

Thane nodded, and signalled Dawson to stay. In turn, Radd beckoned, and his moon-faced sergeant climbed out to join them. Then, Radd leading the way, they set off. The alleyway emerged on Atbara Street, where the houses were local authority blocks of elderly two-storey apartments, the garden spaces mostly trampled back to waste ground but with satellite TV dishes growing out of every roof.

'Here.' Tom Radd led them along one broken-slabbed path to a door, thumbed the doorbell, waited, then thumbed the doorbell again. They heard a man's footsteps plodding downstairs, then Thane was conscious that they were being scrutinised through a tiny security lens set in the door.

'Who's there, eh?' asked a wary voice.

'Police,' said Radd impatiently. 'Don't mess about, Slider. Lower the drawbridge. And tell Angela to put the kettle on — I could use a cup of tea.'

There was a heavy sigh, a key turned in a lock and a security chain rattled, then the door swung open. The man who looked out was middle-aged, thick-set and grey-haired.

'Hello, Slider.' Radd beamed. 'Keeping fit?'

'Hello, Mr Radd.' Sullenly, Slider Laird thumbed at the narrow staircase behind him. 'Better come in, I suppose.'

Again they let Tom Radd lead the way. As soon as all four were in, Laird closed and locked the door again. Then, as they reached the top of the stairway, Thane blinked in surprise. After the grey, shabby exterior, the inside of Slider Laird's home was an eye-opening surprise. The spotlessly clean entrance hallway had thick wall-to-wall carpeting, a slow-ticking long-case Victorian grandfather clock, and a sideboard with a rich array of silver behind its glass doors. Half-open doors gave him glimpses of a modern kitchen and a gleaming bathroom.

'In here.' Their reluctant host opened another door and ushered them into a tastefully furnished living-room where chairs were upholstered in tan hide and faced a home cinema sized television set. Laird looked past them. 'Visitors, Angela.'

'I'm no' exactly blind, Uncle Slider.' The girl who rose from one of the chairs was slim, with long, dark hair worn in a single pigtail. Angela Laird, the girl from the Paddy's Market witness statements and video, might still be in her teens but she was hard-faced with it. 'What do you want this time, Mr Radd?'

'That cup of tea,' suggested Radd again. 'You know what cops are like.' He nodded at Thane. 'You don't know my friend — '

'Do I want to?' she sneered.

'Maybe,' said Thane neutrally.

'More than maybe,' declared Radd. 'This is Detective Superintendent Thane, Scottish Crime Squad.' He grinned at the way her eyes widened. 'Angela, you and your uncle are moving up a league. This time, you're dealing with the heavy mob. Now will you put that damned kettle on?'

Scowling, chewing her lip, she went out of the room. They heard a kettle being filled in the kitchen then banged down on a worktop.

'Suppose we sit down, folks?' Radd dropped into one of the armchairs and waited until the other officers did the same. Only Slider Laird remained standing. 'If you want to know about Angela, superintendent, her ma and pa are doing time in a Spanish jail for liquor smuggling. They won't be out for another couple of years. Then — well, maybe you want to know how Slider got his nickname?' He chuckled. 'Simple. For a spell he worked in a post office parcel sorting office. Except that when Slider went to work he always took along a supply of stick-on labels, labels addressed to himself or his pals. Any time he saw a parcel that looked interesting, he'd take a label out of his pocket and slide it on to stick over the original delivery address on the parcel.'

'Then the ordinary postal system did the rest,' contributed his sergeant, grinning. 'No extra charge!'

'Except it couldn't go on for ever,' murmured Tom Radd. 'So he recruited a few little helpers. When Slider was caught, he did time. But the little helpers took over — nothing left to chance. Labels all different shaped, different coloured. No substitute address used more than twice in one week. Know how to pick your parcels, and there's a good living in it.'

'Nothing to do with me — not now,' said the man hoarsely.

'Just a consultant, are you?' Radd gave a smooth smile, rose, and slowly walked around the room. He took his time, stopping to admire an ornament here, lingering over a piece of furniture there, as if he'd time to waste. 'This house says different. Suppose I turn the place over — '

'Where's your search warrant?' demanded Angela Laird sharply. She had been listening at the doorway.

292

'Haven't got one.' Radd thumbed at Thane. 'He wants to talk, that's all.'

'Talk about what?' The girl glanced quickly at her uncle, who gave a fractional headshake.

'These.' Thane reached into a pocket and brought out three of the security camera prints — one of Angela Laird looking up as Jane Tamsin passed her at Paddy's Market, another showing the two bikers passing, and a third showing the girl with her uncle. 'Taken two days ago.'

'Taken by the security cameras outside the High Court,' contributed Phil Moss acerbically. 'When you witnessed a murder, Angela. Remember?'

'You knew her,' said Thane softly. 'And you knew them — didn't you? Just like you knew Old Aggie. Old Aggie, killed exactly the same way — did you know that?'

'Dear Jesus, no!' The teenager was no longer hard-faced. She was pale, there was raw fear in her eyes. She made a plea for help. 'Slider — '

'Keep a grip, girl.' Slider Laird, equally pale, swallowed hard. 'We don't know anything, mister. You hear me? Right?'

They tried again and separately, Thane first, then Moss, with the two Strathclyde CID men a purely listening audience. It was a bad time for Laird and his niece — but their fear still ruled. Their stance was still that they knew nothing.

'Hold on,' said Tom Radd suddenly, frowning. A strange, growing noise was coming from outside, getting nearer. He crossed to a window which overlooked Atbara Street, then scowled. 'What the hell . . .?' He turned to Thane. 'You'd better see this!'

Thane went over, looked, and swore under his breath. The noise had become a chorus of shouts from an approaching crowd still growing in numbers. Between eighty and a hundred men and women of all ages with a fringe of excited children were marching towards Laird's door. The shouts became louder and clearer. Fists waved, then there were angry howls as Slider Laird and Angela appeared at their window.

'Murderers!' yelled a heavily built man in overalls, brandishing a stick. 'They did for Old Aggie — let's have them!'

'Square it for Aggie,' screeched a woman who had a child clutching her skirt. 'And stuff the polis! You stinking Lairds, come out!'

An empty beer can sailed out of the crowd and smacked the window. A whisky bottle followed and smashed against the sill. The yelling grew.

'Do something, Mr Radd,' pleaded Slider Laird, his face now ashen. 'You're the polis, it's your damn job, isn't it?'

Another hurtled beer can clattered against the house wall, and the baying continued. Angela grabbed Thane by the arm. 'Get them to stop — '

'My patch, Superintendent Thane,' reminded Radd with a deliberate formality. He gave a mild curse as a clod of earth broke against the window. 'We're talking a potential group disorder — '

'Potential?' Phil Moss stared in disbelief. 'What more do you want?'

'Potential,' repeated Radd. 'With respect, superintendent, we'll handle it our way.'

'Then do it.' Thane sucked his teeth. The baying outside was nearing lynch mob proportions. But in police politics, he still had no option. 'Just do it, man.'

'Right.' Tom Radd pointed at Moss. 'Inspector, there's a back way out. Angela will show you. Oblige me. Get your dog man and his dogs, then wait with them in the alleyway — you'll know when we need you. But warn your dog man there are women down there, some probably pregnant. Women — and kids. You understand?'

Moss nodded. 'What about uniformed back-up?'

'My worry.' Radd spun on Slider and the girl. 'You two, listen. I'll shift these people. But they can come back — remember that. Think about it.'

They nodded. The girl beckoned Moss and they left the room as the steady volume of menacing noise continued outside and other missiles rained against the building. There was a crash, and the window smashed in.

'That's it,' said Radd harshly. 'Fancy a walk, superintendent? Better come too, sergeant.'

The three men went back down the stairway to ground level. Radd opened the front door and was first out; the shouts became a solid roar as he was seen. Face empty of expression, the Strathclyde chief inspector walked towards the crowd. When he stopped, one of the nearest men, truculent and unshaven, pushed aggressively forward.

'Benny Macphee,' murmured Sergeant Paulson in Thane's ear. 'A local trouble-stirrer. The big swine is good at it too!'

Some of the crowd were still shouting, but most were watching the two men now arguing face to face.

'About now, I'd reckon,' said the moon-faced sergeant placidly.

There was a brief flurry of movement, a thud, then Chief Inspector Tom Radd stood exactly as before. But Benny Macphee lay on the ground.

'I wonder what happened,' mused Paulson. 'Do you think he tripped, sir?'

'What else?' asked Thane gravely.

Stunned by what had happened to their leader, the crowd had gone silent. Then a new gathering rumble began and they started to shuffle forward.

'Hold it,' bellowed Radd in a parade ground voice. 'Listen, you bunch of stupid bastards!'

The crowd froze again, staring.

'Good, Tom — sir,' whispered Paulson almost under his breath. 'Now . . .'

'Some of you know me,' declared Radd in the same bellow. He swung an arm, pointed. 'You do, Lewis! You do, MacKenzie!' His manner hardened. 'Well, this time you've really landed in the muck. Because you're fouling up a murder investigation, you maniacs!' He thumbed at Thane. 'His investigation, which is why he's here!'

Someone in the crowd made a protest. Radd scowled him down. 'Shut up and listen — all of you! I'm going to give you a choice, and a minute to make up your minds. You can get back where you came from — '

'Or what?' demanded a voice.

'Or this doesn't end as a police court case

and a fine. Not this time!' Now Radd had their total attention. 'We'll go after every last one of you! If you've a job, we ask Inland Revenue to take a close look at your tax returns. If you've no job, we ask people like the Benefits Agency, then Housing Benefits, even Social Security to dig out your files. We tell them things we know about — those little undeclared cash-only earnings, the jobbing window cleaning, the minicab driving, even the grass cutting.' He bared his teeth in a wolfish grin. 'Women too — the part-time barmaids, the home helps, the wee domestic cleaning jobs. Then we get more officials in to check for TV licences and car tax discs, all the rest of it — and we help them find out things!' He paused, and some of the crowd were already edging back. Then he reached a totally fictional climax. 'You morons, we've even had you on video ever since you came here. So move — now!'

Someone dropped an iron bar and ran. Someone else followed. Then it had become an exodus — an exodus which speeded even more as Moss and Jock Dawson erupted from the alleyway. Rajah and Goldie came too, both dogs barking and snarling, tails thrashing. Two men stopped long enough to pick up Benny Macphee and drag him along. Another side-stepped Tom Radd and made a dive towards Thane, swinging a bottle. Dodging the blow, Thane kicked him in the groin in a way that brought a scream of pain. Still moaning, the would-be attacker lurched away.

Then it was over.

'My way, superintendent,' said Tom Radd apologetically. 'Who wants a battle and a great load of paperwork? So maybe we — uh — sometimes exaggerate a little.'

'Or someone trips,' murmured Thane. He left it there as Phil Moss joined them, the street miraculously clear again.

'That's it,' reported Moss. 'Jock and his dogs will do a prowl around, to make sure they keep their heads down.' He faced Radd, a suspicion of a grin creasing his scrawny face. 'You know, I'd give a lot to hear the way these people knew we were here, and why we were here.'

'I'm not sure.' The Strathclyde chief inspector gave a heavy frown. 'You're not suggesting we would tell them?'

'Like just to put the fear of God up Slider and the girl? Never crossed my mind!' Moss gave a small, cynical laugh. 'That wouldn't be your style, chief inspector.' He glanced at Thane. 'Would it, superintendent?'

'Definitely not,' said Thane, his voice totally empty of emotion.

He saw the brief flush that crossed Tom Radd's face and knew that Phil Moss was on target. It would have taken only a few words dropped in someone's ear, and the rest could almost be guaranteed — even down to when it would happen.

They went back into the house, and up to where Slider Laird and Angela were waiting. While they settled, the dark-haired girl brewed the tea that Radd had demanded, poured the steaming liquid into mugs, then found some biscuits.

'That's better.' Radd sipped happily for a moment, then set down his mug. 'We've a deal. We kept our part, now it's your turn. Anything ordinarily illegal you tell we'll forget — drugs apart.'

Sitting side by side on a couch, Laird and his niece exchanged a glance, then a reluctant nod.

'So go back to where we started,' said Thane grimly. 'Angela, you stay in an expensively furnished house like this. Yet you were there at the market, sitting on the ground, just one roll of cheap cotton to sell. What was going on?'

'It — ' She stopped, moistened her lips and glanced at her uncle. When he nodded again, she shrugged. 'It's cover, superintendent. People talk to me, they tell me what they want to buy or sell, maybe a car radio or a TV. I know who is buying, who is selling. You could . . . ' She hesitated uneasily. 'You could say I'm in the middle. I fix things.'

'Fix as in fence?' suggested Thane bluntly. He cut her protest short. 'Angela, I don't give a damn. But think Jane Tamsin. You knew her, she knew you?'

She nodded nervously.

'But she walked past you.' Suddenly, Thane understood. 'She came to the market to clinch a deal to buy antique door handles.' He swung round to Slider Laird. 'Not with Angela this time — she was just a spectator. You were the fixer — weren't you?'

'You've got it right, mister,' said the man resignedly. 'I thought I'd fixed a meet. But straight up, honest — ' he swallowed — 'that was all! I told Angela about it, yes. Mainly because we'd both done those salvaged antiques deals before with the Tamsin woman.'

Started, the rest came in a flood. Someone he'd worked for before had spelled out exactly what was to be done.

'Does this someone happen to have a name?' asked Thane caustically.

'You'd better believe me, mister.' Sadly, Laird shook his head. 'We've done jobs for him for over a year — but all I know is he phones, he pays cash, he uses a biker messenger.'

'You've never seen him?' Tom Radd didn't hide his disbelief.

'Not the way you mean. Hell, mister, he could even be one of the bikers himself.' The man shook his head. 'But I know his voice on the phone — cold like crushed ice, the kind that says don't mess him about.'

'Does he sound local?' asked Moss.

Laird shrugged. 'Maybe yes, maybe no. These days, even the kids around here talk like John Wayne.'

The way he'd been ordered, Slider Laird had got word to Jane Tamsin about the antique handles. Again, the way he'd been ordered, he'd told her the handles were being offered by someone named Peter. If she was interested, she was to come to Paddy's Market.

Jane Tamsin had arrived, Laird had met her the way they'd agreed, but the seller hadn't turned up. She had been angry when she left. Minutes later, she was dead.

'I was told she knew this Peter,' said Laird uneasily. 'But the man I was working for said they'd had a mega fall-out. So he reckoned it would be safer if I set things up.'

'Do you know a Peter Sonas?' asked Thane grimly.

Laird shook his head.

'Angela?' Thane switched to the girl.

'Never heard of him.' She avoided Thane's eyes.

'All right.' Thane looked at the market girl, seeing her unease growing. 'But you knew the other one, didn't you?'

For a moment she didn't answer, fingering the end of her long pigtail. Then she gave in. 'Yes.'

'Who was he?' It was like drawing teeth.

'A bampot character called Bushy Bramble, from Paisley.' She scowled. 'I called hello, but he stared straight through me like I wasn't there.'

'He had more on his mind, and be glad,' grunted Moss. He groaned at her puzzled look. 'Look, girl, if friend Bushy had really noticed you, you could be dead.'

'What about me?' It came from her uncle like a squeak.

'What about you?' Thane felt his patience slipping. 'You did your deal. As far as you know, this Peter didn't show. You didn't see the bikers?'

The man shook his head.

'Then I wouldn't worry.' Thane reached into his inside jacket again and brought out two more photographs. One was a copy of the Edinburgh collect photograph of Peter Sonas, the other was an SCRO head and shoulders of Bushy Bramble. He laid them both in front of the girl. 'What about these?'

She looked at Sonas's photograph, and shook her head. 'Not this one.' But she tapped the second picture with a fingertip. 'That's Bushy. He was riding the bike.'

'You're sure?'

When Angela Laird nodded, she had just cleared Bramble of murder.

Then it was the turn of a totally demoralised Slider Laird. He identified Bramble, but not Sonas — and he hadn't seen who was riding the Ducati.

'That's it for now.' Thane tucked the photographs away. 'We'll want statements later.' He glanced stonily across at the two Strathclyde detectives. 'And Chief Inspector Radd will let the neighbours know how things stand — so there's no chance of more misunderstandings.' He paused. 'Won't you, chief inspector?'

'My word on it,' declared Tom Radd righteously.

* * *

They went back to where they'd left the cars. While the two Strathclyde men departed to

304

continue searching for the Rocket Scientist, Colin Thane looked at Phil Moss and sucked hard on his lips.

'Are we thinking the same thing?' asked Moss tonelessly.

'Peter Sonas probably killed her.' Thane nodded. 'And killed Old Aggie.'

It had been shaping that way. There were still things he didn't understand, answers that could maybe only be supplied by Sonas, the man Jane Tamsin had maybe loved too well. But they had a breakthrough.

They got into the Ford again. Jock Dawson was waiting in the dog van, ready to head for home. But a light on the Ford's Crime Squad radio was glowing, meaning a message was waiting. Wearily, Thane called in and spoke to the Squad's night shift supervisor.

'Two messages for you, sir,' said the supervisor in the relaxed tones of a man who had most of the night shift still ahead. 'DC Lennox checked in from Paisley. No movement at his location. I've arranged for him to be relieved and off watch in another hour.'

'Make it a two-man relief, and warn them it's for observation only,' ordered Thane. 'They check in immediately anything happens — and they do nothing without back-up.'

'Sir.' The duty officer made it clear he

wasn't impressed. 'There's also a message for you from a Mr Frank Alder at Sonnet-Bytes, East Kilbride. Says you know him.'

'Go on.' Thane frowned at the microphone.

'He wants you to meet him. Like this evening. Says it's urgent.' The supervisor made the kind of on-the-air noise which meant he was eating as he spoke. 'He's entertaining a bunch of Nips — uh — Japanese business executives at the Glasgow Hilton, and he'll be there until midnight. Can you join him?'

Thane swore under his breath. 'Did he say why?'

'No, sir.' The duty officer waited.

'I'll be there.' Thane ended the call, tossed the radio handset back on its shelf, sighed, and glanced at Moss. 'Damn. Any ideas?'

'None. Except he told me he would be flying out tomorrow.' Moss huddled his thin frame deeper into his jacket, shivered a little. Dusk was greying outside, the air was cooler. 'I could go if you want.'

'He wants me, he'd better get me.' Thane resisted temptation. 'I'll do it, then head home.' He grinned. 'Jock can give you a lift back to headquarters — if the dogs don't object.'

'Enjoy,' said Moss bleakly, and climbed out.

At twenty-two storeys — if anyone really goes counting — the Glasgow Hilton is the only five-star hotel in the West of Scotland and is located in the very heart of the city, close to the Clyde and the Kingston Bridge. When Colin Thane arrived, it was around 10 p.m. Leaving his car in one of the underground parking levels, he went straight in.

At that hour, the broad lounge and reception area was quiet, almost deserted. But even before he reached the hotel's main desk Thane had been spotted. One of the hotel security team, an ex-cop who knew his job well, gave a slight nod but otherwise stayed clear. When Thane spoke with a duty manager, he was already expected. A snap of fingers produced a receptionist who steered him past the public restaurants, up to the first floor, and along to a wood-panelled private function suite.

'Take a seat, superintendent.' The receptionist indicated one of the armchairs in an otherwise empty bar area. She hovered as Thane sat down. 'Can I get you anything?'

'Just Frank Alder,' said Thane.

She smiled, nodded, and went in through a screen door to one side of the bar. Thane had a glimpse of diners, most of them Japanese, eating and talking around two long tables. He caught a glimpse of Alder hosting at one table and Abbie Carson at the head of the other. Alder was in a dark business suit, but the big, fair-haired woman was in a sleek green silk dress which sported a sparkling diamond brooch like a battle honour. An instant later, Abbie Carson caught a glimpse of Thane and gave him a deliberate wink across the room.

Then the door closed. But only for a few moments, then the receptionist came out again.

'Mr Alder thanks you for coming, superintendent.' She switched on her smile at full beam. 'He'll be with you within a couple of minutes.'

Then she had gone. Thane sighed and settled back, listening to the muffled sounds coming from the other side of the panelling.

Japanese VIP guests usually ended up in the Hilton, where there was a whole floor dedicated to Japanese needs. He caught himself yawning. The hotel had another claim to fame — as the only Hilton in the world which was haunted by a dead gangster. The ghost was confidently believed to be a top Glasgow gangland figure known as Mad Archie who had disappeared in the early 1970s, rumoured to have been killed off by a rival thug. Legend was that Mad Archie had been given a 'concrete jacket' then dumped into the foundations of the Kingston Bridge, still being built.

Taking down one of Britain's busiest bridges to discover the truth wasn't a practical option — and Mad Archie's ghost began appearing on the thirteenth floor of the Hilton soon after the hotel opened. When the alleged ghost ambled around, his shape seemed covered in what staff and guests claimed looked like wet cement.

But Mad Archie knew his manners and was a friendly ghost. His main activity was wolf-whistling after female staff late at night. And far from the alleged haunting by Mad Archie being a liability, the Hilton management found that they were never short of bookings for their lucky thirteenth 'ghost floor'.

Thane switched back to hard reality as the partition door to the dining area opened and Frank Alder came out, closing the door quickly again.

'Thanks for coming, Thane.' The Sonnet-Bytes sales director came over, shook him firmly by the hand, then dropped down into another armchair. 'You're probably wondering what the hell this is all about.'

'True.' Thane considered the shrewd-eyed

gnome-like man with his protruding ears and that early pot belly straining under his carefully buttoned suit jacket. 'But here I am.'

'I hope you'll still see Abbie as arranged tomorrow.' Alder bared his teeth in a quick, partly apologetic grimace of a smile. 'But you know I can't be along, and that worries me. Abbie has her executive area but — ah — I have mine.'

'And there's something you want to tell me?' suggested Thane woodenly. 'Something she might forget?'

'No, that's not what I mean!' The man bristled. 'But my executive responsibility includes security. Do you know what we have to protect? We're talking about a world-wide semiconductor market worth up to £170 billion — if you want it in dollars, over $250 billion!'

'But not all of it out in East Kilbride,' murmured Thane mildly.

'I'm making a point,' snarled Alder. 'How much we matter as an industry, the kind of competition that exists between firms. Sonnet-Bytes are mostly into R and D and special development projects — sensitive areas, superintendent.' He nodded towards the muffled sounds coming from the dining area. 'These people are important. They

310

matter, they bring orders, jobs — '

'And you don't want them to think there's any kind of a problem at East Kilbride,' suggested Thane drily. 'Because that could be bad for business?'

'You're damned right it could.' Alder gave an emphatic nod. 'For appearances as much as anything else, I'm increasing our plant security. There's a general tightening up of all procedures. All I want from you is — well, low-profile policing.'

'Agreed,' murmured Thane. 'Anything else?'

'I've to report back to our US head office.' The small, tight mouth twisted a fierce attempt at a smile. 'Give me something I can tell them. What about the Tamsin girl's murder? Give me something!' He made it a plea. 'What about this Peter character she talked so much about? Any progress there?'

'Maybe more than little.' Thane thought of the photographs in his pocket, but decided against showing them. 'Tell your head office we're satisfied with how things are going but we need time.'

'And this Peter?' pressed Alder.

'Is a Peter Sonas, who very much exists.' Thane held up a hand to stop it there. 'That's all I'll give you.'

'Dressed up, it's enough to keep head office

happy. Thank you.' Alder bounced to his feet. 'Sayonara or whatever, superintendent — and I'll get back to work! Goodnight.'

The man disappeared back into the dining area, leaving Colin Thane frowning. After a moment he got to his feet and made his own way back down to the reception lobby.

The ex-cop security man was waiting. He went out with Thane to the car-park, and used his management smart card to get the Ford through the exit barriers without having to pay.

Sometimes, being police was almost like being in a private Mafia.

★ ★ ★

It was dark enough to need headlights as he drove back along the M8, heading for home, and he'd travelled a couple of miles before he noticed the light-coloured coupé which had appeared behind him. The coupé stayed there, not far behind, for the best part of another half-mile, then it closed the gap and the glare of its full beam lights struck his rear view mirror, almost blinding him.

Thane cursed, knocked the mirror aside, then the other car was level. There were two people in front, the passenger window was down, and a hand was reaching out,

312

clutching what could only be a sawn-off shotgun. He swung the Ford's steering wheel to swerve, braked — and the shotgun fired.

He ducked, still swerving the car, while shotgun pellets lashed the Ford's bodywork. The front offside tyre collapsed, ripped away, and the Ford went into a wild skidding dance across the road. That ended as it slammed into a barrier rail. Glass and torn metal tinkled, his engine stalled, then there was only the spitting coming from the car's cooling exhaust.

The seat belt had saved him from slamming into the steering column. He had banged his head against a door pillar and hurt a knee. But that was all — and although he was dazed, he saw the light-coloured coupé disappearing ahead, exiting the motorway without slowing. The number plates were obscured.

Within the next couple of minutes a young couple with a Fiat pulled up to see if they could help, then a friendly tanker driver. The Ford's radio was still operational, and Thane put in a breakdown call. He waited beside his crumpled wheels until a Crime Squad car arrived, then a Strathclyde traffic car which had been diverted because he'd been spotted on a CITRAC control screen.

Once he'd told the Strathclyde crew where

they could put their breathalysers, Thane left them to arrange for the Ford to be hauled away. Then he commandeered the Crime Squad car to run him home.

The house was in darkness when they dropped him off. Mary and the other two were asleep. Thane quietly went into the kitchen, sat down, poured himself a stiff malt whisky, and sipped it until his hands stopped shaking. Clyde came out of his basket, and a querulous boxer mouth nuzzled his lap.

He rubbed Clyde gently down the front of his nose. When his hands were steady, he poured himself another whisky. What had happened had been too crude to be any attempt to kill him. It had been meant to worry him, distract him . . .

And it certainly had.

Thane swallowed his drink, got Clyde back into his basket, then limped up to bed. He undressed while he listened to Mary's quiet, regular breathing, then got in beside her. She stirred and half wakened.

'All right?' she asked drowsily.

'All right.' He kissed her forehead.

A minute later, he was asleep. Chased by a nightmare that was a light-coloured coupé.

7

By dawn the weather had changed. The wind was from the west, and strengthening, there were long ribbons of dark, threatening clouds marching the sky and more than a hint of a fine drizzle of rain hung in the air.

Colin Thane was collected from home at 6.30 a.m. by a Crime Squad car. It was driven by the transport pool sergeant, who wasn't often seen anywhere at that hour, and who wanted to hear first-hand why one badly grunched pool Mondeo had been hauled in from the M8. The sergeant, considerably more concerned about the car than about its driver, delivered his passenger to an almost empty Crime Squad headquarters before 7 a.m.

Thane had wanted the early start. Mary had wakened when he did, and by the time he had showered and dressed and limped downstairs there was coffee and toast waiting. He gave her a shortened version of why he was home without a car, with a worsened limp, and with a new livid bruise on his face. It was enough. He knew Mary would know the rest of it quickly enough via the Maggie Fyffe grapevine. When he left, Tommy and Kate were still asleep and Clyde hadn't stirred from his dog-basket.

At headquarters, he checked in with the orderly at reception, and hobbled up the stairway to his office. He had some aspirin in a drawer and swallowed a couple. It was the second time in as many days that he'd injured the same knee, and twice was enough for anyone.

Seated behind his desk, flexing the knee to soothe the ache, Thane savoured the peace of the partly sleeping building and caught up with some of the reports and faxes that had come in overnight. Most were additions for the stack of prepared folders spread on his desk — a separate folder for each name on even the fringe of the Jane Tamsin stabbing. He hadn't forgotten Old Aggie. He wouldn't. But her death had been almost a brutal extra involving the same cast of people.

Phil Moss appeared at 7.30 a.m., yawning and groaning about it being still the middle of the night. But things were noticeably different this morning about the scrawny detective inspector. He was wearing a clean white shirt which had its buttons intact, and he seemed to have managed a better job of shaving.

'How do you feel?' asked Moss gruffly.

Like most in the Squad, jungle drums had already told him about the M8.

'Like the car. I need some panel-beating.' Thane allowed himself a twisted grimace. 'They played rough.'

'Superintendents shouldn't be allowed out on their own.' Moss grunted his verdict. 'Not after dark.'

'Say 'sir',' suggested Thane.

'Go to hell — sir.' Moss punctuated it with a belch. 'Reckon they probably picked you up when you left the Hilton?'

Thane nodded.

'Why?'

'I don't know. Maybe just to rattle my cage, give me a scare.' Or equally worrying, how had they known he was there? Thane sighed. 'Well, if they wanted to scare me, they did.'

Moss frowned. 'What happened at the Hilton meeting?'

'Mainly Frank Alder trying to score executive points. Wanting to keep level with Abbie Carson on the Sonnet-Bytes pecking order. He said they're boosting security.'

'Hooray.' Moss wasn't impressed. 'How about Paisley?'

Thane shook his head. Glasgow Rangers had lost their game against Hearts in Edinburgh, but so far the night shift watch on Wilson Bramble's home had seen no sign of him returning. Backed by photographs of both men, there was now a general alert out for Peter Sonas and Bramble on a 'report but do not approach' basis.

Detective Sergeant Sandra Craig arrived at exactly 7.45 a.m. She was yawning, and she had a shaky grip on a polystyrene cup of black coffee. Her make-up was smudged at the edges, her copper-red hair was tousled, and she was neither bright-eyed nor bushy-tailed.

'How was the Navy, sergeant?' asked Thane, trying not to grin.

'I can't speak for him, sir,' she said demurely. 'But I'd no complaints.'

'And now you've finally arrived, maybe you can do some work,' grumbled Moss. He shoved some of the case folders across towards her. 'Start with these.'

A steady stream of people, including Jack Hart, began arriving to start work. Within minutes, the Squad commander stuck his head into Thane's room.

'My office, now,' he said, then had gone.

Thane sighed, grimaced at Moss and Sandra, then went through to Hart's lair. Maggie Fyffe had just arrived, looked him over carefully, and nodded.

'One thing, Colin,' she said grimly. 'If

you'd been killed last night, would Mary know where to lay her hands on your insurance policies?'

Thane grinned, but the thought stayed in his mind as he went past her into Hart's office. He wasn't totally sure.

'Classy limp,' greeted Hart from behind his desk as Thane entered. 'Close the door and sit down.' He gave his second-in-command a careful scrutiny as Thane sat down. 'You were lucky. I'll need a formal medical examiner's report on you, including the knee. Then the usual incident report.' The Squad commander settled back, hands clasped behind his neck. 'Fit for duty?'

Thane nodded.

'Good.' Hart showed his teeth. 'So — as of now, tell me how things stand.'

Thane did and Hart listened, his thin, leathery face staying impassive until he gave a fierce snort at the end.

'Nuts and bolts,' he said dispassionately. 'Tina Redder's target operation is cooling down for a couple of days. I've told her that means a couple of days when she gives you any help you need.' That, guessed Thane, hadn't made the long-legged Tina's day. From the wintry chink of a smile that crossed his face, the Squad commander had already learned it. 'Next, I called Forensics.

They found buckshot in your car bodywork. Buckshot we don't play about with, Colin! On top of your Bushy Bramble's two armed hold-up convictions, it settles another matter. I'm authorising firearms and an issue of body armour for your people.'

'Body armour including for Sandra?'

'Particularly for Sandra,' emphasised Hart. 'You can tell her. Your turn for a hard time — I coped with Tina.' He brushed the matter aside. 'What's your next move? The Glencoma estate house?'

Thane nodded. 'I'll give Bramble another hour to show. Then if he still hasn't appeared, we move in.'

Hart broke off as Maggie Fyffe arrived with coffee in two of Hart's 'using' mugs — china cups and saucers were for visitors only. But Maggie also brought in a plate of Hart's favourite doughnuts, enough to mark this as no ordinary meeting.

'Agreed on the house,' said Hart eventually, through a mouthful of doughnut. 'And we presume that the other biker known as The Man is probably Peter Sonas?'

'I'd put money on it,' said Thane simply.

'Sonas.' Hart frowned. 'We're weak on background there.'

'So far.' Thane couldn't argue. 'We're still waiting.'

An Interpol tracer request, emphasising South Africa, still hadn't brought a reply. Another route to information, through tax and insurance records, had met a dead end. Peter Sonas had been on an emergency tax code when he had been on the Edinburgh electronics firm's payroll. Without earlier tax records there was no way he could be traced further back — and from the moment Sonas left his Edinburgh job, he had officially ceased to exist.

'The Paisley pattern at Empire Lines.' Hart sighed. 'That's one package on its own. Then there's East Kilbride — ' he checked a scribble of notes on his desk — 'and this local architect, Ken Hodge.'

'Hodge is still a possible. But on the fringe — and that's probably as far as it goes.' Thane took a swallow of coffee. 'I'm having another try around East Kilbride later.'

'A warning, Colin. Be gentle with Sonnet-Bytes — they've some important friends.' The Squad commander signalled the session over by reaching for another doughnut. 'Keep me informed. And — ah — one last point . . . '

'Sir?' Already out of his chair, Thane paused.

'This secondary thing that Moss and Dunbar are pursuing — going well, is it?'

'Almost tidied,' said Thane smoothly. 'A

time-waster, nothing more.'

Jack Hart seemed ready to say something more, but didn't. There was still one doughnut on the plate, and Thane lifted it as he left. He was still chewing when he reached his own office.

'Happy meeting?' asked Phil Moss drily. 'While you were putting the world right, we've firmed a little more on Sonas. Stage one, East Kilbride says his photograph matches someone who was sometimes seen out and about with Jane Tamsin. Or was, until about two months ago. Stage two, we've Sonas now firmly identified as a biker. Also confirmed as being known as the Big Man because he loves talking about himself.'

'Credit Jinty Shaw?' guessed Thane.

'Yes.' Moss nodded gloomily. 'The woman is good. I'll give her that much.'

Listening in the background, Sandra Craig shaped a suspicion of a grin but stayed quiet. Sensible new sergeants quickly learned when to keep a shut mouth. A little later, she was out of the room when Francey Dunbar came in. The equally new detective inspector leaned on his antique silver-topped cane and eyed Moss.

'Told him?' He indicated Thane.

'No chance.' Moss grimaced and shook his head. 'It's all yours.'

'What is?' demanded Thane, frowning.

'The Tyndall Black business.' Dunbar sucked an end of his thin bandit moustache. 'You've other things on your mind, but . . . '

'But what?' snarled Thane. 'Get on with it, Francey. Or I'll use your damned cane to commit an arrestable offence.'

'I think Tyndall Black had things right, yet had things wrong.' Dunbar grinned weakly. 'We've been looking at a bank manager. We've been thinking that the way he's spending money has to mean he was tied into the same embezzlement scam that put his assistant manager in the dock . . . '

'So?' Thane was suddenly ready to listen.

'It could be totally separate,' said Dunbar softly. 'I got the idea when I heard how Jane Tamsin's will had been lodged at her bank. Then I found a couple of old newspaper stories suggesting that there were a few loose ends about the original case left outstanding. Complaints from relatives after old ladies died and wills were read. They were left legacies where the money had already been spent.'

'Phil?' Thane gave a surprised glance at Moss.

'He could be right,' murmured Moss. 'We might be talking forgery, Colin. Now, if we gave the Forensic mob some bits of paper to play with, like cash receipts and will documents lodged for probate . . . '

'Do it,' decided Thane.

Dunbar gave a wolfish grin and went out, his cane tapping a brisk new rhythm. Thane watched him go. It would be good if Dunbar's guess could be right. It would mean there had been nothing wrong with Detective Inspector Tyndall Black's last investigation. It had been complete on its own. What was left over had been a matter of separate, unfinished business.

And chalking up the success would also be good for Francey Dunbar.

Thane was sorting out some of Jack Hart's orders with Moss when Sandra Craig returned. His sergeant was munching an apple, had repaired her make-up, and had brushed more of the usual glint back into her hair. As she came in, there was a surprise tattoo of heavy rain on the window. That came at the same time as the telephone began ringing. Moss answered the call, listened, then passed him the receiver.

Tom Radd was on the other end of the line, and the Strathclyde DCI knew about the M8 shooting. He demanded, 'How are you, Thane?'

'Intact,' said Thane wryly. 'But the car is pretty sick.'

'Never joke about sawn-off shotguns,' declared Radd bleakly. 'This might interest you — there's a story that you were tailed out of our area last night by a biker. No description, except that he had a red crash helmet.'

'Damn,' said Thane softly. Now he knew how he'd been targeted.

'I know the feeling,' sympathised Radd. 'And sorry I couldn't call earlier. But I've been chasing my tail again on our Rocket Scientist caper. Did I say caper?' His growl came over the line. 'There was another head-to-head last night — one ned slashed across the head with an old cavalry sword and damned nearly decapitated, the other knee-capped when the latest of his bloody rockets went off course.'

'And you're no further forward?' Thane stayed patient while rain whipped the window again.

'I'm floundering,' snarled Radd. 'Hardly any description for him except he's early twenties and has fair hair. Outside of that, and a story that when he's not building his damned rockets his hobby is rebuilding old cars — like for real, everything authentic.' He swore viciously. 'He'll need some personal rebuilding when I lay hands on him. And I will! That's a promise!'

Radd ended the call. As the line went dead, Thane hung up his phone then sat for a moment, thinking. Then he gave a lopsided grin, checked in a Glasgow telephone directory, then tore a single sheet of paper from his notebook. Writing on the sheet, he folded it over then beckoned to Sandra Craig.

'Remember Babs Riley from yesterday at the High Court?'

'Your girlfriend, sir?' Her green eyes danced with amusement. 'Could I forget her?'

'Just hope that Babs remembers you.' Thane handed his sergeant the folded note. 'Go out now, give her this personally — to Babs, nobody else. Tell her the bottom line is drugs. Then you forget about ever being there.'

'You mean do it right now, sir?' She sighed as the window rattled again. This time it was more hail than rain.

'Like really right now,' agreed Thane. 'Move. We'll be heading out in an hour. You're invited.'

Satisfied, Sandra Craig smiled and left.

★ ★ ★

Phil Moss was first to leave, setting off as arranged for East Kilbride and taking a uniformed constable along for the ride.

By the time the main group was ready to go, the sun had returned and was chasing away the last of the rain and hail. There were still storm clouds around, but the roads were drying as two police cars and Jock Dawson's dog van set off for Paisley. The lead car, a red BMW, was driven by Ernie Vass with Thane beside him in the front passenger seat. Sandra Craig, her task completed, had made it back with time to spare and shared the rear seat with a spare detective constable. As Jack Hart had ordered, all four were armed with Colt .38 automatic pistols.

Behind the BMW came a big blue Nissan four-wheel drive station wagon. Dougie Lennox was driving, an Armed Response marksman sat beside him, and his rear-seat passengers were the Beauty and the Beast CID twosome from Tina Redder's team. Beauty — a small, china-doll blonde — was an honours sociology graduate. By comparison, The Beast was built like a gorilla. When on his own, he was also known as The Animal and sometimes almost frightened his colleagues. Behind them were stacked the anonymous canvas hold-alls which contained the team's body armour. Beneath the hold-alls, a locked steel box padlocked to the vehicle floor contained a brace of Savage pump-action shotguns and a flanking pair of Heckler and Koch automatic rifles.

In the last firearms evaluation, the Armed Response marksman and Sandra Craig had tied for best score. As Squad commander, Jack Hart had never believed in playing about.

Three vehicles became four. As the little convoy reached the Crazy K divisional boundary, a green Peugeot van slotted in at the rear. Strathclyde had been asked to provide Scenes of Crime assistance, and everybody knew Boomerang, tall and thin, and The Pawnbroker, small and fat — specialist plain-clothes sergeants who were among the best in their painstaking trade.

'Now,' ordered Thane as the little convoy reached the start of Glencoma territory.

Sandra Craig murmured into a radio handset and the three vehicles behind them dropped back. Then it was up to Ernie Vass to be guide. Chewing an unlit cheroot, humming, he drove the red BMW with only a gentle purr coming from its six-cylinder power plant.

'We'll circle in behind our lookout point, boss,' he explained, his lips shifting the cheroot to one side of his mouth. He nodded at a four-storey housing block ahead, and chuckled. 'There it is. Top floor right — with a window that overlooks Bramble's place. The tenant's name is Vera. She's a widow, friendly by nature, non-stop cups of tea, and likes cops!' He winked at Sandra Craig. 'Vera's in her sixties, sarge — in case you wondered!'

Sandra Craig used the car's radio again to check ahead. Two Crime Squad night shift men at the lookout window had been asked to stay on, and her call was answered immediately. There was still no change, still no sign of any new movement around Bramble's home.

'Then let's do it,' ordered Thane.

The BMW murmured round the bulk of the four-storey block, then Bramble's home was ahead — small and cottage style, the left-hand side of a semi-detached twosome, part of a row of identical steel-frame, chalet-roofed houses. Planners loved them for 'aesthetic reasons' — breaking up the visual horror of lines of high-rise blocks. But in bad weather, when the high-rise blocks acted like canyon walls, the little cottage chalets were regularly battered by hurricane winds.

'Don't worry about neighbours, boss,' beamed Vass. 'Our Vera says the people through the wall from Bramble are heroin users — half the time they don't know what year it is. Across on the far side, they've a couple of single mums who make a career out of staying out of things.'

Which was typical of Glencoma. Just as much as was the friendly widow with the window and her non-stop cups of tea.

The BMW stopped a stone's throw along the street from Bramble's home. Getting out, Sandra Craig strolled towards the house then up the short, weed-covered garden path. The curtains were closed. The front door, long starved of paint, had a simple, badly tarnished cylinder lock. Outwardly, the street was deserted apart from a tan-and-white mongrel dog trying to stalk a half-asleep ginger cat. There would be watchers behind some of the windows. There were always watchers around Glencoma — but they knew how to keep out of sight.

Sandra rang the doorbell, then rang it twice, and nothing happened. Glancing back towards the BMW, she beckoned. Thane got out and came over to join her, the spare detective constable close behind him. Reaching into a hip pocket of her denims, the redhead brought out a small slip of printed plastic. Like a credit card but slimmer, originally printed by the thousand by an enthusiastic police traffic department, the plastic cards had been given away to advertise a confidential Police Hotline campaign telephone number to use to report drunk drivers.

Then it was discovered that the Hotline cards could have another use.

Sandra Craig fed her piece of campaign plastic into the tiny space between door frame and door, eased it up, and the cylinder lock clicked open. A push with the flat of her hand, and the door swung back.

Thane led the way into a dull hallway where the interior doors lay open. Instinctively, he touched a hand on the Colt .38 holstered at his waist, then glanced back and saw that Sandra and the detective constable were already crowding in behind him. Artificially dark with the curtains closed, the little house was silent. The first room he looked into held two beds, each with its tangle of unmade sheets.

The bathroom was opposite. Then came a smaller bedroom and a stale-smelling kitchen. That left what was obviously the main living-room at the rear, in darkness like the others. Thane looked for a light switch, couldn't find one, and made to cross towards the closed curtains. He bumped into what felt like a table, swore to himself, took another stride, then kicked something else and stumbled, almost tripping.

'Dear God.' Immediately behind him, Sandra Craig gave a half-gasp and was staring. Looking down, Thane swallowed. Then the detective constable went past them, opened the curtains, and daylight poured in.

The body of a man lay at Thane's feet. He was tall and thin, bald — and dead. He lay in the middle of a thick pool of blood, and most of the back of his head had been smashed in. The dead man wore a slate blue suit, had fallen face down on the threadbare carpet — and whatever the weapon had been, it had crushed his skull like an eggshell. Brains, blood and bone fragments had sprayed out over furniture and carpet and up across the nearest wall. A first few flies were already gathering.

'Do we know him, sir?' Sandra kept her voice under control.

'Maybe.' Thane had a grim suspicion that he did. Avoiding the worst of the gore and stains, he squatted beside the dead man then carefully lifted that head just enough to be certain. He looked up at his sergeant and gave a reluctant nod. 'Yes.'

They had found Kenneth Hodge. A dried rivulet of blood streaked down the architect's beak-nosed face from that terrible damage at the back of his head. His small eyes still stared blindly, his mouth sagged. Thane laid a hand against the dead man's neck. It felt cold to the touch, and he rose to his feet. They would need a police surgeon and an autopsy to give a final verdict. But Hodge had been dead for hours.

'I don't understand.' Sandra Craig moistened her lips.

'You don't understand!' Thane's anger boiled over in a snarl which he immediately regretted. 'What the hell do you expect from me, sergeant?' He saw the way Sandra's face had gone red, he sighed, and he shook his head in almost an apology. 'This, believe me, I didn't expect.'

But now they had another violent death. One that threaded between Jane Tamsin's activities at East Kilbride and then at Paisley.

Ken Hodge had been murdered in Wilson Bramble's living-room — yet what had brought him over to Glencoma? The bald, thin East Kilbride architect, so deliberately targeted towards Mary Russo by Jane Tamsin yet still secretly meeting her, had played an uncertain part in what had happened. Maybe a more important part than anyone had realised — but who would answer questions about it now?

An old tablecloth was lying on top of a sideboard. Thane used it to cover the architect's head and upper body, swatted again at some of the flies, then stood back with his lips pursed. He had felt no liking for the man, wouldn't have trusted him. But Ken Hodge had mattered a great deal to Mary Russo, mattered in a way that had grown even stronger after Jane Tamsin's murder.

Now, yet again, the widowed schoolteacher was going to be hurt.

'Well, let's get to it.' For the moment he pushed thoughts aside and switched his attention to Sandra Craig and the unhappy detective constable. 'Sandra, bring everybody in. Organise medical and forensic back-up — the usual.' He paused, then put a grim emphasis into his words. 'But we've an officially unidentified victim. For now, he stays that way. Understood?'

'What about Phil Moss?' Sandra frowned. 'If he doesn't know, and he's out at East Kilbride — '

'Exactly.' Thane cut her short. 'Then he won't need to tell anyone. Tell — or lie.' It could be cruel, but it was practical. 'Worry you, sergeant?'

She shrugged, beckoned the detective constable, and set to work.

There was a telephone in the kitchen.

Colin Thane used it to call Jack Hart at Crime Squad headquarters. When he told Hart what they had, there was an initial silence on the line, then an angry rumble of near-disbelief.

'So we blew it. We've a watch on the place and we still end up with another body!' Hart made it a snarl. 'How the hell did this happen?'

'I'm still trying to find out,' said Thane wearily. But there was a back door in the kitchen, and he was standing beside it. 'And for now, I don't want him named.'

'Then we don't.' Hart was thinking as he spoke. 'We say we've an unidentified body. Police — um — found him when they answered an anonymous tip-off.' He made a tooth-sucking noise over the line. 'Anyway, we wouldn't normally release a name until a body had been formally identified and next of kin informed. So we just take our time about it.' He grunted to himself. 'I'll square things with Strathclyde — if I've any credits left there. Anything else?'

'Not for now.'

'Then do me a favour, Colin.' It came like a sigh. 'Don't find any more bodies — not before the weekend. Please.'

The line went dead, but Thane hardly realised it. He had found the murder weapon — a heavy duty work hammer lying propped against the kitchen sink. Both wooden handle and bright metal head were stained with blood and speckled with fragments of pulped bone and tissue.

One vicious swing of it would have been enough to kill. But from the damage to Ken Hodge's skull, there must have been more than one blow. This killer had been cold-bloodedly determined not to make a mistake.

He suddenly realised he was still holding the telephone receiver in his hand, and hung it up. By then, the rest of his team had arrived. Some, like Ernie Vass, had taken part in the viewpoint watch from across the street and were uneasy and puzzled.

'I know there's a back door, boss,' protested Vass. 'But there's a ruddy seven-foot high fence all round the backyard!'

Thane had seen the fence, a solid timber structure. A well-meaning local council had fitted them at one time to cut down on vandalism — and the vandals had burned most of them. Coming in at any speed over that fence would have needed Commando training.

Others among the arrivals included Boomerang and The Pawnbroker, who went straight into their normal work mode. While they started, Thane made another tour of the house. With drawers lying emptied, contents dumped on floors, there was an air of people leaving who had no intention of returning.

Thane was in the living-room when shouts and the sounds of a struggle came from the direction of the kitchen. When he got there, the rear door was open and Sandra Craig was dragging a thin and frightened man in from the tiny patch of overgrown back garden.

'Playing at Peeping Tom outside the kitchen, sir.' His sergeant had the stranger squealing in an arm lock. 'This is Jimmy Boyd, the through-the-wall neighbour.'

'I just heard noises, mister,' the man protested. 'I came roun' like a good neighbour, right?' Then he made a struggling attempt to break free.

'Behave,' snapped Sandra, and swung the man round in a narrow arc which rammed his face into the nearest wall. The struggling ended in a yelp of pain. Her prisoner was wearing a long-sleeved jersey. When she shoved back the left sleeve the thin white arm revealed was covered in a pin-cushion of needle marks.

'How did he get round here?' Thane walked over to the open rear door, looked out, and swore as he saw the answer. The apparently high and solid fence now had a gap, where two planks of wood had been lifted out. He came back to the frightened, unshaven man, and considered the needle marks. 'You're a user, Jimmy?'

The man shrugged, avoiding his eyes.

'Personally, I don't give a damn,' Thane told him. 'But how many people use that gap in the fence?'

'Hard to say, mister.' Jimmy the Neighbour tried to move, gulped as Sandra tightened her grip a fraction, then tried again. 'I mean it — me an' my partner, we sleep a lot. Honest, we don't know. Bushy made the gap, paid us — that's all.' He shrugged.

'What about yesterday?' asked Thane grimly.

'Yesterday?' The man licked his lips, probably calculating that they were with him and Bushy Bramble could be far away. 'One or two people came an' went. Like they'd done the usual first, of course — parked a car down the street somewhere.'

'Did you see them?' demanded Sandra.

'Uh — no.' The man gave her a foxy, sideways look. 'But — ach, they were noisy.'

'Noisy like what?' Deliberately, she brought the reluctant Jimmy's head round towards the wall again.

'Like — ' he swallowed — 'like two, maybe three men were arguing. Then I think I maybe heard someone scream. After that . . . ' He licked his lips. 'Me? I suppose I went back to sleep again.'

'When?' pressed Thane.

Early afternoon was the best he could manage. Twice again, patiently, they took Jimmy the Neighbour through his story, with no real changes.

'Get rid of him,' said Thane resignedly.

'Mister — ' querulously, Jimmy put up a token resistance — 'what's it about?'

'Someone died,' said Thane brutally. 'Goodbye, Jimmy.'

The thin face drained of any remaining colour. Then Jimmy the Neighbour was shoved into the waiting arms of Jock Dawson, and the dog handler marched him off. Dawson's dogs were already prowling the enclosed yard, ready to discourage any new sightseer.

There were more arrivals, including a K Division police surgeon who performed his usual macabre tricks, used a rectal thermometer, then gave a possible time of death as around 3.30 p.m. the previous day — not long before Ernie Vass had logged Bramble as boarding the football minibus bound for Edinburgh.

The other help Thane had been hoping for arrived a little later, when Detective Inspector

Francey Dunbar limped in. The new stage of the Tyndall Black fraud inquiry was now with Forensic, and Francey had come out to Glencoma for the simple reason that his nose was itching.

Two minutes after Dunbar's arrival, Thane put him in charge of the murder locus and collected Sandra Craig and Dougie Lennox. He let them leave first while he spoke with Boomerang and The Pawnbroker.

'This is one where we need anything you come up with,' he told the Scenes of Crime sergeants bluntly. 'We've got problems.'

The two shared a pleased beam as they finished sealing a used set of plastic evidence bags.

'We like problems, superintendent,' murmured Boomerang. 'Don't worry. We'll — uh — get back to you.'

'Just leave it with us,' agreed The Pawnbroker.

Their cherished routine accomplished, the tall thin man and the small fat man exchanged a grin as Thane left.

★ ★ ★

He used the car pool's flagship red BMW. A court had confiscated the BMW from the previous owner, a drugs baron, when he was

340

sentenced to ten years and it had come to the Crime Squad, awarded like Brownie points.

When he got the chance, Thane always liked handling the BMW. He drove with Sandra Craig in the front passenger seat, Lennox in the rear. The roads were quiet, and a few minutes' travel took them out of Glencoma, back into Paisley, then round to the Empire Lines warehouse.

The churchyard lot was empty, which wasn't good news. But they drew in and parked the BMW. The old building was open for business as usual, except that there was no sign of Michael Spring or Dirk.

'Not today, Mr Thane,' said the plump brunette secretary in the gallery office. 'Mr Michael said he had some things he wanted to do at home. Dirk — ' she shrugged — 'he's gone off on a buying trip up north.'

'For how long, Joan?' asked Dougie Lennox mildly, his best smile in place.

'Hard to say.' The admiring brunette gave the baby-faced Lennox her full, wide-eyed attention. 'But maybe I can help . . .'

'Detective Constable Lennox will stay with you to sort out a few things,' said Thane blandly. 'They're mainly about Empire Lines casual workers. While you help Dougie that way, we'll go visit Mr Michael at home.'

'Does Dirk live with his father?' asked Sandra.

'Dirk?' The brunette's eyes were still on Lennox and his smile. But for a moment her face showed that her boss's son wasn't her favourite person. 'No, Dirk has a place of his own — not that he always uses it.'

They obtained Spring's home address and directions, then left Dougie Lennox with the brunette — something akin to presenting a cheerful fox to an already hypnotised rabbit — and set off.

Michael Spring's home was a large two-storey villa on the outskirts of the town in an avenue where, starting with the cars on runways, most things looked and were expensive. Thane drove into Spring's monoblock paved runway, stopped behind the man's old silver-grey Mercedes Benz, then walked to a glass and oak house door with Sandra Craig at his heels. When he rang the doorbell, a set of chimes pealed like cathedral bells. A minute passed, then a dyed blonde in her early forties approached from somewhere in the house. She was casually dressed in shorts and a well-filled sports top.

'That's Mother?' whispered Thane, surprised.

'Second wife — stepmother,' hissed Sandra. 'First name Barbara. It's in his file. The one on your desk.'

Which he hadn't got round to reading. Thane made the introductions when Spring's wife opened the door. She greeted them in a cautiously friendly style, then took them through to a small, well-furnished sitting-room.

'I'll go find Michael — he's around.' She waved them towards a couch. 'He's catching up on some household chores. The kind that won't wait any longer.'

They were left in the sitting-room, looking around it. Thane saw his sergeant eyeing a sideboard set of red Venetian glass goblets which Mary would have sold him to own. There were some exquisitely carved wooden animals sharing a shelf with a modest collection of silver sporting trophies, then the room door opened again and Michael Spring came in.

'When the law comes looking for me, I reckon it has to matter,' said the grey-haired man drily. He seated himself in an armchair version of the couch, and considered Thane carefully. 'What's it about this time, superintendent?'

'These.' Reaching into his pocket, Thane produced the photographs of Bramble and Sonas and handed them to the Empire Lines owner. 'Recognise either of these men?'

'Wait.' Spring reached into his shirt pocket,

produced a pair of horn-rimmed spectacles, and put them on. He took time studying the first photograph, almost too much time, his eyes not meeting Thane's gaze, then nodded. 'This one. Wilson Bramble, a salvage scout.' He took even longer with the second photograph and lightly moistened his lips with the tip of his tongue. 'This other character — I'm not sure. You've got a name?'

'Peter Sonas.' Thane waited.

'Bramble teamed with a new partner a few months back. I don't always hire angels.' Spring shrugged. 'Could be him, I don't know. The hair is too long, I've only seen him from a distance, and maybe my eyes aren't as good as they used to be.'

'Would Dirk know?'

'He might. He handles most of our scout deals.' Spring gave a short laugh. 'But you're out of luck, superintendent. Dirk left here this morning, heading north. Part business, part pleasure for a few days — just drifting around maybe doing some fishing, maybe some sailing.' He nodded approvingly. 'The boy deserves a break.'

'Could you contact him?' asked Sandra.

'I doubt it, sergeant.' The man shrugged. 'Does it matter?'

'It can wait.' Thane leaned forward, his manner staying reasonably casual. 'What about your architect friend from East Kilbride?'

'Ken Hodge?' The humour wiped from Spring's face. 'What about him?'

Thane shrugged. 'He gets involved in these architectural salvage projects.' He indicated the photographs. 'That way, I wondered if he knew this pair.'

'Can't say.' Spring's eyes had narrowed. 'Ask him.'

'Could he have met either of them yesterday?'

'Not when he was with me.' The Empire Lines owner shook his head. 'We met at the warehouse, we went out for an early lunch, then back to the warehouse — that was all.'

It was a change of story, but Thane decided not to press it — not yet. 'How about after that? When did he leave here?'

'Around 2 p.m.' Spring shrugged. 'He said he'd things to tend to back in East Kilbride.' He gave a humourless laugh. 'Which probably meant his other woman — Jane Tamsin's cousin. You know about Hodge and the cousin, right?'

'We do.' Thane glanced at Sandra Craig, and they got to their feet. 'Thanks for your time, Mr Spring.'

'No problem. Now I'll get back to my

chores,' said Spring.

His mood had apparently thawed again. He walked with them back to the BMW, saw them aboard, then stayed at his open front door and waved a farewell as they drove off.

★ ★ ★

'What do you think?' Thane asked the redhead beside him as the house behind them faded from sight.

'That he's anything but happy.' Sandra Craig didn't hesitate. 'But . . . ' She paused.

'But?' probed Thane.

'Depends what's worrying him, sir.' She produced a chocolate bar but only looked at it for a moment, frowning. 'Maybe he doesn't know himself.'

It was as good an answer as any.

Chocolate temptation won over willpower. Sandra broke two squares from the chocolate bar and gave them to Thane. Then she got to work on the rest.

Their first stop was at the Empire Lines warehouse, to learn that Dougie Lennox had taken the plump brunette out to lunch. Knowing Lennox, it was the way Thane had thought things might shape. But a lunch receipt for two would be in the baby-faced

DC's next expenses sheet.

It was back to Crime Squad headquarters next. There he caught Jack Hart ready to be visited by two Members of Parliament who sat on one of the purse-string government committees. But the Squad commander still managed to squeeze enough time to listen to another quick update. In turn, Hart could contribute that Interpol had at last come through with something from South Africa.

'Cape Town police are more than interested in our — ah — your Peter Sonas,' said Hart almost smugly. 'If we get him, please can we let them know?' His leathery face shaped a humourless grimace. 'They want him on one count of murder and two of armed robbery. Also for questioning about other killings.'

'No surprise,' said Thane softly.

'Nor is this.' Hart searched through the telex messages lying on his desk and passed one across.

Thane read it and cursed under his breath. Peter Sonas had disappeared from South Africa during the frequent confusion that followed the end of apartheid. In particular, he was wanted for a murder in which a female bank messenger had been stabbed to death.

The weapon had been a sharpened motor-cycle wheel spoke.

'Nail the bastard,' said Hart soberly. 'Let's get the lot of them, Colin. They're trouble just waiting to happen again as long as they're on the loose.'

On the way out, Thane briefly visited his own office. A stack of telephone message slips were lying on his desk, but none — even one from Mary — seemed end-of-the-earth urgent. He left them there, found Sandra Craig queuing at the service counter in the new basement restaurant, and beckoned. She obeyed, but was in a near-mutinous mood.

'Tighten your belt and hold on, sergeant,' he said stonily. He considered her hard, flat stomach. 'Don't worry. I won't let you starve — we'll eat in East Kilbride. My treat.'

She gave a blink of surprise, grinned, and the mutiny was over.

As they travelled, they used the BMW's radio to arrange the East Kilbride meeting with Moss and Jinty Shaw. The rendezvous was a quiet farmhouse restaurant, on the outskirts of the new town, and they arrived to find that a Strathclyde police car and a Crime Squad pool car were already parked outside with their drivers gossiping beside their charges in the sunlight.

The two inspectors had arranged a small private room at the rear of the restaurant. They sat side by side at a table, Moss

348

looking uncomfortable, Jinty Shaw relaxed and smiling, wearing a lightweight civilian jacket over her uniform skirt and tie.

'Eaten?' Thane asked them, smiling a greeting to the immaculate woman inspector, wondering who cut her grey hair in that expensively sculpted look.

'Not yet.' Moss fingered a menu. 'We decided to wait. Uh — have we time?'

'I don't think I've a choice.' Thane indicated Sandra Craig. 'The Federation are calling a lunch break.'

'A waiter came and took their orders for drinks and food. Once he'd gone out again, Thane settled back in his chair.

'Finished interviewing?' he asked quietly.

'Finished,' confirmed Moss. He strangled a belch in mid-birth, reddened, and glanced at Jinty Shaw. Her face hadn't as much as twitched. 'Not much luck, Colin. There's damned little to show.'

'You talked with Mary Russo?'

'We did, sir. A lot.' Jinty Shaw nodded. 'She's very gradually admitting that even if Peter Sonas was the only man Cousin Jane cared about, the same Cousin Jane also led a busy sexual social life. But I'd say she genuinely doesn't know that Ken Hodge was still courting them both, and we haven't suggested it yet.'

'Anything more about Hodge?'

Phil Moss scowled and shook his head. 'Just that he's not around. He left for the north — or so he claimed — yesterday afternoon. A business trip — he warned Mary Russo he'd be away a few days.'

'When was that arranged?' asked Sandra Craig sharply.

Moss and Jinty Shaw exchanged a puzzled glance then a shrug.

'Some time ago, sergeant.' Jinty Shaw gave the answer. 'It's inked in her kitchen calendar.'

'Right.' Thane took over again, thinking it through. Sonas and Bramble had vanished. Dirk Spring had packed a bag and taken off. Now the East Kilbride architect could have been added to the list. He looked at Moss and the grey-haired woman and rubbed a fingertip over the wood-grain table-top. 'I've news for you both. Ken Hodge didn't get far. He's dead. We found him this morning.'

Moss swore. Jinty Shaw stared at him.

'When?' demanded Moss.

'When we raided Bramble's place. His skull had been smashed in.' Thane pursed his lips. 'It made sense to keep you out of it.'

'Maybe.' Moss recovered first. 'Saved a few lies, I suppose. You're still sitting on it?

350

Even to Mary Russo?' He scowled at Thane's nod. 'Then who explains it to her?'

'A uniform, Philip,' said Jinty Shaw with a bitter resignation. 'As usual. It goes with the job.'

The waiter returned with drinks and their orders a moment later. They'd chosen a light meal — thin, pan-fried beef with tossed salads for both Jinty shaw and Sandra, smoked lamb for Thane, grilled trout for Moss. Afterwards they finished off a pot of coffee. They'd talked during the meal, but now it was over there was work to do.

Something had to be about to happen. Somewhere. And probably soon. Colin Thane had one growing suspicion in the back of his mind, but for the moment he wanted to keep it there.

'You first, Phil.' He pointed a finger at Moss. 'Use a radio patch from one of the cars. Shake the local trees again and see if anything more falls out. Then check if Dougie Lennox got anywhere with Spring's secretary — ' he gave a warning glare, and Sandra's grin vanished while it was still forming — 'including this northern trip he'd planned. We've enough of a file on Father, but we need a lot more about Dirk — anything we can get. And I want to know how many people knew about Ken

Hodge planning his trip. If you need more people, ask Tina Redder to chip in.' He switched to the two women officers. 'You two are with me at Sonnet-Bytes. I'm seeing Abbie Carson, you concentrate on another fast trawl through the workforce.'

'Asking more about Jane Tamsin?' Jinty Shaw nodded. She had a full police harness belt round her trim waist, hidden under the civilian jacket. Opening one of its equipment pouches she took out a lipstick and compact. 'Give me a moment, superintendent, and I'm ready.'

'We'll take a Federation comfort break, inspector,' said Sandra Craig, rising and pushing back her chair. 'That will give a certain superintendent enough time to settle the bill!'

★ ★ ★

Abbie Carson had said two o'clock, and Thane and the two women officers walked through the Sonnet-Bytes front door with a couple of minutes to spare. There were several signs of the enhanced security promised by Frank Alder. A new barrier system had been installed at the vehicle parking area and there were more security TV cameras in place around the reception area. Two new uniformed security men were now visible in the front hall area.

The three visitors were put through the photo-pass routine at reception, then Thane was taken off on his own.

At first, he was taken along the same rubber curtains route with their pressurised air seals and round corridor portholes. But this time he wasn't taken to Abbie Carson's office. Instead, he was left alone in a small classroom which had two rows of desks and chairs, teaching aid screens, and an observation window. On the other side of the observation glass, protective-suited, helmeted staff moved in what was more like a science fiction laboratory setting than any production area Thane had ever known.

'Yes, it's different, superintendent.' Abbie Carson's attractively unobtrusive American drawl came from behind and he turned. The tall, corn-silk haired Sonnet-Bytes managing director had entered the little classroom behind him. Her strong mouth shaped a warmly friendly smile and those large, sea blue eyes twinkled. 'Well, you wanted to know about microchips — and this is where we do our teaching!'

Thane watched her come over. The Saxon princess was dressed in a simple cream-coloured linen dress, a bright red silk scarf at her throat. Only someone with her height and build could have carried that dress so well, only someone with those magnificent legs could have got away with teaming that dress with embroidered flat-heeled moccasins.

'Sit down,' she invited. 'Anywhere. I'm ready to collapse!' She dropped into a chair beside a teaching lectern and gave a mock groan. 'I was with our Japanese friends until 2 a.m., they were at the plant at eight this morning, and we got rid of them less than an hour ago! Still, I'm ready to start.'

'I need to know something first.' Thane crossed over and looked down at her, the light perfume she was wearing teasing at his nostrils. 'It's about Frank Alder — '

'Our much-loved sales director. He's not here.' She raised an eyebrow. 'What about him?'

'When will he be back?'

'Hey, superintendent!' She gave an amused laugh. 'If you're worried about Frank bursting in on us, I can always lock the door!'

'This is for real,' said Thane patiently.

'Well, it's simple enough.' Abbie Carson frowned and looked at the gold watch on her wrist. 'Right now, he's aboard an executive mini-coach with a couple of our security men. They're giving about a dozen of our Japanese a courtesy escort back to their hotel.' Her frown lingered. 'Satisfied?'

'Satisfied.' It seemed safe enough. Thane nodded and sat at one of the desks.

'So . . . ' She spread her hands. 'What do you want to know?'

'How you select staff, how you train them.' He was feeling his way.

'From the start?' Abbie Carson settled back in her chair. 'We consider all applicants — some can be university graduates, some can be straight out of school. They pass medicals, they sit educational tests. Every step is pass or fail. Depending on the vacancy we're filling, training can be weeks or months.' She raised a hand in emphasis. 'There are two things to remember. First, that a microchip is the most important part of any computer memory.

'We talk about how many bytes of information a microchip can hold. Each character in a word is a byte, the word 'police' would be six bytes — and the most powerful microchips handle umpteen million bytes.' She paused. 'With me so far, superintendent?'

'Holding on by my fingertips,' he admitted.

'Good.' Abbie Carson smiled and gestured at the observation window. 'The other is that microchips in the making are incredibly fragile, and a major part of our job is quite simply to protect them from people!' She laid a hand on Thane's arm. 'Look out there, superintendent. Men or women, almost everyone out there is under thirty years old. They're working in a young people's world, they probably think of me as an ancient relic.' The big woman watched a trio in their protective suits pass on the other side of the glass, then added softly, 'What you're looking at is pure space age technology — or the next best thing.'

She went on, explaining why, like all its fellows, Sonnet-Bytes was a non-smoking facility — even a trace of tobacco smoke on a production operative's breath could destroy some embryo microchips. The same went for alcohol.

Starting a shift, production line operatives had to shower and scrub up using a special soap. Hair nets had to be worn by men and women alike, they dressed in suits without pockets, suits sewn with carbon thread to avoid static. They wore special boots and safety glasses, a polythene hood and polythene gloves.

'Superintendent, we're a hell of a sight cleaner than a hospital operating theatre. We have to be!' The sea blue eyes were serious. Abbie Carson was selling an enthusiasm. 'But would you like to guess what our

356

biggest single problem is with people? We're everyday dirty, shedding our skin like snakes — and the manufacturing process suffers all the time.'

So the Sonnet-Bytes rules were tough. On the production lines, women couldn't wear make-up. Men and women alike had to use a special daytime moisturising cream so that facial skin stayed in place longer. All staff had regular medical checks.

'And if they don't pass?' Thane was suddenly interested.

'They're out.' Abbie Carson shrugged. 'Off the production line. Maybe they get some kind of office job, maybe not. A lot of them fail because they've developed a skin condition or something like — well — ' she shrugged — 'maybe plain, scratch your head dandruff or a scalp dermatitis. They are yeast-based conditions and . . . ' She frowned at him, realising he wasn't listening. 'Something wrong, superintendent?'

Thane took a long, deep breath. In his mind, he was back at Empire Lines, talking with Dirk Spring, recalling the way he scratched at his head, the way he regularly used that pocket comb. It was a mad long shot, but it was mad enough to matter.

'Superintendent?' she asked again.

'I need to get back to my people.' Thane rose as he spoke.

'Why?' She moistened her lips. 'I think maybe I should know, superintendent.'

'Because of something you said. Because there's been another murder linked to Jane Tamsin.'

'Another?' Abbie Carson took deep breath and didn't hide her anxiety. 'Hell. But why did you ask about Frank?'

Thane gave a small shrug. 'To make sure he was safe.'

'That makes sense, superintendent,' she said in a suddenly tight voice. 'More than you know.' Face pale, she rose from her chair. 'I'll phone the hotel.'

Abbie Carson swept from the room and almost sprinted along the outside corridor with Thane hurrying close behind and ignoring the way his knee had begun aching again. The woman executive grabbed her phone as soon as she was in her office.

'Abbie, what's going on?' demanded Thane.

'Wait, superintendent.' Abbie Carson dropped into her chair and punched telephone buttons. 'Give me a minute.' Her call connected, she spoke quickly and quietly with the voice at the other end. Hanging up the instrument, she glanced at her watch again. 'They haven't arrived.' She bit her lip.

'But — yes, it could be all right. I've left word he's to call me as soon as they arrive.'

'What's wrong?' Thane grabbed her by the shoulder. 'Come on, Abbie. Out with it!'

'Superintendent, give me a chance. I'm thinking.' She was silent for a moment, then sighed. 'All right, I could be fired for breaking absolute company confidentiality, but to hell with it.' The sea blue eyes looked up. 'Frank is on that coach, the way I said. But after they unload the Japs, the coach and the security guards will take him straight to Glasgow Airport. He's booked on a London flight. From London, he's booked on a Cathay Pacific flight to Hong Kong.'

'And?' Thane knew there had to be more.

'It was his own damned fool idea. He called it real-time security.' She bit her lip. 'Frank is carrying a briefcase. The briefcase is filled with our first advance production run of a new generation microchip.'

'Valuable?'

'Hong Kong think so.' Abbie Carson said it simply. 'The Sonnet-Bytes asking price was $20 million, superintendent.' She took a deep breath. 'None of these microchips is bigger than your thumbnail. Any one can hold twelve gigabytes of data. That's like being able to store an eighteen-storey stack of double-spaced typed pages in less than an inch of space — more than any maker has ever managed to store before.

'Gigabytes — but they're beginning to seem more like Death Bytes.'

The tall, big-boned woman fell silent, looking drained.

★ ★ ★

There was a lot to do and critically little time in which to do it.

Inspector Jinty Shaw and Detective Sergeant Sandra Craig joined Thane first, then Moss arrived by car. Thane had put out a priority search request for the executive coach, a sky blue Mercedes Benz, and an armed Crime Squad protection team were on their way to the Hilton for the coach's still hoped-for arrival.

There were negatives in plenty. Dougie Lennox's investment in buying lunch for the Empire Lines brunette had failed to extract anything more about Dirk Spring's holiday plans. Tail slightly between his legs, Lennox had been chased back to her again with more questions. A standard door-to-door check at the Glencoma estate had uncovered the expected three wise monkeys approach — no one had seen anything, heard anything, knew anything. The post-mortem report on Ken

Hodge confirmed time of death but failed to add anything new of significance — and Strathclyde's K Division were screaming to know what the hell was going on in their patch.

The executive coach-load of Japanese moved into the officially missing category, overdue by half an hour.

There were fragments on the plus side. Abbie Carson, hearing Ken Hodge's name, thought that the architect might have done some private work on a house for Frank Alder. Working with Sonnet-Bytes' personnel department, Phil Moss was digging out a list of any of their employees who had failed health checks in the past five years. At Bushy Bramble's house, the murder hammer had been wiped clean of fingerprints. But elsewhere in the house other prints had been found. Some belonged to Bushy Bramble, but others were a positive match to record prints belonging to Peter Sonas and satellite-linked in from South Africa.

Then, after just over an hour, the sky blue Mercedes Benz was found. Driver and passengers still aboard it but individually tied to their seats. The executive coach had been abandoned in a country lane near the town of Hamilton, miles off its intended route. The briefcase with its $20 million worth of microchips had been taken.

Jack Hart broke the news to Thane by telephone.

'The Japs are squeaking like budgies, but, thank God, at least they weren't hurt,' was the Squad commander's summing up. 'We're talking an armed hold-up, shots fired by three men. And surprise! Two of them were wearing your favourite motor-cycle helmets.'

'Colour red, with two white stripes?' asked Thane resignedly.

'You win a prize,' growled Hart. 'Frank Alder and his tame security heavies were knocked about, but nothing worse. Tina Redder is the DCI looking after that end, and I want you back to the ranch.' He forestalled Thane's protest. 'That's an order, Colin. Don't argue. I'm not in the mood.'

Thane left Phil Moss and Jinty Shaw running the East Kilbride end of things, drove back with Sandra Craig through a thin drizzle of rain, and reached the Crime Squad compound before 4.30 p.m. As soon as he arrived, he was summoned through to Jack Hart's office. Hart greeted him with a scowling nod when he walked in and Tina Redder, already there, gave him a sympathetic grimace.

'Better you than me, Colin,' she declared, gulping at one of the mugs of tea brought

362

in by Maggie Fyffe. 'I'm not laughing, but it's still one of the craziest sights I've seen in years. There are these VIP Japs, all being desperately polite, all offering their business cards — '

'Tina, I don't bloody care if they offered you work as a Geisha girl,' snarled Jack Hart. He stood glaring at the wall map beside his desk. 'Out there somewhere there's around $20 million worth of those — those damned things, whatever they are.' He turned on Thane. 'We're getting phone calls direct from God knows who all in the US and the Far East, I've the Scottish Office and the Foreign Office frothing at the mouth. Thank God for just one thing, that I can tell them we are already working on the case — ' his leathery face twitched with impotent rage — 'except next I've got to explain why it still happened!'

Tina Redder had a first draft report ready. Thane nursed another of the mugs of tea while he scanned her summary, precise and neat, not a word wasted.

A Lanarkshire patrol car, alerted by a farmer, had been first on the scene after the executive coach was found. The patrol car crew had called for back-up help, had forced the coach doors, and had freed the occupants. The most badly beaten of the two security guards had been taken to hospital by ambulance with concussion and a possible fractured skull. The second guard had gone with him for a check-up and Tina Redder had brought Frank Alder back with her to the Crime Squad compound.

In the hold-up, an old white-coloured van had suddenly blocked the coach's path on a lonely stretch of road. When it stopped, the two men wearing motor-cycle crash helmets and armed with sawn-off shotguns had forced their way aboard. Two shots fired as a warning, followed by Alder and the two security men being knocked about, had ended any suggestion of resistance. The coach driver had obeyed when the third man, wearing a balaclava mask and armed with a handgun, went back to the white-coloured van and he was ordered to follow.

When they reached the lane, the coach occupants had been systematically tied and dumped on its floor. Then the white van had driven off . . .

'Smooth,' said Jack Hart grudgingly. 'I've done all the usual from warning airports onward.' He folded his arms and considered Thane. 'We know about the hired help . . . Bramble and Sonas. Do we label Dirk Spring as leader?'

'Dirk, Dirk, the Dandruff Man,' murmured Tina Redder.

There was a watch on Empire Lines, another on his father's home. Details of Dirk Spring's car, a black Saab, had gone out to all forces . . . and the brunette secretary now confirmed that Spring's jacket collars regularly showed white speckles of dandruff.

'Label him,' agreed Thane resignedly.

'What about Father?' asked Commander Hart. 'We could haul him in for questioning — '

'Wait,' suggested Thane. 'I'll go to him. Where's Alder now?'

'Downstairs, Number Two interview room.' Tina Redder finished her mug of tea. 'Want me along?'

Thane shook his head. 'Thanks. But no thanks.'

He left them and went downstairs then in past the constable on guard outside the small, plain confines of the interview room. Frank Alder was sitting at a table, head clasped in his hands, and his middle-aged face was miserable when he looked up.

'Come to see the resident idiot, superintendent?' The Sonnet-Bytes sales director's North of England accent was bitterly resigned. 'Visiting the security whiz who came unstuck?'

'Depends why you did it,' said Thane unemotionally.

'Why?' Alder's small mouth twisted. The man had a scatter of cuts and bruises on his face and a deep gash showed on his scalp among his pepper-and-salt hair. He laid his hands flat on the table and looked at them. An ugly bruise circled one wrist. 'Simple, superintendent. I wanted to play with the big boys, to be a vice president — Sonnet-Bytes has a Main Board vacancy coming up. At my age, I knew it would be my last chance.'

'You thought you'd get it this way?' Thane stared.

'If it had worked.' Alder nodded. 'Our company sales policy is twinned with absolute commercial secrecy and security. Microchips are in that kind of world, superintendent. I thought I had a hell of a smart idea, using the Jap buyers as cover. Head office loved the notion. But now . . . ' He gave a brittle, defensive shrug.

Thane sat on the edge of the interview room table, looking down at him, sensing this was truth. For a moment, he glanced at the statement he'd brought with him. In it, Alder said that he hadn't recognised any of the trio of raiders. All the time he'd been with them, they had hardly exchanged a word.

'When did you decide to use the Japanese buyers' coach?' he asked.

'Two days ago,' answered Alder wearily.

366

'But a few people knew.' Thane took Alder's silence as his answer. 'Including Ken Hodge, the architect?'

Alder nodded sourly. 'He's been helping me with a house. 'We're friends — or I though we were, the bastard. We'd had a few drinks. We usually had a few drinks.' He paused, then asked hopefully, 'Have you got him?'

Thane shook his head. That Hodge was dead could wait. But another small piece had fallen into place. The prowler spotted around the Sonnet-Bytes parking lot had to have been watching for the pattern of Alder's movements and the vehicles he might use.

He left the man, went upstairs again, and gave a quick report to Jack Hart. The Squad commander had his own piece of update news — the white van used in the hold-up raid had been found, burned out in a field. There were tracks nearby where another vehicle had been waiting.

Thane left Hart, remembered that Mary had been telephoning, and took a moment out in his own office to try his home number. It was engaged. Around 5 p.m., with Tommy and Kate home from school and a whole evening to plan, it was always engaged . . .

And there was another, crucial interview

waiting, this time in Paisley. Collecting Sandra Craig, Colin Thane left the head-quarters building. This time they used her white VW Golf and his copper-haired sergeant drove the direct route through the evening rush-hour traffic until they turned off for Michael Spring's home.

The old Mercedes Benz was parked as before on the monoblock runway at the Empire Lines owner's villa home. But there were a surprising three police cars parked in the street outside. One was the car detailed to watch the villa — the other two surprised him. Francey Dunbar stood in the evening sunlight beside the second in line. The third was the green Peugeot van used by Boomerang and The Pawnbroker, and the two Scenes of Crime sergeants were aboard it.

'What goes on, sir?' frowned Sandra Craig.

'Only one way to find out,' said Thane resignedly as the Golf pulled in at the rear of the line. When he climbed out, Francey Dunbar came towards him, limping on his cane, while Boomerang and The Pawnbroker emerged from the Peugeot.

'I heard you were on your way, boss,' Dunbar greeted him briskly, and thumbed towards the two approaching Scenes of Crime sergeants. 'They reckon they needed to see you in a hurry. And before you saw Spring.'

Thane raised an eyebrow, but he knew the glint in Dunbar's eyes. This was a moment that belonged to the two Scenes of Crime sergeants. He nodded as they reached him, and waited.

'We said we'd get back to you, super,' reminded the tall, thin Boomerang happily. 'So here we are!'

'It's like this,' beamed his small fat companion. 'We went gathering routine dust and grit samples at that Glencoma house — with our own kind of dust collector, right?' He gave a small, triumphant gesture with his hands. 'And what did we find?'

'Something pretty unusual,' declared Boomerang. 'Fragments of old ceiling plaster — like from where a ceiling had fallen down. We found them on the dead man's shoes, even traces on his clothes. Then other fragments on carpets and discarded clothes. Like whoever lived in that house had been at the same place.'

'You said unusual,' said Thane slowly. 'What do you mean?'

'Victorian or older,' said The Pawnbroker patiently. 'There was a time when the recipe for ceiling plaster included binding it with chopped cattle hair. We found plenty of cattle

369

hair, superintendent. A common source.'

'Architectural salvage?' suggested Sandra Craig.

'Well done, sergeant,' murmured Francey Dunbar. 'How are you at joined-up writing?'

Colin Thane didn't hurry the rest of the way to the villa's front door with Sandra Craig just behind him. He sensed he was already being watched, and before he could ring the doorbell the door was already being opened by Barbara Spring. She stood looking at him for a moment then moistened her lips.

'It's about Dirk, isn't it?' she asked.

Thane nodded.

'Damn him,' said his stepmother, her voice wiped of emotion. 'It would have been better if he'd been drowned at birth.' She beckoned them into the house then closed the door again. 'Michael is expecting you. What he doesn't know, he guesses.'

Barbara Spring took them to the same room as before but didn't follow them in. Michael Spring was sitting in his chair. The man had changed into a tweed suit and a white shirt with a knitted blue tie, his feet in his ankle-length lacing boots. He looked at them in silence for a moment, his round face grave.

'I expected you back, superintendent,' he

said quietly. He sucked at edge of his neat moustache. 'My son?'

'Yes.' Thane sat on the couch and Sandra Craig joined him. 'Do you know where he is?'

'No.' Michael Spring ran a weary hand over his close-cropped grey hair. 'What charges will you arrest him on?'

'Complicity in the murders of Jane Tamsin, a woman known as Old Aggie, and the architect Ken Hodge — '

'Hodge!' The man stared in near-disbelief. 'You're sure?'

'And a count of armed robbery,' went on Thane. Remorselessly, because it had to be that way. 'Hostages taken, shots fired.'

'What did he steal?'

'$20 million worth of microchips,' said Sandra Craig. She paused. 'Mr Spring, you said you expected us back. Why?'

'I suspected things. Things I didn't want to believe.' Michael Spring looked at Thane. 'I've a criminal record — nothing major, but a record, superintendent. I always hoped it wouldn't be like father, like son.'

Thane waited, saying nothing, hearing Sandra's quiet breathing at his side. 'You're sure?' pleaded Spring, hurt in his eyes.

'One question,' said Thane. 'Did your son ever have a job in a microchip plant?'

'A job?' Spring bristled. 'He came out of university with an honours science degree, microchips were his total interest.'

He described with a tattered remnant of pride how his son had walked into a high-flying research laboratory post with a major American microchip company — then how it fell apart after less than a year.

'Medical grounds, seborrhoeic dermatitis,' said Spring in a flat, bitter voice. 'Damned fool high-class dandruff. He can't shift it. They said they'd move him into something else, but he was too proud. He didn't want to know.'

So Dirk Spring had come back to working with his father, who had turned a blind eye to some of the things he soon knew were going on, like the way his son began organising the steady stealing of computer parts for overseas buyers.

Peter Sonas had 'just appeared'. Then Jane Tamsin, who had been thieving for him. But for months Dirk Spring had been hinting that something big was going to happen, that he was watching and waiting, his contacts in place.

'These killings.' Michael Spring drew a deep breath. 'Why Jane Tamsin?'

'I'm still guessing,' admitted Thane. 'Tell me about her. It could help.'

'Jane?' Spring pursed his lips. 'Likeable enough, even when I knew she was thieving. Totally infatuated as far as Peter Sonas was concerned — even after they had a major fall-out because of another woman she caught him with. Sonas stayed well clear after that — but I knew he was still tied in with Dirk.'

Thane nodded grimly. 'She could have been making threatening noises.'

Threatening enough to be silenced. Until she was lured to a meeting with Peter Sonas, a reason for wearing his microchip pendant. To be murdered.

Old Aggie had been different, simply in the wrong place at the wrong time. Then there was Hodge, who had served his purpose. A weak link, no longer needed.

'So what now?' asked Spring bitterly.

'We need to get them,' said Thane simply. 'They could be holed up — at that derelict mansion we talked about. You know where it is?'

The man opposite bit hard on his lip. 'You're asking me to shop my own son?'

Thane nodded. 'Before someone else is maybe killed.'

Michael Spring gave a long sigh. Then nodded.

'Two conditions. I take you, and first I

have five minutes alone with Barbara.'

'You've got them,' said Thane softly. He met the man's eyes and nodded. 'You're doing the right thing. The only thing.'

★ ★ ★

They left in just over the five minutes, travelling aboard Michael Spring's old Mercedes Benz. Spring was driving, as he had insisted. Whatever passed between the man and his blonde wife was private to them, but she came out to see them leave and was still standing at the roadside when they drove off.

By then, too, there were five Crime Squad cars behind them. One was Francey Dunbar's transport, the blue Nissan four-wheel drive, and another had brought Detective Chief Inspector Tina Redder and some of her team.

Michael Spring drove slowly and in total silence, grim-faced in a way which discouraged conversation — not that any of his passengers felt inclined to talk. It wasn't a long journey. First there were the few miles to the neighbouring town of Barrhead. Then on into the network of farm roads which criss-crossed the mix of low green hills and small lochs which lay behind the town. It

374

ended on a winding stretch of narrow road.

The road was flanked by hedges and trees, and Michael Spring let his car coast to a halt where a builder's sign pointed to a gap which was an overgrown lane.

'Pirnin Hall,' he said simply, nodding towards the gap. 'This is as near as you'll get without being seen.'

The rest of the convoy pulled in. As they got out, the occupants of the other vehicles followed their example.

Cautiously, Thane walked a short distance through the rutted weeds and grass of the sunlit old lane. A lot of traffic had used the same route in recent weeks, some of it big enough and heavy enough to damage the tangled hedging on either side. He saw the outline of a house ahead, stopped, then cursed as Sandra Craig cannoned into him from behind.

'Get off my back, sergeant,' he hissed and half heard her muttered apology.

His main interest was the house ahead. Pirnin Hall — or what was left of it — was in the old Scottish manor house style, three storeys of rough stone with small windows and a dark slate roof. The stonework had once been painted white, the glass in most of the windows had been broken, and he could see where clearance work had already reduced outhouses and part of one wall to rubble.

Demolition equipment of all kinds lay around, beside large metal skips and piles of salvaged wood and slates. But what mattered most was an edge of yellow van protruding from behind the old manor house — that, and a glimpse of someone moving behind one of the broken upper windows.

Signalling to Sandra, he moved back to where the others were waiting.

'They're there.' Thane glanced across at Michael Spring for reaction, but the grey-haired man turned away. He beckoned the others nearer. 'They probably don't plan to move until darkness, but we won't wait. We do this in stages, we use any cover we can. This isn't World War Three, so no frontal attacks. They've firearms, but we return fire only if necessary. Everybody going in — ' he looked deliberately at Sandra Craig — 'everybody wears body armour.'

'What happens if you're shot in the head?' muttered The Animal.

'With some, it won't matter too much,' growled Thane. 'Get on with it.'

In five minutes they were ready to move out, Sandra Craig and the china-doll Beauty complaining that the bulky body armour left them feeling like overstuffed bears. But it was only as the thin line of armed officers began to spread out and advance that Thane realised something was wrong.

Michael Spring was missing.

No one had seen him leave and he hadn't gone back. Which meant he'd gone forward.

Cursing, keeping low, Thane hurried towards the old Hall at a rapid trot, with others doing the same around him. Then he froze as a single shot sounded somewhere within the building. A moment later there were two more shots, close together and sounding from the same weapon.

A plain-clothes man over to his right sprinted forward, abandoning cover — and there was the immediate flat double boom of a shotgun. The man yelped and went down, rolling behind a pile of bricks and clutching his leg.

Someone else on the left moved, and another shot barked, the bullet whining off the side of one of the metal skips. Then there was silence. Dougie Lennox had reached the injured plainclothes man and was tying a bandage around his leg, other people were cautiously crawling and moving about. But all waited for Thane to decide what came next.

The decision was taken for him by a

sudden bark of engines from behind the old Hall. Seconds later, the yellow van came out, travelling fast, jolting and swaying, driven by Dirk Spring. With it came two bouncing, skidding motorcycles, travelling at full throttle, their riders wearing red crash helmets with twin white stripes. One biker clutched a sawn-off shotgun across his machine's handlebars. As they came on, Dirk Spring pointed a revolver out of the van's side window and fired wildly. Shots came back from several police weapons, and the van's wind-screen vanished. Choosing his moment, the Armed Response marksman, complete with trademark blue beret, jumped out from behind the shelter of a cement mixer and fired a single aimed burst from his Heckler and Koch rifle.

The van's nearside tyre disintegrated. The vehicle lurched, dipped, and began to spin towards the giant metal shovel of a bulldozer blade. For a moment, the van's driver tried to recover it. Instead, his vehicle hit one of the fleeing motorcycles, and threw the biker flying. Spinning, now totally out of control, the van crashed head on into the bulldozer's armoured steel. Metal screamed as the van body was ripped open as if by a giant can-opener.

The second motorcycle slowed for a

moment. Then, engine roaring, it started off again — and the The Animal, roaring howling, jumped out swinging a long, heavy plank of wood. The scything plank took the motorcycle just below the handlebars, unbalancing it into a skidding crash — and sending the biker tumbling and rolling along the ground straight towards Sandra Craig. He crashed hard into her and they fell together.

For Thane, running to get there, it was like a moment of grotesque, almost slow-motion horror. Snarling behind his helmet, the fallen biker rose up on his knees, and straddled the winded redhead. His right arm rose up, sunlight glinting on the thin stiletto-like steel of the long metal spoke he was gripping, then the weapon stabbed hard down into Sandra Craig's chest. She screamed. The metal swung up to strike again — and Thane triggered two shots from his .38.

But Tina Redder had also fired. So had Ernie Vass and a limping, cursing Francey Dunbar.

Peter Sonas jerked, twisted, then fell clear of the redhead and lay still. There was only the drifting smell of gunsmoke in the evening air and the spitting metal of cooling exhausts.

But Sandra Craig was sitting up, opening her jacket, staring in disbelief at the puncture hole in her body armour. She stripped back another layer and looked at a small surface scratch on the firm flesh just below her left breast.

'Dear God!' She shook her head in disbelief. 'The things work!' Then she was shaking, and looked up at Tina Redder. 'Tina — hold me a minute.'

'Let me park my broomstick, girl,' grinned Tina Redder.

Then she made a grab as Detective Sergeant Sandra Craig slumped in a faint.

Wilson 'Bushy' Bramble had survived, now handcuffed and with a broken leg. Peter Sonas was dead. So was Dirk Spring, inside the mangled wreck of the van.

Colin Thane was among the first into the old mansion. They found Michael Spring lying in a corner of the ground floor, shot three times in the chest. He was still just alive, as if he'd been waiting. He managed a rasping breath as his dulling eyes recognised Thane.

'I tried . . . ' he managed. 'I asked him to give up.' The greyhaired man coughed painfully, blood came from his mouth. 'He . . . ' Michael Spring died without being able to finish.

They found a bulky leather briefcase in an upstairs room. Its $20 million worth of microchips were intact.

★ ★ ★

There were aftermath situations. Wilson 'Bushy' Bramble, as sole survivor of the murder trio, was ready to talk about anything if it helped his position. Like why he'd broken into Jane Tamsin's locker after her murder. The motive had been simple greed — Bramble knew she hid any money creamed from her float inside her locker and he'd found and stolen close on £500.

Yes, Peter Sonas had killed Jane Tamsin. Because Jane Tamsin's feuding with Sonas had become what Dirk Spring saw as a high-risk threat — and Peter Sonas, tired of her, hadn't resisted the idea. Jane Tamsin, drawn in at the beginning by her feelings for Sonas, had eventually died for them.

Old Aggie had been killed by Sonas as a simple precaution.

Ken Hodge? Recruited through Jane Tamsin because of his Sonnet-Bytes connections, Hodge had been enticed to a pretended meeting with Dirk Spring in Bramble's home. He had gone in the back way — and it had been Peter Sonas who had smashed in his skull with a hammer.

Or that was Bushy Bramble's claim while he daily added more detail to his original story. Whatever happened, Bramble would face major charges — in the dock of the High Court, so near to where Jane Tamsin had died.

Elsewhere, leads were opening into an international network of outlets ready to deal in stolen microchips. Inevitably, there was a mountain of paperwork to sort out. Lawyers could decide the final results all round. Given time, a lot of time.

While other people including Mary Russo and Barbara Spring were left to mourn.

Other things refused to stay still. At the end of a week, Detective Inspector Francey Dunbar beamed from ear to ear as he announced that the unfinished business inherited from Tyndall Black was completed. Soft X-ray treatment of suspect receipts and will documents showed evidence of figures altered and signatures forged. The bank manager could forget his dream of that retirement villa in Spain. Where he was going, sunlight was limited.

Tyndall Black might never know, but it would matter to plenty of other people.

A second week passed, then came an evening when Phil Moss visited Thane at home. He found himself drinking Thane's best malt whisky, enjoying it in a way that wasn't supposed to accompany stomach ulcers.

'Are we celebrating again?' he asked Thane.

'Maybe.' Thane grinned. 'And old acquaintance didn't forget.'

There had been a telephone call that morning, from Tom Radd at Strathclyde's Eastern Division. Detective Chief Inspector Radd had a triumph — and a puzzle.

'We've pulled in the Rocket Scientist,' he had pronounced happily over the line. 'He's a twenty-year-old university student with big-time delusions. A call from a woman named Babs dropped his name in my lap.'

Thane had made a congratulatory noise, but Tom Radd cut it short.

'I owe you,' he declared. 'Babs said to tell you it took a few days, but she delivered.'

Thane wasn't too surprised. He knew Babs Riley.

Mary looked in, poured herself a whisky, then considered their visitor with some care. After a short period of clean shirts and pressed suits, Phil Moss seemed to be sliding back to his old ways again.

'Phil, are you still seeing Jinty Shaw?' she asked carefully. 'I mean — '

'I know what you mean, woman.' Moss grimaced. 'She's still a friend.'

'Nothing more?' Mary Thane was disappointed.

'Nothing more.' Phil Moss took a defiant swallow of whisky from his glass. 'She got too interested in my damned health — and she's into acupuncture. Nobody, but nobody, sticks needles into me!'

He winked at his two friends. Then, for emphasis, he gave a thunderclap belch.

★ ★ ★

Footnote

This story is fiction. But as it was nearing completion it was announced by Strathclyde police that an armed raid had taken place on a computer manufacturer's factory in East Kilbride. Four men held up staff, loaded a van with an estimated £10 million worth of computer equipment, and drove off.

At the time of writing, there have been no arrests and there has been no trace of the computer equipment.

Books by Bill Knox
Published by The House of Ulverscroft:

THE INTERFACE MAN
LEAVE IT TO THE HANGMAN
BLUEBACK
WITCHROCK
LIVE BAIT
DEVILWEED
DRAW BATONS!
PILOT ERROR
THE TALLYMAN
LAKE OF FURY
AN INCIDENT IN ICELAND
PLACE OF MISTS
SALVAGE JOB
A BURIAL IN PORTUGAL
A PAY-OFF IN SWITZERLAND
CARGO RISK
ISLE OF DRAGONS
NEST OF VULTURES
THE COUNTERFEIT KILLERS
A CUT IN DIAMONDS
MAYDAY FROM MALAGA
DRUM OF POWER
A PROBLEM IN PRAGUE
CAVE OF BATS
BLOOD PROOF
BLOODTIDE
WITCHLINE

THE WORLD AT NIGHT

Alan Furst

Jean Casson, a well-dressed, well-bred Parisian film producer, spends his days in the finest cafes and bistros, his evenings at elegant dinner parties and nights in the apartments of numerous women friends — until his agreeable lifestyle is changed for ever by the German invasion. As he struggles to put his world back together and to come to terms with the uncomfortable realities of life under German occupation, he becomes caught up — reluctantly — in the early activities of what was to become the French Resistance, and is faced with the first of many impossible choices.

BLOOD PROOF

Bill Knox

Colin Thane of the elite Scottish Crime Squad is sent north from Glasgow to the Scottish Highlands after a vicious arson attack at Broch Distillery has left three men dead and eight million pounds worth of prime stock destroyed. Finn Rankin, who runs the distillery with the aid of his three daughters, is at first unhelpful, then events take a dramatic turn for the worse. To uncover the truth, Thane must head back to Glasgow and its underworld, with one more race back to the mountains needed before the terror can finally be ended.

ISLAND OF FLOWERS

Jean M. Long

'Swallowfield' had belonged to Bethany Tyler's family for generations, but now Aunt Sophie, who lived on Jersey, was claiming her share of the property. It seemed that the only way of raising the capital was to sell the house, but then, unexpectedly, Justin Rochel arrived in Sussex and things took on a new dimension. Bethany accompanied her father and sister to Jersey, where there were shocks in store for her. She was attracted to Justin, but could she trust him?